SKY-BIRDS & RAVISHERS

Musa Kheswa

Published by Liyasa Publishers 2020
www.liyasapublishers.co.za

Cover Design by Yenzi Mpila
Editing by Chuck Sambuchino (USA)
Typesetting: Book Lingo

Email: publish@booklingo.co.za
Set in 11 point on 15 point Minion Pro

ISBN: 978-0-620-86138-0
e-ISBN: 979-8-663-41823-2 (Epub edition)

DEDICATION

This book is dedicated to the loving memory of my beloved father, Mnyayiza Basil Kheswa, my dear paternal grandparents, Zephried Maxhegwana and Katherine Victoria Kheswa (née Strydom); my great-grandparents: Frederick Strydom and Lina Strydom (née Ndumo); Ali Mlahlwa and Violet Ntonjana Kheswa (née Hadebe) … and their glorious clans: NoZulu, Mpangazitha, Ngelengele, Liyasa Liyasibekela, Mnguni omuhle wakwaMchumane, iZulu eladuma ekuseni kwathi ntambama laphangalala, Amaqhaqhambi eZulu eliphezulu, Amazala Nkosi, Izimpofana ezawela uThukela noMlazane neza nimacocombela njengekwindla.

Not forgetting this great man, Jonathan Khanyile: Ngwane.

And to my maternal grandfather, and grandmother, Agnes Nxumalo (née Zulu): Zwide KaLanga, Ndwadwe, Mkhatshwa.

May your souls rest in eternal peace.

A special thank you goes to my family: noting my loving mother, Ncane Kheswa (née Nxumalo), my caring siblings and cousins, and our adorable children. Last but not least, Simon Maginn (UK), and the man above. In God We Trust.

1

ENTERING THE DEVIL'S PLAYGROUND: THE PRISON

Sosobala NoZulu stood in the courtroom, his gaze locked with that of his attorney, Billy Thornton. He wiped his face, his hands moist and warm. He fixed an image of himself as he had been at sixteen, the lean sportsman at soccer practice. Striking, he had thought at the time. And in a courtroom with a nasty draught, a thousand miles from that soccer practice was a twenty-one-year-old gangster, about to face the wrath of the law. The judge with a baby face that complemented her silver ponytail delivered her sentence. He kept himself from screaming at her as her lips pursed with every word: "Sosobala NoZulu, you have been sentenced to a maximum of ten years imprisonment for the first-degree murder of Sifiso Mkhize, two years suspended. You will be eligible for parole in the third year."

The public gallery was filled with faces both familiar and unfamiliar. His mother looked distraught as she sputtered syllables that lingered in the air like an early-morning river fog. His tender wrists felt almost crushed as an officer, the kind who looked like he'd eat and sleep gym, tightened the handcuffs behind his back. Sosobala's brow furrowed. They bounded down the stairways of the court, escorting him through an underground tunnel past the cells like a racing horse in a harness. The cells were occupied with men of all ages—some clearly at home here, others plainly scared.

They stopped behind a police van. He was hustled in through the back door, followed by the others. It was locked from the outside and the flaps on the sides of the mobile cage's barred windows were wound halfway open. He crouched in there, crammed together with other offenders like rubbish in a dump. The odour of rotten eggs and dragon breath fouled the stifling air. He frowned. The van careened out of the Umlazi Magistrate's Court onto the Mangosuthu Highway. He peeped through the barred window, screwing up his face and squinting like an old grumpy woman. He took in the sidewalks. They had tall trees, as green as its grass, lined up in formation, and billboard advertisements of different brands with cool and dashing models. And the streets bustled with vendors in their brightly painted mobile containers flashing by. Passers-by, young and old, congregated from all angles to flock to this spot near the four-way traffic lights in V Section, the mouth of Umlazi. He sensed in the pit of his stomach that, maybe, this would be the last time he ever saw such a vibrant sight.

Maybe.

He was a bucket of emotions as the van sped onto the highway. They bounced like softballs around every inch of the mobile cage as it skidded down the road. It cranked up a steep hill before they pulled in at the gates of the prison. The way the driver's foot revved the accelerator was as if he was late for his wedding.

He peeped again, wide-eyed, through the barred window and there stood a sign engraved in yellow, above the colossal aluminium gates: WELCOME TO THE WESTVILLE PRISON: A PLACE FOR NEW BEGINNINGS.

The outside of the prison consisted of multiple storey red brick buildings trimmed with beige paint on the windows, doors, and roofs. It had a high double-row fence of galvanised security chain-link topped with concertina wire. Its heavily armed warders looked constipated, dressed in uniforms, as brown khaki as a walnut, with matching hats and bullet proof vests. They patrolled the area like ants swarming a dead worm. The driver aggressively sounded his horn, as if he loathed everything about the world.

Sosobala sighed, pondering the inevitable.

"Guard," the driver shouted, honking once more. "Open up."

The guard appeared and pulled on the gate. It opened wide as the van drove in, racing like a Formula One car until it pulled in at an isolated building. The driver blew the horn again and the steel gate opened with a creak. A warder carrying a large hoop of keys fumbled with the back door. It unlocked and opened wide.

"Bring those cocksuckers in here," a hoarse voice said.

Eyes bulging, he jumped out of the van with the others, like sheep into a shearing shelter. The warder gave the convicts their first orientation at the Westville Medium B prison. His nostrils were assailed by the stench of a thousand dead squirrels. He flushed in disgust at the offending convicts, some mere inches away from him.

"My name's Montie. In here, we're your Vaders," a warder said in an Afrikaans accent. "If you behave, we won't have problems. Hear me, convicts?"

Sosobala took him in. He was in his fifties or so, lofty with hands the size of a bull skull, and sporting a neatly trimmed red beard.

"Listen carefully. One at a time, come forward, strip naked and do a Tauza dance like this." He stooped and mimicked exposing his butt-hole. "After that, pick up your clothes, you go there and collect your stuff. You'll get a foam mattress, a sheet and a blanket, a bar of bath soap, a towel, a roll of tissue, and a uniform."

Montie pointed to the next cell, his eyes growing more intense, "Don't make me repeat that. Hear me?"

While being escorted along the corridors, floor to floor, steel gate after steel gate unlocked, clanged, and locked. His bladder weakened at the sound of the warder's boots. His shadow moved on the linoleum. Very shiny, the linoleum, and so are the boots. They passed the guardhouse for the middle floor. Two guards sat inside, feet up on the desk, behind the thick glass walls of the office. They seemed annoyed.

"Here's your cell," Montie said, unlocking the gate. "You take that bed over there." He pointed at the steel bed frame metres away from the entrance.

Sosobala nodded like a boxer stepping into the ring to begin the fight of his life. He took his first step. His cell was a hall, spotlessly clean, with about forty prisoners or so. Some convicts looked hardcore, others scared. The beds were laid out side by side on both the walls. Very orderly.

Westville Medium B, the maximum security prison holding dangerous convicts, comprised different cell blocks: A, B and C. It also housed the various prison gangs. Every cell block had its gang leader and his lieutenants, with the lower ranks following. And then there were the sky-birds, men fit only to wear women's panties. They had no privileges, not even to carry their own stuff: money, cigarettes or dagga, or any valuable goods—laughing stocks of the prison. He put his stuff on his bed.

An inmate approached him with a killer look:

"Moth'fucker, let's see your prison card."

A blue card with full names, prison number and the conviction. Sosobala fiddled in his back pocket and stole a glance at his interrogator while taking it out. He was a one-eyed man with tattoos of playing cards on both sides of his scrawny neck, which looked like it could snap under the weight of his gigantic head. The prison clothes, as orange as the sunrise, hung from him like wet clothes from a line.

"Another killer," one-eyed man said, twitching his eyebrows. "I need soldiers like you, you feel me, who aren't afraid of spilling blood."

A prisoner with tattoos of an ace of spades and a king of diamonds would be the highest ranking member in the 26 gang. For every kill, whether a sky-bird or a gang member or a prison official or even a gang leader, a tattoo of the appropriate playing card was inscribed onto that convict's body. Just like the medals of honour bestowed on a soldier.

"Call me Chopper, moth'fucker. In here, you either join my soldiers—the 26s," he said, "or you become a sky-bird. You wouldn't want that, right?"

It was more of a directive than a plea. Pledging to be part of a gang was most sacred, yet a cursed oath in jail where you chose to live or die by it. To take up the number lore of the prison gang was to accept that your gang leader was your god, that his word was final. And his orders were to be executed to a T with no questions asked.

The 26s crouched and raised their right fists, thumbs up, in front of their faces when engaging each other. They were the capitalists of the prison who would give anybody, even prison officials, a bloody fight if they dare stood in the way of their money-making. The 27s, they were the assassins who took no sides and only looked out for number one. The 28s were the ravishers who preyed on anything, young or old, quick to poke a hole in anybody they thought deserved one.

"My lieutenants will fill you in on the 26s' number lore straight away," Chopper said. "Thereafter, you'll have to earn your stripes, moth'fucker."

Sosobala nodded like a child as he realised that earning his stripes had everything to do with spilling blood.

As the days went by, he picked up the monotonous prison routine. At four-thirty in the morning, the lights came on. At five o'clock, it was roll call. Convicts stood to attention next to their beds whilst the warders counted heads. After that, the sky-birds did their beds and cleaned the cell. They would place rags under their hands and knees, and then kneeling on the linoleum would shuffle backward and forward like horses. Some of the soldiers would hop onto their backs and ride them as if they were in a Horse-Ball competition. Thereafter, it was shower time, at your own risk.

At nine o'clock they walked in twos, marching downstairs with their plastic containers and cutlery to the cafeteria for breakfast. It was porridge with one teaspoon of sugar, two slices of plain brown bread, and cold tea. After that, it was recreation time where they chilled outside the corridors of their cell blocks, in the four-by-fifty metre courtyard. During that time, some convicts who had influence were allowed to exercise at the gym facility centre. And the soldiers would be hard at work relieving the sky-birds of their valuable possessions, or engaging in low-key drug dealing.

At two o'clock, again, they marched to the cafeteria to be dished up with an afternoon meal. It was pork, or minced fish, and meat curry with no condiments, served with samp or mealie pap. It would be accompanied with five slices of plain brown bread. Chicken and rice were luxuries served only at Christmas.

If there was a smell of uncertainty in prison, like a gang war where the stabbings took place on the ramp or in the cafeteria, or if their rights were rescinded, they were lined up outside the cells. And by three o'clock another head count was done, and then they were locked back in the cells. The sky-birds would be compelled to do their washing, using the barred windows to hang it out. They did the ironing too, by putting clothes in their beds between the sheets and the blanket, and sliding on them until they were ironed.

On weekdays the gang leader flanked by his most trusted lieutenants would summon his soldiers to the chambers, in the far end of the corner of the cell. They crouched in a ring for briefings. It took three hours or so. That was where the soldiers placed their daily takings-money or valuable stuff relieved from the sky-birds, or traded-in the centre of the ring. The gang leader would then educate them about the number lore or talk about new strategies to control merchandise flowing in and out of prison. Or he would discipline those who challenged his authority. It was not a pleasant sight. It was gruesome until Sosobala got used to the stabbings and the reek of blood. And then the gang leader would keep what he desired from the daily takings, and the rest was traded off to other cell blocks.

It was more like economics: Who was it who'd made that statement, where in a comparative advantage, the first party traded for what they had less of, with the second party that supplied more of that, in ex-change for what the second party had less of. Then a carry-bag, using sheets, was used to transport those goods to the upper and lower blocks whilst lieutenants guarded the trade-offs like hyenas hunched over their kill. After business was concluded and all parties satisfied, it was time for some entertainment. That was when the sky-birds stooped to their lowest levels—singing karaoke and performing dance moves or acts beguiling the gang leader and the soldiers until the night lights were switched off at ten o'clock. Soon after the lights go off, high-pitched sex sounds, reverberated in the dark of the cell.

By the end of the second year, Sosobala had shown his rough thug side which made Chopper take note, even hinting about promoting him to the rank of lieutenant—the top echelon of the gang. It was more like being the most trusted advisor of an army general.

It was a Tuesday afternoon when the cell gate unlocked and a young inmate entered Sosobala's prison cell. These youngsters believed prison was some exotic hotel. Well think again, Bozo. Who was it who'd said that?

Sosobala took a lingering look at him: he had a boyish face, plump and a bit taller than himself. There were some similarities with his late childhood friend, Boyi. Chopper advanced towards the young inmate with a slow shuffling intimidating 'don't mess with me' rolling gait. He then left with a devious grin after a minute or so. He wondered what Chopper said to the young inmate.

The following morning they walked in formation going to the cafeteria, steel gate after steel gate unlocking, like kindergarten kids marching to the hall. One prison warder stood out from the rest, Montie. The convict behind Sosobala heaped praises upon him:

"Vader has thirty years as the warder, I tell you. He has seen it all, gangsters, real hardcore, come and go. Some taken out by other convicts in gang wars, or by prison warders. He's really something that Montie. I tell you, his rehabilitation programmes do wonders, some of 'em repent for real and leave as new men."

The young inmate in front of Sosobala had a roving eye as they entered the cafeteria: It was a hallway with 10-seater steel tables lined up for face-to-face seating arrangements at the far end. Just like a school cafeteria. Opposite the entrance was a long steel counter, and behind it were the sweaty cooks dishing out. The cooking equipment seemed dilapidated as if there was a special technique, like a bang on the side needed to get them to work. Was it the reason they were served cold meals?

His first days in prison, Sosobala had hated the smell, like expired milk, and the sour taste of the mealie porridge. The pork, sticky and rubbery, and the minced fish studded with bones, and the meat—horse or donkey—smelled as if it were boiled and left for days in the pot. But in time his taste buds and smell had succumbed to his stomach's demands, he was munching it like it was Kentucky Fried Chicken.

A young inmate took a seat next to him. Couldn't he find another seat? He frowned and looked away like a kid not wanting another kid to come within ten feet of his toys. After the young inmate forced a few swallows of porridge, Sosobala chuckled a bit at his suffering.

"What's your name, convict?"

"Madubula."

"Why are you in here?"

"I stole my teacher's car last year at school. A real bitch she was," Madubula said proudly. "The judge gave me two years. Can you believe that shit? I only wanted to teach the bitch a lesson. Anyway, I'm eligible for parole in six months or so. Me being in here now, I tell you, my gang's going to salute me when I get out."

The young inmate was ill-informed about prison. Just like many other youngsters in the township who begin crime as an exhilarating play with tangible rewards, until the wrath of the law corners them and shows no mercy. Why he was not sent to Medium A? That was where they sent prisoners who had committed lesser crimes.

"So how did you end up in here?" Madubula asked. "Can I call you Sosobala?"

"Soso will do."

He sighed.

"Life, just one fucked-up bubble. The guy I'd thought was a friend raped my girl, and another gang member and I smoked him in broad daylight. Days later I get arrested. The captain was some loony. He had been after me, made a vow or something that he was never going to rest until I was fuckin' dead or behind bars. Real lunatic. So anyway, I'm in the slammer and this jackass, my gang member, real jackass this guy, he takes all my stuff, and boom, he's gone. Who gets thrown into the hole?"

Sosobala paused.

"So they fuckin' bury me with ten years, you know, I'll be eligible for parole in three years or so, almost there," he said. "So, months later I heard from an old friend, the jackass died in a Pietermaritzburg prison. Hope he rots in Hell. I'll never forgive him, fuckin' jackass. You know, my heart doesn't forgive that easily, it's like trying to catch a speeding train."

"So where's your girlfriend now?" Madubula asked, mesmerised.

"A real babe that one! She moved to Cape Town to finish her law degree, haven't heard from her since," Sosobala said. "Maybe we'll reunite someday. Or maybe not."

Days went by, and Madubula was associating more with Chopper, puffing his dagga and cigarettes and munching his food. The first lesson Sosobala learned from the streets: Never—not even if the convict showed genuine sincerity—eat or puff anything from anybody in the prison. There were some 26s who doubled-up as the 28s—the ravishers. The young inmate could not tell the difference between a mouse and a cat. So he tried to warn him.

"Madubula, you be fuckin' careful in here. Convicts have their protocol in any slammer. You see, when you chain smoke with them their cigarettes and dagga, and munch their food, you know, you are accepting their favours. You don't want to go there, alright?" Sosobala said, seeing the naivety in Madubula, "They'll knock on your door for a payback someday."

"Don't worry about me, Soso," he said. "I can watch my back, besides, Chopper digs me."

Weeks went by, and Sosobala got used to the young inmate sitting next to him at the cafeteria, or coming over to his bed for friendly chats. Madubula was warming up to him, just like the time he had developed a friendship with the late Boyi. But Chopper's facial expressions showed that he did not like that one bit. He had other things in mind.

"Listen, moth'fucker, I want you to stash this under Sosobala's bed," Chopper said, showing him a small plastic bag.

"But, Chopper?" Madubula said.

"Don't worry, nothing's going to come of it. Besides, you do want to join my gang, don't you?"

Madubula wanted so much that ultimate recognition in prison since he would have authority over the sky-birds. Sosobala was with the 26 gang, doing that little job would earn him Chopper's respect. He would walk the prison corridors, his head held up high when associated with the most feared man, the 26 gang leader.

"Why hid the stash in Sosobala's bed?" one lieutenant asked.

"A little birdie told me, the warders are going to surprise us, tomorrow morning," Chopper said, his tone demonic. "It's time for payback. With that moth'fucker out of the way, the sky-bird is all ours."

That afternoon, the cells were locked and Sosobala was held up in the chambers. Madubula saw his chance, perspiring as he sneaked to Soso's bed, he hid the stash. Relief and fright assailed his conscience like a kid who had taken a bite of his sister's surprise birthday cake. After this, Chopper would be proud of him. Maybe, with his wittiness and Chopper's fearless demeanour, together, the prison would be theirs to rule.

The next morning their cell was awoken by the prison warders doing a roll call and ransacking the entire cell for contraband.

"What's this doing in here?" Montie said, holding up the small plastic bag as the prisoners lined up against the wall.

Sosobala's blood clogged his brain, ready to burst out of his ears, when he realised that it came from under his bed.

"Ahh, don't know, Vader." He shuffled closer, shaken and confused.

"You've got drugs in my prison, you scumbag?"

"Vader, it's not mine," he said, his breath caught in his throat.

His eyes locked with Madubula's. The young inmate had guilt written all over his boyish face. Chopper watched with a devious grin as Soso was removed from the cell in shame.

"This moth'fucker won't be coming back anytime soon," Chopper whispered in Madubula's ear.

Before the prison cells could be locked that afternoon, Sosobala came back shuffling in a slow gait like a monster ready to feast. Chopper's face told a tale of a thousand years.

"I don't understand why this moth'fucker's back so soon."

The cell was strangely dark that night. Sosobala covered his head with a blanket as the thunder kept him half-awake. He rattled his brains, trying to understand the reasons for being set up. He concluded that Madubula was a victim. He somehow felt sympathy for him, but Chopper, what would he gain?

The shuffles sounded. Soso peeped from under his blanket and concentrated, screwing up his face and squinting like a monk. Four wriggling figures stood next to the young inmate's bed side.

For fuck's sake. What is going on here?

The thunder struck, and terror cascaded in his brain. As a seven-year-old asleep in his bedroom, he was awoken by thunder that made him wet his bed. The fear of thunder had laid itself a solid foundation in the pit of his heart. It had caused him to lose his father, and his childhood friend, Boyi. His eyes widened. Madubula's wrestling prostrate form was pinned to the bed. He zoomed in and caught a glimpse of a familiar figure wrestling his pants down.

Holy moly. It was… and they were…

The moans grew louder as if from a wounded cub. The impact of Madubula's behind being thrust into was like waves slapping on the seashore. His heart beat faster, the blood in his head felt like spewing out of his nose. Sandy's agony resurfaced, his lost girlfriend, who was also raped. Each and every second that went by, a germ of sadness and anger became more and more inflated like a balloon. He suppressed the terror of thunder out of his brain.

Do something!

He flinched, heart pounding, thoughts racing. But that was Chopper and the number lore forbade him from challenging his authority. And he was eligible for parole in his third year, quite close, he counted, mere weeks away.

As the victim's moans grew louder, so the balloon was inflated bigger and bigger until it burst, breaking the terror and flooding his conscience with the desire to act fearlessly. He sprang into action, skipping a few beds like a 100-metre sprinter. He hurtled towards them, fists clutched. He jumped at the leader who was glued to the young inmate's behind.

"Fuckin' bastards."

Sosobala opened his mouth and shrieked. A primitive scream came from him, sickeningly loud in the dark of the cell.

"Get this moth'fucker off me," the leader grunted, breathing heavily.

Hands dug at his flesh as he fought back. He was losing momentum, overwhelmed. Someone new had just entered the fray.

"Finish him off, bloody sky-bird."

"Ahh, they've poked me, Soso," the voice said with a girly squeak.

"Madubula." His voice hung in the air like smoke as he lay on the floor, bloodied.

The coldness of the linoleum sent shockwaves down his spine.

Click.

The cell lights came on, the cell gate unlocked.

"Roll call," a warder said, approaching. "Fuck, what's going on here?"

Sosobala pulled himself up, holding his lower abdomen and tasting blood in his mouth. He stared with failure flickering in his dull eyes at Madubula's writhing body, and the cream sheets stained bold red. Tears ran down his cheeks, warm and salty. Chopper together with the others, were positioned against the wall like sheep. As soon as their eyes connected, he knew that this challenge of his authority would come at a price.

"Who did this?" Montie asked, his look aimed at Sosobala. "Are you deaf or what, tell me who?"

Sosobala held back from pointing at the culprits. If, God knows by whose power, he could let his fingers do the talking, but then he would have signed his death warrant.

"You don't want to talk," the warder said, frowning. "We'll see how you going to like spending a week in G7."

The mention of G7, solitary confinement, was gut-wrenching to any inmate, hardcore or not. The muscles in his face twitched, his stomach churned and held back the retch at the smell of blood as the warders carried out Madubula's helpless body.

"I don't know why you're protecting these scumbags," Montie said as he dragged him out of the cell. "It might be you next time."

Sosobala averted his gaze as they passed through steel gate after steel gate until they reached solitary.

2

A NO MAN'S LAND: SOLITARY CONFINEMENT

Sosobala shivered like a wet dog. This was G7: solitary confinement on the top floor of the Westville Prison. It was his new home for a week.

If he had not helped Madubula, he would not be there. His heart skipped a beat as the warder's keys ground in the lock. He took deep breaths, his chest and stomach feeling heavy, as did his orange prison clothes. The door was steel with a small gap at the bottom for sliding in food. It opened wide; the smell of a dead rat and misery hung in the air like smoke. He blushed in disgust.

If he had not joined the gang, maybe he would not have been caught in between the number lore and morality. If he had not refused to reveal the culprits, he would have been toast, and there was not a bloody thing Montie could have done to protect him.

He took in solitary. The roof was high and its light bulb shone faintly. It was tiny inside and only allowed him to stretch his arms, no more. It had a spume mattress placed against the wall. Directly opposite the door was a concrete slab with a built-in stainless steel toilet and a roll of tissue.

"Inside," the warder said, cold as a stone statue.

Sosobala felt afraid, his feet becoming wobbly like jelly, and then the hands the size of a bull skull shoved him in. He flew inside. All because he had refused to dig himself deeper than what he already was: a member of the number lore.

"Please, Vader," he said as he swung his body around. But the steel door slammed shut.

His heart beat wildly when he sensed more darkness than light. The footsteps of the warder's boots stomped away from solitary. He choked, his breath caught in his chest as his eyes flickered.

"Vader." He banged the door.

He sensed that the boots would not stomp back anytime soon and his voice succumbed to the silence. Banging against the cold steel of the door caused his palms to throb. He knelt against the wall, hands on his head, a trickle of tears running over his chin, warm and salty. His mind raced with unanswered questions: Why? How did it all go wrong? Drowned by silence, he dozed off.

Clink. The baton rapped the steel door.

"Breakfast," the voice said as the food skidded inside.

His body felt sore and cold. He had fallen asleep on the concrete floor. He heaved himself up against the wall, stretched. There was not much room for that. He took a small step towards his food. The usual smell of porridge and brown bread were swamped by the smell of solitary. But something was missing.

"Vader," he said. "No tea here."

"No tea today, sonny."

He tried to breathe, feeling nauseated, his throat dry.

"Come on, Vader," he said behind the door. "Let me have tea."

The footsteps of the warder's boots stomp away until they stomped no more.

"Vader, give me some fuckin' tea."

His gut ripped apart thinking how his noble intentions to help Madubula were now poison eating him alive. He kicked and punched in the air, swearing and cursing. The porridge plastered the wall and the bread slices were strewn across the floor. He threw himself on the spume mattress, curled his body and sighed.

The first day he met Madubula, his upper lip twitched when he talked, and he smiled as if he was screwing up his face. Boyi, his childhood friend had risen from the dead.

He battered himself with some more questions: if he had looked away at the cafeteria and not taken a chance to get to know him, would his life have turned out differently? If, for crying out loud, he did not get too close and personal with him, would he have avoided being set up by Chopper? If, God knows, he had not interfered with his rape, would he have felt OK about himself? If he'd had the courage to point the culprits out to Montie, would he have felt like a hero? He accepted that Madubula's blood was on his hands. He failed him just like he had failed his father and Boyi. Guilt ate at him.

His eyes closed as he recalled that night of his father's tragedy, and his burial that had shattered him. It had been the spring of '81. The primroses and the wallflowers had bloomed beautifully that month in the west of Umlazi neighbourhood. He was lying in bed, which sat against the wall next to a sash window, when he sneaked a quick peek through the gap in the curtains. He concentrated on this like he had X-ray eyes, squinting. The dark velvety sky cast shadows around the bright circle of the street lights. He counted sheep until he reached La-La Land. And then it rained buckets with loud crashing thunder. He woke up abruptly, wetting his bed in the process.

"Soso, gimme a hand, the damn roof's leaking again," his father said, opening his bedroom door.

The wooden ladder was old but still had life. His father scaled to the top. He had secured the ladder as best as a seven-year-old could while his father climbed. The striking of the thunder caused him to let go of the ladder and cover his eyes and ears, shaken.

"Look out. For Christ's sake."

The ladder slipped and his father must have felt it too as he turned seemingly in slow motion. Soso froze in place. Then a sickening crash: His father thudded to the ground, arms stretched. He had rushed towards the motionless, supine figure.

"Father. Are you—?"

Sosobala was not able to bring himself to say it. He stared at his father, helpless. The rain flooded down and over him, drumming fear in his heart. He knelt beside him, a hand behind his back, but his father's moans said it all... he had failed him.

"Ma."

His father was whisked away to the local Prince Mshiyeni hospital, with his mother by his side. The next bleak morning brought sorrow to his soul. His mother returned from hospital.

"How's Father doing?" he asked.

She avoided eye contact like a thief caught in action. Her shoulders slumped, and tears rolled down her cheeks, soaking her blouse.

"What's wrong, Ma?"

"The doctors rushed him into surgery." She hid her face. "The operation went horribly wrong. He didn't make it," she said. "Your father's gone. Mlahlwa's no more."

An overwhelming grief sneaked underneath the door frame causing a chill to run up his spine. If he had held the ladder and not be distracted by the thunder, his father would still be alive. Guilt began eating away at him like a slow poison. His home had become the sad sanctum of sobs that week with neighbours and relatives taking turns to give comfort.

On that crisp, dark Saturday during a night ceremony, his grieving mother, a scarf wrapped around her head, blanketed in the corner of a sitting room on a mattress on the floor, ringed by slow-burning candles. She looked intently at the coffin without blinking an eye. The love of her life lay lifeless in there, mute, with no word of comfort for her in her time of sorrow.

The gray sky announced Sunday morning with dark curtains of clouds hanging in the cold dawn. It dawned on him that it was the day they would lay his beloved father to rest. A heat that could melt a glacier crept up his chest and restricted his breathing. He heard the loud melodic cries inside the house while gospel hymns were sung outside in the tent. The tree branches and the birds mournfully sung nature's sad farewell.

His father's coffin was carried away by the hearse. He said a silent prayer for his mother who could not put one step in front of the other. Disheartened, the convoy went to his father's last resting place at the Seventeen Cemetery, to the south of his neighbourhood. His body felt paralysed, his hands moist just by looking at his father's easy-on-the-pocket coffin aligned on the green straps of the grave. He took in the gospel hymn realising that when death came knocking on his doorstep, he would want it sung at his burial.

"Be still and know that I am God."

At that moment he felt empty. His eyes found his mother, her shrieks sounded as if she was watching a horror movie. He gazed with sadness clouding his dull eyes as his father's coffin sank in the grave. He scooped a handful of the red soil and sprinkled it into the grave. He had to live with knowing the terror of thunder lay like a solid foundation in the core of his heart.

* * *

He snapped out of it when his stomach grumbled. Nothing he could do about the porridge but the two slices of bread, they could be preserved. He rolled off the spume mattress and wiped them clean. He exhaled deeply, closed his eyes, opened his mouth, and began chewing, grinding them—one by one—like paper in a shredder until his mouth was left wishing for more. He stretched a bit as he focused on the wall. There was much graffiti. He moved closer and tried to focus but with difficulty. Why have a light bulb if it had little effect at brightening the place? He zoomed in some more and concentrated, squinting like a cop. The writing on the walls was dark brownish. The composed message in English did not make sense at all.

He tried to read, 'Joe as her I ad to ill at wad I as a ode anada medl fo me anada kiln of te wad wud mak me lutenat I m aged in her lik a nimal no to do no solds to tal it jus ark an old alls I ill rat be ded dan liv ike is.'

He looked at the artwork next to it. It was a fist with a thumbs-up. How did the inmates write this? He deciphered the sentence by feeling word after word like he was reading Braille. After hours of attempting it, he finally read the sentence aloud, 'Joe was here. I had to kill that warder. It was an order. Another medal for me. Another killing of a warder would make me lieutenant. I am caged in here like an animal, nothing to do, no soldiers to talk with, just dark and cold walls. I would rather be dead than live like this.' Then the sign of the 26 gang.

He imagined Joe's agony and what tattoos of playing cards he was inscribed with after the killing of the warder, and he fell asleep.

Clink.

"Lunch." The plate slid inside and the footsteps disappeared.

"Come back here," he shouted.

He hauled himself up, stretched warily, and picked up the plate. He leaned against the wall and ate. Sticky and slimy-pork stew and stamp mealies. He put the plate down and rolled on the spume mattress. Suddenly, his stomach churned, and he became nauseated. It grumbled with no apologies. He sprang up and rushed to the toilet, and his jaws opened in a flash. He leaned on the toilet seat and spewed pile after pile, moaning with self-pity. He screwed up his face as he spat the last drop, and wiped his mouth. He used the toilet paper, frowning, and threw it in. He pulled himself up and shuffled back to the mattress, still feeling the stomach cramps.

The last time the food was bad, it had caused half of the cell blocks to battle each other for the use of the toilet. It was when the cooks put Epsom salt in the stew as a replacement for condiments.

He clutched his body and tilted his head; his eyes locked at some other graffiti on the side wall. He began zooming in on the words; this time around he just concentrated, taking his time for his eyes to adjust to the faint light from the bulb:

"Solly was here these warders think by beating me and throwing me into solitary that would stop blood from being spilled in here. I was born a killer and will die a killer. Anyone who challenges my authority dies a slow and painful death. Salute to my lieutenants, I will be back," and then a sign of the 26 gang.

Sosobala realised that the author had been a gang leader put into solitary for killing somebody who had challenged his authority. Chopper flooded his mind, filling the pit of his heart with panic.

The first day Chopper had advanced towards him: his one eye, his speech, his slow shuffling 'don't mess with me' rolling gait, all cried for blood to be spilled. He made a deal with the devil's favourite demon, and soon it would be knocking on his doorstep.

He pondered on the devious ways Chopper would use against him when he got out of solitary. Would he suffer the same fate as Madubula, being attacked in his sleep, raped and then stabbed to death?

Maybe he would be attacked as they lined up in twos going to the cafeteria. Or in the cafeteria, as he dug into his plate, maybe somebody would sneak behind him and plunge a knife in his neck. There was no inmate he could trust.

If Boyi was in there with him, oh what a powerful force they would be. When his world had been under a dark cloud after he was fired from his job at Transco, left only with a car, and no money to pay the rent, Boyi took him under his wing. He pulled a stunt that left his heart beating many times faster on their first ever hustling job. Sandy had invited him for an opening night party at varsity. He and Boyi pulled in at the varsity's main gate in Francois Road, in Glenmore. It was jam-packed as Sosobala searched for the time on the dashboard's clock: it read eight-fifty.

"Let's park here. Sandy's building isn't far from here," Sosobala said, as he pointed at the sidewalk just across the road. "I'm sure she's at the gates wondering where I am."

Campus was bustling. Boyi was going to have a field day, his tongue hanging out like a cat's, its owner thrown into confusion about which plate—milk, honey, custard, or chocolate—to devour first. He grinned at the sight of a petite figure strolling towards him. He rushed up to her and gave her a squeeze. But then as he turned, Boyi was already linked with a group of scantily dressed chicks at a distance. He beckoned him but Boyi gave him a 'do not disturb' look.

"Meet up later dude," Boyi said.

"Stay out of trouble," he said, clutching his sweetheart and disappearing into the residence corridors.

"Yes Dad." Boyi had waved, his voice trailing behind.

He made sure that every minute with Sandy counted. Later a knock sounded at the door and a voice called to him. He opened the door. A chubby form on the doorstep sported the weirdest smile. That very rare smile that would incriminate any man who was found in a house alone with another man's wife.

"What happened to you?" he asked, searching Boyi's eyes.

"I scored big time," Boyi said, "what an ass, couldn't keep my hands off her."

Sandy gave him the look that meant, 'Gross.'

Boyi continued, "Ready to go, Soso? Let's bounce".

He said his goodbyes as he headed out of the door. Boyi suggested they stop for burgers in the CBD at a 24 hour KFC, in a bustling Point Road. The hookers loitered in the streets, as the drunkards frolicked with them like they were playthings. After downing their meals, they jumped into the car and cruised along the Esplanade, on the harbour side, greeted by all the colours of the traffic lights. But before they exited the city, Boyi insisted that he pulled over. Boyi's eyes looked like a vulture's spotting a dead carcass. Boyi jumped out and crouched under his passenger seat, and then pulled out a small leather handbag. His stomach fell when he saw the shiny pistol inside.

Boyi winked at him and slid it under his jacket, and walked to the traffic lights a short distance away. The Jaguar, white as snow, had just pulled up, idling. Boyi pulled out the gun, like a seasoned shooter, and aimed it at the driver's window.

"Get out, I said out," Boyi said with loathing in his voice.

Boyi dragged out the driver, a tubby man, shoved him to the ground, slammed the door behind him and then took off in the Jag. Sosobala tailed him closely. On the way, he turned on the radio, anxiety eating him as he changed between stations, impatient, and then switched it off. Boyi sped into the quiet snaking roads of Umlazi until he stopped at the house in the north of Umlazi.

"It's me. Are you up?" Boyi asked, pressing the intercom.

The gold plated aluminium gate engraved on the centre with

'THE DUKE', automatically slid open. A slender man appeared with eyes that could fill his face, beckoning them behind the high walls of his mansion. Excitement hovered over him just by looking at this double-storey house.

"I don't sleep," the slender man said, "money flies at night. Guess what, those who sleep never get to taste it."

He was envious of the man in a white silk robe with matching fluffy sleepers, glittering in gold.

Duke meant a member of the highest rank of nobility, and indeed that Duke was a member of the highest rank of the criminal underworld.

"Jaguar XKR, nice," Duke said, nodding. "Boyi, follow us, I'm driving with you. What's your name by the way?"

"Sosobala, but Soso will do," he said, overwhelmed. "You've got a beautiful house. It'd put to shame some of the houses in the suburbs."

"I always say, Soso right? Why move to the suburbs," Duke said, his big eyes wandering, "when the township has so much to offer."

"You're right, don't know why we don't think like you."

Boyi tailed them until the drop-off point in Isipingo Hills.

"Wait for me here," Duke said. "I won't be long."

He jumped into the Jag and drove away like it was his own.

"That's going to be our ticket to good life now," Boyi said.

"We'll get killed doing the hijacking thing, you know that, right?" Soso said.

"People die every day, Soso. You'd even hide under a rock, but when your time's up, there's no cheating death," Boyi said.

He had nodded shyly as the car headlights approached and Duke had alighted.

"Let's go home, boys," Duke said, chuffed. "If you'd bring me more of these, I tell you, you'll make a killing."

They drove back to Duke's home. In the driveway, Duke pulled out an envelope from his robe front pocket. Duke counted out thirty thousand grand in crisp hundred rand notes, and took his own split of ten grand.

"Here's your share, boys," Duke said, jumping out of the car. "Go home now, by this afternoon, the Jag will be crossing the border gates to Zambia."

Duke winked and walked on as if the aluminium gates sensed its master. Twenty grand split two ways amounted to a cool ten grand each, tax free. What he earned at Transco in a month was not even half of what he had made in one night. Boyi split the spoils like a kid who had just learnt to read, 'That's yours, this is mine. Yours, mine.'

Fear and excitement all bundled together as he sensed a new life was on the cards. And that was how being acquainted with Duke led to the birth of their gang, CMB—Cash Money Brothers.

* * *

His eyes flickered in the darkness thinking their lives had taken an unexpected turn. He felt the stomach cramps again, and his eyes heavy; he dozed off.

Clink.

"Breakfast." the voice sounded, the plate and tea skidded inside and then silence.

The smell of solitary had become a familiar stench in his nostrils. That time around, he guzzled his tea like it was spring water that flowed on some exotic island (Who was it who'd noted that?) and ate his porridge and bread with vigour.

As he slid his plate out, he stretched a bit. Their new prospects of making money frightened him, so he had gone and seen a sangoma. It was on a chilly afternoon that he navigated his car until dust lingered in the air like smoke at the wooden gates of the homestead in Umbumbulu, the south of Durban. Ndosi—a tubby sangoma with a pot belly—communicated with the ancestors and gave him muti and a lion tooth necklace made of bright beads, with powers to protect and bring him wealth in his new prospects. He had been startled by Boyi as he urged him to go and see a sangoma too. Boyi laughed it off, saying he did not believe in the sangoma or God for that matter, he made his own destiny.

Clink.

"Lunch."

Sosobala tossed and turned on the mattress after ignoring his lunch, thinking how much it would mean just to have a tiny conversation with another person, or enjoy fresh air. But solitary became darker and quieter. The effects of his grumbling stomach had not subsided as he rolled off the mattress to spew another pile. He leaned on the toilet seat, feeling dizzy and drained.

He had felt that same way, dizzy and drained the night when the CMB had decided to christen his first debt-free taxi at the shopping centre's parking lot, in the west of his neighbourhood. By the time the owl hooted, the celebration was in full swing. A VW Golf GTI, as pink as the flamingo, an unusual colour for a car, parked a few metres away with two forms entangled in the front. And then a beefy man alighted with a fearless look as he charged towards them.

"Fuck off from here, I'm not asking you," the beefy man said. "You hear me? I parked here first for peace and quiet."

"What? It's you who must move your jalopy if you think we're disturbing you," Boyi said.

He and Soso were both intoxicated. The beefy man brandished his gun.

"Split or else?" the beefy man insisted, striding arrogantly back to his jalopy.

"Fuck off," Boyi said over the music. "Or else what, tough guy?"

The beefy man turned, and pounced at Boyi. Seeing his friend overpowered, Sosobala entered the fray, and the three of them ended up wrestling on the tarmac. He was very strong, as they rolled back and forth on the tarmac. The beefy man pulled out his revolver again. Boyi ducked out of the way whilst he wrestled the hand with a gun with every ounce of his strength. And then the gun went off.

Bang.

Sosobala felt dizzy and drained as the beefy man's body writhed next to him. His heart throbbed, and the blood clogged his brain like an inflated water balloon. Boyi screamed his name and hauled him up as they dived into the car, tyres screeching and vamoosed.

Pain, anger and sadness, piled up all at once, realising it could have been him lying on the tarmac in a pool of blood.

Duke had been helpful in making that case go away without it even reaching the courts. Furthermore, Duke found out that the deceased was a younger brother of the notorious leader, Sgola of the Dube gang from KwaMashu, in the north of Durban. The Dube gang were made infamous by the ambush of the KwaMashu Police Station where arms were stolen, leaving carnage behind. To avoid gang wars, Duke had facilitated a meeting with a recently released jail bird, Sgola. But to his surprise, Sgola reiterated that prison had changed him; he was no longer a killer, but the child of God.

* * *

Sosobala sat up, perspiring, and breathing heavily realising that the night Madubula was raped and stabbed, that could have been him stabbed to death in his futile attempt to help him. His heart beat uncomfortably thinking: What if, when he got out of solitary, Chopper was no more a killer but the child of God as well?

What if Chopper handed himself over and pleaded for his sudden release from solitary?

What if…

Sosobala pulled a stop on the brakes in his mind games knowing that Chopper was the devil's obedient son... he would be itching for his blood when he got out of solitary.

He stood up to stretch. His eyes itched, his throat itched, his mind itched, and so his butt. He screamed aloud, but solitary was dark and quiet. An immeasurable guilt ate him away for being a failure. He closed his eyes hoping he would not wake up and face guilt and failure ever again.

Clink.

"Breakfast."

Clink.

"Lunch."

Sosobala stared, his eyes dead, at the faintly shining light bulb: It hypnotised him. His supine figure went into spasms like a zombie in a horror movie. The sound of the clink, the baton tapping the steel door, for breakfast and lunch during the following days were like scratches on a video recorder tape, playing his pitiful recollections over and over again. Boyi's face appeared, sad and angry. He shivered pondering about how he failed him in the moment of need. That week played in his mind: The CMB had met at the shopping centre's parking lot.

"Gents, I got a tip-off for tomorrow, a bloody good one, to hit-down a microloan bank in Clairwood," Boyi said.

"Tell us more, my hustler," said Bonga, a gang member.

"The woman reckons it's about two-hundred grand in a safe," Boyi said, getting all worked up.

After Boyi painted a vivid picture of what was what, the CMB concluded it was like taking candy from a kiddies' store.

On that night it had begun to drizzle. The planned robbery was at eight o'clock the next morning. By then it was drizzling, with periodic peals of thunder. A worried frown on his forehead revealed his fears when the CMB came for him.

"The weather is bad. Let's postpone this for another time," he said, his stomach upset.

"Don't fret," Boyi said. "I'm here, Soso, trust me."

It was an affirmation of their true friendship that whatever he feared, Boyi would always come through for him. Bonga took the steering wheel as they headed to the would-be spot. His watch read seven thirty-nine. They surveyed the intended spot; it was sandwiched by old buildings in an L-shape comprised of factory clothing stores and motor spares.

"Let's not park too close," Boyi said.

Sosobala monitored the time: it was seven fifty-five, when his side mirror reflected two white males pulling out of a sedan. The original plan was that Boyi and he would pounce on them as soon as they fidgeted with the keys to open the glass door. He reminded himself, his worried frown revealed on his face.

"OK, go now," Bonga said.

As peals of thunder struck in succession, Sosobala felt his body heavy as if bound with chains. He took deep breaths, hoping the panic would recede.

But Boyi—gun in hand—hurtled himself towards the entrance. He blinked once as he suppressed the terror and followed on his hooves. They slunk towards the entrance and burst the glass door wide open. The thunder struck with a loud crash just then. He panicked, covering his eyes and ears.

"Dammit."

Half way through Boyi emitted a girly squeak realising there was a solid locked gate that could not be shaken even by Samson.

"We're being robbed, take cover," a voice said.

Sosobala froze in place when Boyi called for him to make a sudden retreat.

"Come on. Soso, let's bounce," Boyi said, shoving him from behind.

But then a volley of bullets flew their direction. He clenched his jaws and kicked up his legs, and then the terror broke as Boyi shoved him hard. Boyi covered him, firing back whilst he made his way out of the door. As he flew out, he heard a shriek. Behind, Boyi had taken a dive. He called for him to help, but the thunder struck once more, paralysing him. Bonga reversed towards him, pulling him inside the car, and sped off.

"No, don't leave him, go back!" he said.

"That hustler's dead, you hear me? Forget about him," Bonga said.

Sosobala sank in the seat, shrilling and moaning like a heart-broken widow under the full golden moon. Who was it who'd implied that?

"Damn," Bonga said. "We need to get you to a hospital."

"No, no hospitals, the police—" he said, voice fading.

"I know a nurse, don't worry," Bonga said, suppressing his own panic.

"Boyi, my friend." he faded into unconsciousness.

Clink.

The steel door opened.

3

FACE-TO-FACE WITH THE DEMON

"Come. Let's go," the voice said in an Afrikaans accent. "Don't have all day, sonny."

The voice sounded like the captain's, the loony, who released him from jail after a wrongful arrest. It all played out like an action movie in slow motion.

It was a breezy Thursday morning. Sosobala decided to surprise his mother with a load of groceries that could feed the village. The terrace of his neighbourhood, west of Umlazi, comprised of red-brick four-roomed houses, with an exception of the few that were plastered and painted. It had inner roads snaking to the main Mangosuthu Highway like different streams meandering into a lake. Across the terraced slopes, just a short distance away, lay crammed together an array of squatter shacks. Beyond that, there was a hillside with a view of other neighbourhoods also crowded with shack dwellers. Sosobala had pulled in up the short driveway of his home, a yellowish painted four-roomed house, sitting off the main road.

"Take me to church, will you? I'm late already," she said.

"What time does it start, Ma?" Soso asked.

"Nine o'clock. The pastor's look when you come late, tells a story."

His wrist watch read eight forty-five. He navigated the car and was soon at the gates of the church, in the east of the neighbourhood.

"God bless you, son," she said, chucking his cheeks.

He rushed to the shopping centre to meet with the CMB to discuss their new money-making scheme. A car pulled in next to him. What a stunner. A BMW M3, like the silver greyhound, with shiny rims. He had seen the eighteen inch rims on the cover of the car magazine.

"Nice glider," he said as the driver jumped out.

"It's my acquaintance's," Boyi answered. "Smooth ride, I tell you, Soso."

"A panty-dropper for sure," he said, mesmerised. "Where are you coming from?"

"In town, had things to do. You know, just stuff," Boyi said with a grin. "I'm in the mood to party tonight. Are you game? My treat."

Sosobala shook his head.

"You, but your pockets always have a lurking mamba somewhere," Sosobala said as they paced towards the entrance of the shopping centre.

Boyi had begun to recite his favourite lyrics, meaning he was loaded, from The Weather Girls: "It's raining men, Hallelujah, it's raining men… Amen."

Nevertheless they went out, and painted the town red after succumbing to his pestering for a night out. On the following morning, an uneasy feeling crept in while Sosobala listened to the radio news.

"Captain Jones of the Durban Serious Crimes and Prevention Unit is urging members of the public to come forward with information about a bank robbery that took place at the Westville Shopping Centre, where a bank teller was shot dead at the scene. You are requested to contact him on—" the voice of a news reader said.

Still feeling the effects of the previous night's partying, he leaned against the fridge drinking a cold, thirst quenching cider, burping. The way Boyi had dished out the crisp hundred rand notes left him with a lot of unanswered questions.

On that freezing Friday afternoon, he lounged on the couch in front of the TV, flicking from channel to channel. Boring, boring.

He grinned, thinking they should start screening porn on open channels, that way the TV would be fun to watch again. But then he was distracted by a hard knock on the front door. He skipped the couch as the playful kid in him jumped up to open the door.

"Boyi."

Boyi gave him a high five. His friend looked very disturbed; his eyes swung back and forth like a pendulum.

"You okay, buddy?"

"Sure," Boyi said. "Need to go to my granny's house. I have to park this ride right now."

"OK, cool," Soso said, taking a quick peek at his wrist watch. "But I've got to be at the shopping centre by two o'clock. Sandy's coming to do her hair at the salon."

"I owe you one," Boyi said.

They dropped the stunner and then rushed to the salon at the shopping centre for his appointment. The cars in the parking lot were conspicuous by their absence on that day. Sandy emerged soon afterwards.

A cool breeze coupled with her vanilla scent ushered through the salon's double glass door as she stepped in. She looked ultra-cool with the beach bag, as red as a rose petal, adding an extra touch of class.

"Hey, Sandy," he said, flitting from the waiting room couch to hug her.

"Hey, honey," she said, excitement sparkling in her eyes. "After I'm done doing my hair, ditch your friend, me and you have an unfinished business. OK?"

He moaned, pleading with the bulge in his crotch to behave. Her finished hairdo: a Mohawk style, accentuated her heart shaped face and round brown eyes.

"She looks wow," Linda, the salon owner, said. "If I wasn't batting for the other team, I'd sure snatch her away from you, Soso."

"Yeah right," he said, and laughed.

"I'll walk you to the car," Boyi said. "The way she's looking, you need a bodyguard."

Sandy massaged his hands while they strolled to the parking lot, Boyi lagging behind. Then the sirens wailed, the flashing blue lights illuminated the indigo sky, and the car tyres screeched to a halt. The smell of burning rubber—the tyres—lingered in the air. A heavily armed squad hurtled towards them like wolves pouncing on a fragile rabbit. Passers-by stood, watching in disbelief.

"No," Sandy screamed.

"Get down. I said down on your knees," a loud voice commanded.

Sandy's hands tightened on his. The sea of police cars in the parking bays, parked facing in different directions. Some with tinted windows, unmarked, and others marked.

"Down on your knees, now," the voice persisted.

If ever there was a time, he could have just begged for the earth to swallow him, it was in that surreal moment. His eyes searched, and found those of Captain Jones with a devious grin.

The captain's black pupils showed no emotions like the eyes of a crocodile. Sosobala's bladder weakened and in mere seconds, and he stained the crotch of his fashionable jeans, as blue as the deep ocean. Time stood still, his mind racing to the Indian Ocean, back to the Atlantic Ocean, then to Timbuktu. Boyi and Sandy were already on their knees as if praying for sanity to prevail. The men in blue pounced on him as if the movie director had screamed "Action!" through a megaphone. His body felt as if pricked with needles whilst being subjected to a brutal search. He came back to his senses when Sandy was whisked away in a sedan.

"Sandy," he said, voice gurgling, the sound hanging in the air like cheap perfume.

"Stay away from these thugs, they're bad news," a policeman inside the sedan said. "I'll drop you off at the taxi rank."

Sandy nodded, shaken, her body in a sedan but the mind wandering at the shopping centre's parking lot.

"Found anything in the car?" Captain Jones asked.

"Nope, it's clean, sir," the assistant replied sharply.

"Take them away boys, need them put in separate vans," the captain said, "we have a long day ahead of us."

The handcuffs almost crushed his tender wrists. Even his ego had been bruised as he was shoved into the back of the van. Boyi was thrown like a sack of potatoes into another van.

Had any of the car hijacking schemes been uncovered? He rattled his brain.

The police van took off at high speed, tossing him around and into all four corners of a mobile cage. It had been a few minutes' drive, as the convoy pulled in and stopped at a secluded area dotted with mobile offices. His mood on that day switched like a flip of the coin. Strong hands dragged him out and shoved him into a room, and then un-cuffed him. He occupied a dimly lit empty office.

"Where the fuck am I?" he whispered into empty space.

Through a tiny tinted window, he spotted his car parked on the far right side of the entrance. But then some more vehicles pulled in. Out of one of them Boyi jumped and was taken into the room next door. Voices and footsteps stomped towards the room like a street band in a parade. A door opened, its hinges creaking. His body cringed as he assumed it was for him, but it was the door to the room next door. Time stood still as he wondered: What has become of Sandy?

The policeman, the kind who looked like a brick shy of a load escorted Boyi into another office block, opposite his. The screams sounded, then stopped for a while, and resumed in a higher pitch. It was Boyi's voice pulling a high note like Pavarotti, maybe even better than him. The weather was cold, but sweat burst out of his pores, from head to toe as if locked up in a hot oven. Suddenly a BMW M3 pulled in, the same stunner Boyi had parked previously at his granny's house.

What did that glider, and them, have in common? His mind froze.

The oncoming footsteps sounded with a choking man. His stomach churned as the door knob turned, the door pulling wide open. Boyi was thrown in like a rotten apple into a bin, his rag-doll figure thudding on the floor. The policeman called him out, his look intimidating.

"You're next my boy, come."

Like an abandoned kid he shuffled towards the door, looked at Boyi, his lips smeared with blood as if he used lip gloss. It was a short walk to the door, but the spasms wracking his body made it feel like a journey of a thousand miles.

"Sorry, Soso," Boyi said, voice trembling.

"What's going on?" Soso asked.

The policeman pulled him out by his waist; he flew outside. In that moment, in mid-flight he remembered the rumours that created the captain's alias, 'The Loony.' That the captain tortured suspected criminals like they were prisoners of war. He tried to put on a brave face but it was like climbing Mount Kilimanjaro.

The room he was shoved into was small and smelt of shit, probably Boyi's. It had a small wooden chair and a wooden table; on top of it was an arm's length, wide elastic tube. There was also a bowl of water, and a long leather strap. There was another wooden chair where the captain rested his right foot. Very gigantic foot in suede ankle boots, a size eleven or twelve. The captain held a cigarette pinched in his right palm between thumb and forefinger.

"This is Bluff, sonny. In here, I'm the judge and the juror," Captain Jones said, his look becoming more disgusted at the sight before him. "You scumbags are going to tell me: Where is the money?"

The word 'money' lingered in his mind when he was on the floor, tasting blood in his mouth. The captain had thrown a hard slap at him in those few seconds he was trying to compose himself. The Loony ground his suede ankle boots hard into his neck, almost choking the life out of him.

"Tell me, where's the money?" the captain asked.

The captain let up on the pressure for a few seconds as he regained his breath, and then shoved him up by his throat onto the chair.

"I don't know, I'm telling the truth, captain," he said, coughing, long enough to stir the fury in the captain's eyes: dark like a killer shark's.

"Why bloody kill an innocent bank teller in cold blood, you piece of shit?" the captain asked.

"This scumbag thinks he's tough, sir," the assistant said.

"Strip his bloody top off," the captain said.

"No, captain," Sosobala said like a schizophrenia experimenting with words.

In the blink of an eye, his t-shirt came out, and then his prostrate form tossed on the table.

"Bloody hold him, you hear me?" the captain said, his tone feisty.

"No, I beg of you," Soso said.

The captain took a leather strap, and he whipped his back. It seemed like eternity, riding the pain as if a monkey had scrubbed his back with a wire brush.

His screams and moans lingered in the air like a light fog, while his flesh was torn by each stroke of the leather strap.

"You're ready to talk, hey, about the Westville bank robbery you scumbags pulled?" the captain said.

The 'Westville bank robbery' words choked him like a loaf of stale bread shoved down his throat.

"I don't know anything about the—" he said, voice clipping.

The captain continued whipping across his back, and eventually lost consciousness and tumbled to the floor.

"He's a tough nut to crack," the assistant said.

"It won't be bloody long, now," the captain said, his grin devious.

The cold water baptised him, slowly regaining consciousness. The assistant shoved him back on the chair.

"Tell me about the bank robbery you pulled on Thursday morning at the Westville shopping centre," the captain said each word with a pause.

Has the captain's fury transformed him into an idiot or something?

"I'd nothing to do with the robbery. Ask m' mother, on that day I drove her to church around nine," he said, voice trembling.

"So, if it's not you, then who did, tell me?" the captain asked, throwing hard slaps.

Sosobala had been left dazed, hearing drums beating in his head like the sound of drum majorettes parading on the streets.

"I don't—" he said, forcing the words out of his throat.

"You don't want to talk, hey?" the captain said. "Grab him."

The captain put a wide elastic tube around his face and tightened it. He suffocated, kicked and wrestled like a writhing snake in a cage. He kissed the floor, hello. In a timeless bubble, voices entered the room. They conversed for a while with the captain, and then vanished.

"Get dressed, today's your lucky day. Take him away," an annoyed captain said as he emptied the bowl of water over him.

"Why are we stopping, sir?" the assistant asked.

"His mother confirmed his story; he was at home when the bloody robbery took place," the captain said.

Sosobala was in dreamland, but he heard the captain uttering those words. The assistant tossed him his t-shirt, and pulled him out in a huff. He and Boyi were shoved back into the van and whisked away. He recognised the Umlazi police station as they entered its gates. They were taken to the holding cells, and then spent the night there.

"Why didn't you tell me about this job?" he asked, feeling the chilly night breeze on the spume mattress.

"Eish, Soso," Boyi said. "These guys roped me in as a getaway driver. It was a quick job, I tell you, didn't know they'd popped somebody's skull in there."

"Do I know these guys?" Sosobala asked, his tone growing more suspicious. "From where?"

"Don't know if you know them. They're the former MK soldiers," Boyi said, "from the hostel in T section."

"Dammit. You became acquainted with those hot-headed killers? I know them," Sosobala said, annoyed. "How could you be so stupid?"

"The morning of the robbery, I bumped into them at the shopping centre," Boyi said, shrugging. "Their driver didn't pitch, so they offered me a fifty-fifty split."

"You're lucky they didn't put a bullet in your head, and dispose of you," Sosobala said.

If ever there was a gang he played very far from them, it was the former MK soldiers from the hostel in T section, the south of the neighbourhood. They killed for fun, and even the cops were easy targets for them.

"So you told the captain everything?"

"I had to, you see, the elastic tube was the final straw for me," Boyi said, his look filled with shame. "The captain made me a deal, you know."

"In exchange for what exactly?" Soso asked.

"My freedom for testifying against them," Boyi said.

"So what, you took it?"

Boyi nodded and said, "I love money, not blood."

The night spent in the holding cell was very cold and seemed longer than usual as the captain came past the cell in the morning.

"Come. Let's go," the captain said, and tossed him his car keys, as the cell gate opened. "Don't have all day, sonny."

He exited the police station like a 100 metres sprinter unsure whether the captain would change his mind. During that day, he went to his mother's. He reckoned he would see Sandy afterwards. The west side of his neighbourhood had not changed that much, as he reached home. It still had a mixture of painted and redbrick four-roomed houses with no yards, and no fences. He entered the kitchen door, and his eyes met with those of his mother busy doing the dishes. She had a despondent look. He sensed her mixed emotions.

"What's got into you, hey?" she asked with a frown. "Neighbours are gossiping about your arrest."

"I can explain, Ma," he said.

"So it's the truth, you and Boyi, being gangsters, just like the rumours are flying around here?" she asked.

He realised that she could not understand even if he tried to explain his way of living. The sweet obedient boy she raised was gone like a silver coin hidden under the dark waters. That hard truth would dilute the mother's love with venom if it shot out through his mouth.

"No, it's all a lie, Ma," he said. "On that day it was a case of a mistaken identity. That's why the police had to confirm it with you, and release me the next day."

"Your father brought you up to be a good man, to live with integrity, and take responsibility for your actions, okay?"

"I know, Ma," he said, protesting as he changed the subject. "Need anything, like groceries or money?"

"The vegetables are almost finished," she said, opening the vegetable rack. "Oh and the utility bill has gone up, again, this month."

"Don't fret about that, I'll take care of it, Ma."

His mother was now a bit calm than before as he headed to see Sandy. She must have been livid and confused about the recent unfolding events. He pulled in at the parking and paced briskly to her residence, the Mabes. He tapped on her door, anxiety stomping on his every nerve. She opened and her face had a look of disdain coupled with a 'what the fuck are you doing here pose.'

"What do you want?" She blocked the doorway.

"Can I come in at least?"

"What for," she asked with a grim look, tapping her chest, "so you'll just bring more drama into my life?"

"Let me explain, will you?"

"I should've seen this coming, the taxis, your new dress code, the company of friends you hang-out with," she said, "it was all written in bold letters. How could I have been so stupid?"

"You're wrong about this, you know," he said.

"No, I'm not, don't insult my intelligence, Soso," she said like a lizard ready to strike. "I can't have a life where every time I'd get nasty surprises, with wicked looking policemen and their big guns harassing me. No, I damn well don't want that life."

"At least give me a chance to explain what happened," he said, his look and tone hopeless.

She was pumped up for a good reason though.

"Boyi mixed with the wrong crowd, and got involved in a bank robbery. I wasn't involved, OK, the police know that. Boyi will be released soon, well if he cooperates with them," he said, his eyes growing more intense. "I love you, Sandy Gumede."

"I know. Why do you think I'm with you? Money or no money," Sandy said, and shook her head, arms crossing over her chest, "but after this, really don't know, Soso."

"We belong together, Sandy, I know it, and you know it too."

"Let me think this through, okay? My heart says yes, but my mind's saying something else."

He planted a kiss on her forehead, and dashed out of her room. He jumped into his car, and cruised back to his neighbourhood in Umlazi. That day was about damage control with the two most important women in his life.

* * *

His eyes opened as he pulled himself up and shuffled out of the solitary. He gasped for air, confused. Like a puppet on strings, he shuffled feebly past the guardhouse reaching the steel gate of his cell. The cell Chopper controlled as if all the inmates were just puppets for him to play with, or dispose of. The warder fidgeted with the keys, and it opened wide.

"Get in," the warder said, and checked his watch. "It's almost time for breakfast."

He took his first step in, warily glanced at the hall like a kid trying to locate a friendly face on the first day at school. It all came back flooding towards him like an avalanche ripping through the forest: The empty bed... the smell of Madubula's blood... Chopper's satanic smile that could set fire to a thousand forests. Who was it who'd said that? And Madubula's writhing body, like he was a wounded snake. His legs became numb when his eyes locked with that of Chopper.

Just like a soldier who had gone AWOL, was then apprehended to face the music. His breathing became heavy, and he constructed a brave face even though he sensed it would crack soon. He shuffled with a slow gait like an old donkey pulling a wagon, until he reached his bed. He sat on the bed, hands on his thighs, head bowed. The cell was quiet like that night of the rape. Yet if its walls can talk, it could dish out dirt that could pollute the river.

How was Madubula recuperating in hospital, maybe he would be there a month or so? he wondered.

"You're back, moth'fucker," a voice said with a look that said, 'You thought you'd hide from me.'

Sosobala lifted his head, and looked at the skinny man at an arm's length from him in an orange prison uniform that looked like it was hung on his body.

"Chopper," Sosobala said as if gagging.

In front of him stood the man who put fear in everybody, fearless and untouchable. He shook his head, gingerly.

"At the chambers, now," Chopper said, spitting on the linoleum.

His constructed brave face cracked in a flash when Chopper with a swaggering, slow and intimidating, don't-mess-with-me rolling gait, took to the far end corner of the cell—the chambers.

Fear and uncertainty lingered in the air as he tried to pull himself up. It felt like he was carrying a ton of bricks. His eyes instantly brimmed with tears as he remembered the incident where a soldier challenged Chopper's authority. A ring had been formed by crouching soldiers in the prison uniforms, as orange as the desert sunset. And a knife, made of melted plastic cutlery and sharpened, was placed in the centre of the ring. Chopper stood in the middle of the ring, half-naked, like Jesus on a cross, and summoned the guilty soldier to come forward.

"You've two choices, moth'fucker," Chopper said. "Pick up the knife, and see what you do with it?"

Sosobala had wondered shaken about what was the second choice.

"Or I take it, and carve you like wood," he had added with a devious grin.

The guilty soldier tried to reach for the knife, but Chopper overpowered him, and pinned him down.

Chopper was livid, like a tow-truck driver stuck in the mud, as he grabbed the knife and sliced him like he was a tenderised steak. The guilty soldier's screams were drowned out by their singing of the revolutionary songs and the hard clapping. Blood spurted in hot streams onto Soso's face and uniform. The guilty soldier had been left in the centre of the ring, his stomach cut open, and his intestines wriggling like a burnt rubber.

Sosobala crouched feebly in the chambers, shivers running down his spine, his eyes locked on the centre of the ring pondering the knife. He had only a few weeks before his parole review. And after what would happen there, his chances of making it alive were nil. Chopper summoned him to the centre of the ring. He swayed and stood in there like a cripple. Body spasms took-over. His face muscles tightened; he clutched his jaws. If his teeth were ice, they would have been crushed by then.

"Are you a soldier or what, moth'fucker?" Chopper asked, building up momentum, "yes... no?"

"I am a soldier," Sosobala said, his gut shrinking.

Chopper spat on the linoleum once, and then twice, anxiously nodding. The exhaled breath emitted by the crouching soldiers in the ring caused his whole body to melt.

"What then possessed you to challenge me?" Chopper said, pointing at him with the 26 gang sign.

Sosobala averted his gaze like a dog caught eating the neighbour's chicken in its coop.

"Answer me," Chopper said, "you're that sky-bird's ass-kisser, or what?"

Fright flickered in his eyes as Chopper took a few steps closer to the knife. Déjà vu, Sosobala wanted to dive for the knife first, but froze.

"I'm talking to you, moth'fucker," Chopper said, letting out steam.

The sweat flowed over his body like a waterfall splashing down cold rocks on a desert island. He counted the minutes before his life might end, all for trying to help a cocky young inmate. Every shuffle towards the knife that Chopper made, trimmed seconds off his life. The same life he would give his all to build a future with the woman he adored, Sandy. That life he would trade his own for his late father. He lifted his eyes, and they met with that of the one-eyed man, crying for blood.

"Pick up the knife, moth'fucker," Chopper said, stretching his Jesus in a cross stance, topless.

Chopper had a tattooed skinny body with scars all over it as if his upper body was an old patched curtain hung in a ghost house. Who was it who'd teased people about that? The tattoos were all his kills represented by different playing cards.

His attention shifted to the knife on the linoleum, like a hungry pauper glancing at a piece of succulent steak on a dirty floor. He weighed his options, like the last soldier, who had ended up dead. His muscles became taut. His teeth grated, and tears trickled down his cheeks to the corner of his lips. Maybe he would be lucky and stab Chopper first... maybe not, paralysed with fear, anger and sadness all in equal amounts.

The first days Sosobala had entered the prison, he had made a vow never to die without a fight. In that eerie moment, his vow would be tested to the limits. He inhaled once, and then dived for the knife.

"Grab this moth'fucker," Chopper said, advancing towards him.

The lieutenants pounced on him and restrained him. They shoved him back up. The plastic knife fell on the linoleum, next to the spittle. Sosobala glanced at the fallen knife, pity written in his eyes. It was his only hope of fighting to live another day. He tried to break free but the lieutenants' buff figures made it impossible for him to achieve that. Chopper laughed demonically as he lifted the knife and toyed with it.

"Look around you, moth'fucker," Chopper said. "This is my house, I run this place. Not the warders, but me. Whatever I say goes."

He stood a mere inch away from Sosobala. Chopper's demonic laughter quickly turned into a crazed shriek as he clenched the knife tight and lifted it.

Clink.

The steel gate unlocked.

"Breakfast," said the warder as he entered the cell, and threw his glance to the far end. "What's going on there?"

"Nothing, Vader," Chopper said as he hid the knife and stepped away from Sosobala.

Sosobala let loose a small amount of pee, painting his crotch amber. His heart skipped a beat as he thanked his lucky stars.

"It ain't over, moth'fucker," Chopper said, following with a gob of spittle into his face.

4

FIGHTING OFF THE GANG MEMBER

Sosobala walked in formation going to the cafeteria. His eyes and ears alert like that of a werewolf. Everybody kept their distance from him like he had been dipped in a pigsty. His head swung like a yo-yo. The smell of Chopper's gob of spittle into his face was still raw in his mind. How could a one-eyed man put so much fear in everybody? He wondered. Even the warders gave orders to Chopper from a distance.

A story had made headline news, years before Sosobala was imprisoned. It detailed the killing of a white farmer and his five family members from Shongweni, west of Durban. The sentence imposed by the judge, of five life sentences for the first-degree murders, four hundred years for rape, ten years for house-breaking, and fifty years for animal cruelty, was unprecedented. A local newspaper front page showed a headline, 'One-eyed Man Choppers The Farmer's Family.'

The article caught his attention as he read the story:

A farmer and his five family members were killed in a Shongweni farm on New Year's Eve. The police spokesperson, Brigadier Vicky Didi said, "A man in his thirties was arrested in Shongweni on new year's eve after the patrolling security personnel alerted the police of a suspiciously looking man in the area. The police found bloodied axe and stolen goods in the man's possession. After questioning, the alleged murderer led them to a farmhouse, a hundred feet away. The police discovered the body of a Caucasian man in his fifties, in the kitchen, disembowelled. After combing the farmhouse, they then discovered four more bodies: A woman in her fifties, and three young girls, between the ages of ten and fifteen, in the main bedroom, all chopped to death. Their private parts were smeared with a yellowish substance. A dog, a bullterrier, was later discovered in the closet of a second bedroom, hanged with a ski rope. The suspect was taken into custody in the Pinetown police station. He will be charged with five counts of murder, four counts of rape, one count of housebreaking with intent to rob, and one count for animal cruelty. And he will appear in the Pinetown Magistrate's Court on Wednesday for his first court appearance."

A 'Bring Back the Death Penalty' lobby group's president, Mr. Van Wyk, expressed shock in the way the farmer and his family were killed.

"This senseless killing epitomises what we as the 'Bring Back the Death Penalty' lobby group has been campaigning for, all these years. The only way our criminal justice system can send a strong message to the perpetrators of such violent acts of crime, is to bring back the death penalty," said Mr. Van Wyk.

Shongweni prides itself for hosting exclusive polo events. The distraught neighbour of the slain family, Mrs. Koekemoer said, "The Venters were such lovely people, even their dog, Spook, a darling. My husband and I have resided here for forty long years. The Venters moved in about five years later, in a farm, just across the stream. We're terrified of living here now. If such a gruesome killing can happen in this area, you know what, it means we're all not safe. How can a human being do this to another human being? It's absolute madness. I hope the law enforcement act swiftly and bring the perpetrator to book."

Captain Jones of the Durban Serious Crimes and Prevention Unit has been assigned as the investigating officer to this case. He is urging the members of the public to come forward with information that could assist in solving this case speedily.

Could Chopper be the murderer that the article had referred to? Was that the reason why everybody feared him? The footsteps of the convicts and the warders' boots going to the cafeteria were like a band beating a drum in his chest.

In the cafeteria, Chopper and his lieutenants took a seat on a first row bench after collecting their meals. They were seated near the exit. Fear creased his forehead. He rushed to collect his meal, and took a seat alone in the centre row, far away from the entrance. He wondered where Madubula used to sit. Guilt resurfaced for failing him. His eyes swivelled back and forth, his right hand feeling for the slices of bread while his left hand rubbed uneasily on his twitching thighs. His meal had less than the usual amount of porridge, and there was only one slice of bread, not the usual two. He looked with contempt at the cooks. Their faces dripped sweat on their white aprons. So what, everybody was against him now?

The smell of porridge and bread were refreshing in his nostrils. It was as if his sense of smell and taste buds had been suppressed for decades in solitary. He lifted his one slice, took a few quick bites and a long sip at the cold tea.

"What're you fuckin' doing, man?" Sosobala said, caught off-guard.

His porridge had spittle floating on it. He turned to find the source of the spit. He exhaled deeply. It was one of Chopper's lieutenants standing mere inches away. He took him in, quivering like a wet dog: he was buff with a scar crossing his left bloodshot eye.

Sosobala searched for Chopper. He found him staring cynically as if implying, 'I told you moth'fucker I run this place.' His heart pounded in his chest like the horse racing hooves. His stomach churned remembering that that lieutenant had also been involved in Madubula's rape.

"Eat it now, bitch," the lieutenant said.

Sosobala shook his head in disbelief, his eyes misty and his lips twitching.

"Fuckin' no, I won't," Sosobala said as if gargling with vinegar.

The lieutenant snatched up the porridge in a flash, and plastered it on his face. Anger, fear, and sadness all in equal measure cut through his heart like a speeding train pulling out of a subway station. The lieutenant had a smirk on his face. Sosobala perspired, fast, like a racing cyclist.

The last time he had been livid beyond his wildest imagination played in his mind like it was yesterday. It had been a dull afternoon, as they slumped in the couches, him and Bonga, days after Boyi's death.

He had stared, his gaze blank, at the TV set whilst sedated by pain killers. There were no police knocking at his door for questioning, and the swelling was subsiding.

"I've not seen this movie in ages," Bonga said. "What's the movie called again?"

"It was Boyi's old time favourite movie, 'Scarface,' by Al Pacino," Sosobala pointed out, saddened.

But then a forceful tap rapped at the front door. Who could it be, he was not expecting anybody? Bonga stood up and asked through the door, "Who is it?"

"It's me, please, open up," a voice said.

"Don't you have a name?" Bonga said, arrogantly pacing towards the window, a few inches away from the door. He twitched the curtain and peeped through. And then he opened the door wide.

The figure with drooping shoulders slumped in the doorway, stunned. It shuffled in with a slow frightened gait, arms crossed over the chest, and the face purple. His eyes bulged... his jaw nearly hitting the floor. He sprang off the couch. A nasty draught sneaked in causing a chill in his spine.

"What happened, who did this to you?" Sosobala said, spitting fire like a dragon wanting to scorch the village.

The petite figure tugged her torn white shirt into the bottom of her black skirt. He pulled her close, and gave her a tight squeeze.

"It's going to be alright, promise," Sosobala said, freaking out.

Sadness flooded his eyes as he glanced at the door, and then back at her. He wanted answers to the thousands of questions that surfaced in his racing mind: How? Who? Where? When? He ushered her to the couch and took a lingering look at her round eyes, as brown as the forest flood, shadowed with darkness.

"The bastard raped me," she said, choking on her words as she hid her face with her hands.

He listened, upset, as she stumbled through the circumstances that led to her rape.

"He bumped into me this morning in the shopping centre, coming to see you, to tell you—" she said, tears trickled down like steam condensing on a window pane. "The bastard lied to me, baby. He said you were at the Executive Hotel."

The Executive Hotel was the only hotel in Umlazi, and it was central to all the neighbourhoods, their occasional hang-out.

"The next thing," she clutched her body, "we're in some room. I tried to fight, baby, God knows I tried, but the bastard overpowered me."

Sosobala embraced her like a father would his heartbroken daughter. She was too emotional and frightened to go on.

"Talk to me, baby, who fuckin' did this?" Sosobala asked, feeling an inflating balloon of mixed emotions.

"Si—" her voice tore apart. "Sifiso, raped me."

Sosobala's eyes darkened as he imagined Sifiso in his bright baggy clothes, the heavy gold chain around the neck looking as if he was a chained pit-bull. But above all that, at the way he walked: a swaggering, 'don't mess with me' jailhouse roll... mocking him. Blood clogged his brain, nearly bursting out of his nose. He called on Bonga to accompany him; and he obeyed without thinking twice. Sosobala pulled out his gun, hidden in a pot plant next to a TV stand. He tucked it under his waistband as they headed for the door. The words 'Sifiso, raped me' caused a veil to cover his eyes.

"Please, baby, don't do anything stupid," Sandy said, darting in front of him.

He decided to leave her behind but she refused, not wanting to be alone. He sped through the sharp bends of his neighbourhood's winding roads, with Bonga in the front passenger seat, and Sandy in the rear.

"Where are we going to now?" she asked.

"The hotel, Sandy," Soso said with loathing flashing in his brown eyes.

He pulled in and stopped at the front entrance of the hotel. The tyres burnt rubber onto the tarmac surface, and the black smoke soared into the air. The hotel was a five storey architectural design, constructed with grey face brick. Just like any other boutique hotel except that this is where it happened. They jumped out of the car and hurried to search that hotel room first. He held back the need to retch when he saw a thick yellowish substance on the sheets. The bastard must have had the time of his life, his dead eyes glared. Where could he be? He wondered as they exited the hotel. A familiar figure strolled in at the hotel lobby with a woman. Another one of his victims. He recalled the saying, 'Destiny has a strange way of luring mortals to face the consequences of their actions': Which philosopher was it who'd said that?

Before Sifiso could voice out any sound, they hurtled on him like wolves on a kudu, and dragged him to the parking lot, kicking and screaming.

"Bastard," Sandy said, screaming and hitting him.

She freaked out at the sight of Sifiso, reliving the trauma he had put her through.

"Help me," Sifiso said, trying to alert the hotel patrons.

Sosobala struck him with the butt of his gun, lifting it up and down like he was hammering in a nail through a concrete block. A skill his late father had taught him, in his childhood years, to nail portraits to the wall.

Sandy covered her face as blood spattered onto her face. And Bonga in his blond mop and colourful shirt blowing in the wind, stomped on Sifiso as if practicing tap dancing moves.

"No, please baby, he's got the message now," Sandy said. "I want to see him punished, but not like this. Take him to the police station, instead."

She ran to the car, hysterical, wiping her face as Sosobala was hearing none of it.

"Forgive me, Soso, my brother," Sifiso said, his voice echoing in the parking lot.

Sifiso tried to clutch on Sosobala but broke his lion tooth necklace. Its colourful beads scattered on the tarmac. Sosobala stared like a zombie at a kneeling Sifiso, arms raised sky high.

"Your lousy cries are falling on deaf ears," Bonga said.

Sosobala blinked once: a gunshot sounded, and then another one, and then another one, and then...

"He deserves it," Bonga said.

Sifiso's supine figure gushed blood from his forehead. Sosobala turned around, and the eyes of the passers-by and hotel patrons, glued at him with fear.

Like a hero in an action movie, instructed by the movie director to walk away with intense eyes after disposing of the villain, Sosobala jumped into the car and drove away like he owned the world. Silence was the order of the day on their way back. Nobody wanted to raise the issue of Sifiso. He tried to comfort Sandy and reassure her of his undying love for her. But the damage had been done from what she had seen, and the emotional scars she had endured. It would take some time for her to forget.

* * *

The taunting by the lieutenant continued when Sosobala snapped back to his senses.

"Sky-bird ass-kisser."

Being called a sky-bird ass-kisser was just like being insulted by your ex-wife's new hubby about the size of your manhood. His face tightened; he clenched his fists. His sweat broke into tiny particles, regulating his body, just like electrolytes. Who was it who'd made that discovery?

The lieutenant stood with a devious grin, his every part of the body mocking Sosobala. Each second that went by, so was his dignity, his pride, his manhood—tested to the limit. Sosobala lunged at him with no remorse or conscience. He lifted him up and slammed him on the linoleum. They wrestled, rolling up and down. Sosobala kicked and punched; the buff lieutenant was not backing down. He head-butted the lieutenant, choked him, but the lieutenant took it all in like it was just another day's work. The lieutenant caught him with a few shots of his own that rattled his brain. Blood ran from his nose. The warders' whistles blew, and the inmates roared with excitement. He found himself again, and finished off the lieutenant with a Mike Tyson pounding, and ear biting. Who was it who'd beaten people in that sequence?

Pree.

"I'm Soso, you fuckin' piece of shit, I'm not afraid of you," Sosobala said, over and again.

Pree.

The lieutenant was subdued, and left bloodied on the linoleum as he moaned like a wounded bull.

"Inmates, against the wall, now," the voice sounded through the speaker.

The heavily armed prison guards stomped in a rhythm like gumboot dancers, as they contained the situation. And then they pounced on him.

The exact moment when the captain and his heavily armed squad pounced on him, days after Sifiso's death resurfaced. And also the interrogation the captain put him through that made him comprehend how it felt like to be half-dead. It played out, scene after scene: Bonga borrowed his car, more like pleaded for it that afternoon. He dashed out of the living room as if somebody had shoved a hot iron rod up his ass. The next morning, the sun glinted off the house windows as he made himself breakfast. The aroma of the fresh bacon and eggs permeated the kitchen. He wondered why Bonga still hadn't returned his car. That whole day he stayed indoors, occasionally peeping through the curtain window whenever he heard something like a car sound. He grimly counted the events that had unfolded in his life, especially Sandy's relocation. Pavarotti's classical music eased the anxiety of Bonga's total disregard of his feelings, and the pain of losing Sandy. A knock sounded at his door as he was in his pyjamas making his bed, humming along with a high note. But the knocker continued aggressively. He headed to the living room. Probably just Bonga returning his car.

"Open up," a voice boomed.

He stopped in his tracks and felt his heart throbbing. He tiptoed to the window and twitched the curtain. His eyes bulged at the sight of men in blue. Others were in civilian clothes and carrying semi-automatic rifles, encircling his house like vultures converging on a dead carcass. Some even took cover on the neighbours' rooftops on both sides of the road, pointing their rifles at the windows of his house. A helicopter circled the area. He exhaled with a broken rhythm realising the captain could be behind the door. He pulled his bristly hair trying to come up with a plan. Within those seconds he circled the whole house trying to find an escape route. But the whole area was surrounded. He ran back to his bedroom and put on his jeans, as blue as the sky, and the t-shirt, thoughts racing. And then a loud bang sounded as he approached the living room. His eyes locked with that of the captain, his dark eyes staring at him like the eyes of an emotionless shark… his worst nightmare.

"Sosobaal," Captain Jones said.

"Captain—" he said, voice clipping.

He seemed frozen in place as the squad members pounced on him, making his lips kiss the floor… hello. The coldness of the tiles, very shiny, cooled his scorching body temperature. And the tightness of the handcuffs behind his back as they snatched him up again dampened his spirit. His breathing became deeper as he tried to swallow back his saliva whilst being frisked. If ever there was a time he could ask for the earth to open up and swallow him, it was on that precise moment.

"We bloody meet again, sonny," the captain said with a fake grin. "I warned you, didn't I?"

The squad members ransacked his place, leaving no stone unturned.

"Where is it, Sosobaal?" the captain asked. "You're going to tell me, like it or not."

"Don't know what you're looking for?" Sosobala said, chancing a gaze at him.

The captain was interested in finding one thing only… his gun. Why handover the same gun used to kill Sifiso?

"I've found something, sir," one policeman said, interrupting his thoughts.

His heart throbbed pondering the aftermaths of the policeman's 'I've found something, sir' words.

"Did you bloody find it?" the captain said, rushing to see.

"No captain, its cash under the couch," the policeman said, pointing at it.

The captain's sweaty palms sneaked the cash into his back pocket. It was the twenty grand that Sosobala's two taxis had made from that past week.

His other arrests resurfaced momentarily, but this time it felt different like his spirit was headed to a dark underworld.

"What I'm going to do to you", Jones had sniffed, "will bloody make death seem like a kiddy's play." He then ordered his squad to leave.

If ever the captain found his gun, it would spell the end of him. He would be flushed down the toilet. He was whisked away like a terrorist who had just killed the president. On either side of his shoulders, lofty police officers monitored his every step with their rifles pointed at him. The residents of his neighbourhood looked stunned, some clapped their hands, cheering, while others sneered at the police. He was shoved onto the floor in the rear of a sedan—blindfolded—and the police car took off at high speed.

Where was he taken? The driving took long minutes and then the cars stopped. Strong hands pulled him out of the car, and then removed his blindfold. He was escorted a short distance from the parking lot to the entrance. He passed the charge office on the left, with wriggling figures in blue behind the wooden counter. And then he was shoved along a long corridor, and down the stairways. He was at the Durban Central Police Station—the infamous CR Swart.

"No bloody visitors, or food for him, or even to use the toilet, am I clear?" Jones said.

The tiny dimly room he was thrown into carried the aroma of a decayed body. It had a small steel table and a steel chair in the centre. On the floor was a car battery with jumper cables and a bucket filled with water. And on the table, was a wide leather strap. The elephant footsteps came towards the room, and the door unlocked.

"It's going to be a bloody long night, boys," the voice said with a giggle.

He recognised an Afrikaans accent behind the door. It opened wide and its hinges shrieked. He shook in his pants, recalling his days at Transco. He cursed the day he had met an abusive Gordon Botha. He partly blamed, also partly praised Gordon for pushing him to a life of crime. If it had not been for Gordon, he would have passed his trade test and worked as an artisan. Maybe he would have been happier or maybe not.

He wondered why he was not born with a silver spoon in his mouth, why God had allowed him to cross paths with men like Gordon, why his childhood friend had been Boyi of all people, why he had fallen in love with Sandy, instead of... He had no immediate answers to all his questions. Sosobala accepted his unknown fate to be decided by Captain Jones—the Judge and the Juror.

"Sosobaal," the captain asked, "you're going to bloody talk or what?"

His look was sheepish when the captain sat on the edge of the steel table, while he crouched on the steel chair, and the captain's assistant leaned against the door.

"Bloody save time for all of us, will you, sonny?" the captain said, expelling deep breaths.

Sosobala raised his hands, warily, over his chest as the captain moved closer. His closeness gave off more heat than he could handle. The small room echoed as the captain smelt his nervousness. The captain's dark pupils under the faint bulb sent a shiver down to his crotch.

"Tell me about the bloody attempted micro-loan bank robbery in Clairwood?" the captain asked.

The worst was yet to come if Sosobala gave answers not appeasing to the captain.

"Don't know anything about it," Sosobala said.

"So it wasn't CMB, your bloody gang, who attempted it?" the captain asked, faking a grin. "You're trying to make me a mampara?"

Before he could purse his lips, the captain's right hook sent him flying, hugging the floor.

"Captain, I'll talk," Sosobala said, shrinking like burnt rubber, and smelling like it too.

"Bloody talk then, I'm waiting," Jones said.

The assistant's firm grip shoved him back on the steel chair. He kept his weight more centred on his feet, just in case.

"It was Boyi and his other gang that attempted the micro-loan bank robbery," Sosobala said, evoking the dead to come to his rescue.

"And you were not involved, right?" the captain asked, his face a mere inch away from him.

Sosobala pulled back a bit, but the back of the chair made it known to him that it was the end. The captain grinned, and unbuttoned his long sleeved denim shirt at the wrists. He folded them up to the elbow length.

"So, what happened to Shhfiisoo?" the captain asked.

"I wasn't involved," he said, his eyes misty.

The room temperature skyrocketed, caused by the steam out of the captain's big nose. If he had the luxury to go outside for fresh air, he would happily pay a million bucks.

"Sosobaal."

"Yeesh, captain."

"Why you bloody did it, hmm?" the captain said, clenching his fists.

"What—?" Sosobala said, seeing the captain's approach as inevitable towards him.

"Who's the bloody Bimbo Shhffiiiso was with the day he died?" the captain asked.

Sosobala was caught off-guard by the captain's insinuation: Sandy would not on any given day be that. How dare the captain?

But he could not blab that out as he stomached the captain's bimbo word.

The captain's eyes flickered like those of a crocodile in the dark water. Sosobala's heart pounded. The captain turned to his most trusted tools, and signalled at his assistant with a tilt of his head. The assistant attacked him. Sosobala's screams, like those of some wounded animal, echoed in the tiny room as he felt the wrath of his tormentors. He experienced body spasm as the assistant stripped him naked and choked his supine form onto the linoleum. He bellowed like a dying cow thinking it was cold on the floor. The captain paced towards the car battery, and then connected the negative and positive leads. The sparks flew when the captain rubbed the leads against each other.

"You bloody killed Shfiiisooo in cold blood, didn't you?" the captain asked, gauging him.

Sosobala hunched his naked body as the assistant pulled apart his legs. He tried to cover his exposed parts.

"No, sir," Sosobala said, wriggling.

The captain clipped the positive lead to his testicles, and then placed the negative on the positive causing sparks to fly.

"Ahhhh!" Sosobala cried.

His testicles roasted as he realised the end was nearer for him. The small room hummed the tunes of pain and sorrow depicted on his face as the captain continued for a while longer. In a timeless bubble, the lead unclipped. The captain wore a grimace, drenched. Sosobala's lower waist felt numb, as he accidentally messed himself in the process. The captain was counting on that to show the effectiveness of his methods.

Was that the same dreaded room that caused all the other hard-core gangsters to pay much respect to anyone who had survived it? He wondered, choked by blood in his throat: the same room that no one ever talked about how they were coerced to make confessions?

"I'll talk, captain, I'll tell you everything," Sosobala said, his words like a schizophrenia.

"What happened the day Shhiffiso was bloody killed, I'm waiting, sonny?" the captain said, his look growing more disgusting.

"It was Bo… and… me," Sosobala said, mumbling. "Yes, I sh…t him, he… died."

"Bloody good job," the captain said as he covered his nose, and stepped back. "Now, clean up your shit."

Sosobala had an embarrassing look aimed at the floor seeing the aftermath of the battery leads. He felt it for the first time how to be half-dead as he lay helpless on the linoleum. Not so shiny anymore, thinking of the pain he had endured. But he just could not say anything about Sandy's rape no matter what happened to him.

"I'm not done with you," the captain said, looking drained, "take him to the cells."

A trickle of tears ran down his cheeks as he lay on the foam mattress smelling of urine and whatnot.

* * *

Bam.

A baton thumped him on the head. He slumped on the linoleum, very cold, unconscious.

5

SANDY CLOGS HIS MIND

His eyes flickered like a dimly candle, strained by the whiteness of its vision. The smell of disinfectant and alcohol clogged his nose. Where was he? He tried to make sense of his surroundings. His body felt like it was carrying a ton of bricks. It then sank in as he glanced around the hallway with beds covered in white sheets, lined up in formation. And the busy forms with stethoscope in uniforms as white as the ceiling. It was in Westville Medium B—WMB—the hospital ward. It was more like the soldiers' recovery ward.

Ouch. He moaned as he ran his fingers from his head to his torso, and then to his crotch. His dreams must have been tantalising. It had a bulge... the man's best weapon was hidden in there. He grimaced pondering he would not mind paying a million bucks just to have his snake prod into a golden cookie again.

Soso sighed.

It all came back that he had been dismantled by the warders during a provocation in the cafeteria. And then a feminine form walked past his bedside. He concentrated on her, screwing up his face like a weightlifter. She flashed a smile. What a breathtaking smile, just like Sandy's. Memories of how they met, and their intimate moments flooded him like an angry sea wave dashing against the pier. The sun had glinted off the cars on that midday when he had bumped into Duke in the shopping centre's parking lot. The shoppers came out in numbers on that day.

"What're you up to, Soso?" Duke asked. "Jump in, let's go check up on an old flame of mine in the north."

"Sure," he said. "Quite a machine you're cruising with, I tell you."

"Nothing beats a 1968 Ford Mustang. Cool hey."

He nodded gleefully as his butt cheeks were massaged by the leather seats. Soft as a baby's ass. He enjoyed every minute of its thunderous roaring engine as Duke cut through the sharp bends in the neighbourhood roads until pulling in at the long driveway. And it was off the main road. It was an enclosed avocado painted four-roomed house with a sliding aluminium gate. An unusual colour for a house, but catchy to say the least. His eyes caught a figure, young and serene, sitting under the shade and book in hand.

"Beautiful girl." he whispered inside the cabin.

"No, a lady," he corrected himself.

He had been dazzled. At first thinking it was Duke's young hot thing when he paced towards her, warmly embraced her and chatted a bit. Besides, when you're loaded like Duke, money trimmed a decade off your age. But then Duke proceeded to go inside the house. Minutes later he reappeared with a chocolate brown skinned curvy woman. She was his age group, a strong black woman. Somehow he was relieved inside the cabin.

"Soso, bring your ass over here." Duke called him to introduce his old flame, and her daughter.

The daughter's rare vanilla scent lingered in the air like smoke as he gave her a quick, yet seducing, hug. She had a subtle pale complexion and eyebrows like a spider's silk web that accentuated her round brown eyes. Her white dress, short and body-hugging with a matching bandana looked like it had been sewn on her proportionately petite figure. Duke then proceeded to go back inside the house with his old flame. The name Sandy Gumede when she introduced herself had stuck in his brain, more like the first time he had learned to pronounce his own name.

"I'm a third year law student at the University of Natal. Yes I know, boring, you're going to say, right?" she said, flashing her breath-taking smile.

She mesmerised him as she explained her reasons for choosing law as a career: another human rights activist. And then Duke emerged from the house with her mother so soon. He hated him for that. While the old flame was saying goodbye to him, he found a chance to ask for her contact number. She reluctantly gave it to him. Duke pulled out of the driveway. Sosobala grinned like a little boy who had just been offered a sweet. His heart pounded faster every time Sandy had appeared in his head. Cupid's arrow had shot right through his heart.

"Tell me more about Sandy?" Sosobala said.

"Don't even think about it, you don't know her mother. She'll crush you with her own bare hands. That's her life," Duke said. "Sandy is a well cultured girl. OK?"

"You reckon she attends the annual Reed Dance event at the King's Enyokeni Royal Palace in Zululand."

"Bet your ass she does. You know what, I think her mother still takes her for vaginal check-ups in Zululand," Duke said. "So keep that snake of yours in your pants. I mean it Soso."

His mind ridiculed him: Wonder what snake Duke referred to, an anaconda or a black mamba? He chuckled discreetly. He courted her for some time after that, even though her ex-boyfriend bullied him, until she succumbed to his charm. She finally made their relationship official.

"Come visit me for a home cooked meal tonight, will you, at eight o'clock?" Soso said.

"I'd not miss it in a million years," Sandy said.

It was a warm evening: The full golden moon with twinkle-twinkle little stars cast shadows that moved with deceptive swiftness over the neighbourhood of Umlazi. He headed to her home to pick her up. He knocked on her door, all smiles.

"Mom, this is the guy I told you about, Sosobala NoZulu," Sandy said.

"Nice meeting you, again, young man. OK, see you later," the mother said, waving goodbye at her. "Be home by eleven o'clock."

She rocked a mini dress, as red as blood, and a scent of vanilla permeated the car cabin. Her combed hair flowed. After their romantic dinner they did dishes in the kitchen. Sandy naughtily pulled him towards her, and gently massaged his crotch. He followed up, and sucked on her lips. She directed his hands under her mini dress. His hands tenderly massaged her torso, and stroked her perky breasts. The kitchen had been transformed from cool and mild temperatures to hot and misty in less than sixty seconds. She notified him of the damp apex of her legs. He searched her face and made out the tiny words scribbled in her brown eyes that said it all… she wanted him just like he wanted her.

"Make me your woman," Sandy said.

Sosobala gave her a combination of pain and pleasure, but she loved every minute of it. Her tight squeeze and thunderous applause said it all… he had made her a woman.

* * *

Sosobala felt like he was losing a piece of himself when they had a car accident, and Sandy's father insisted she leave him. It all played out like a video recorder on rewind. He had visited her at her student residence. Her small residence room was furnished with new stuff and the wall hung posters of hunky models.

"Babes, you've got new furniture?" Sosobala asked.

"My father decided to surprise me," Sandy said.

He nodded as he took off his jacket, feeling his pistol tucked safely in the inside pocket, and hung it across the chair.

"Juice, babes?"

"That'd be fuckin' nice."

That eagle eye she always gave him when he slipped up with the F-word like a kid rebuked by a parent for using foul language. Her body was covered with a colourful sarong as she opened the mini-fridge and took out a cranberry juice. Her other arm stretched to shift the jacket.

"What's this, Soso?" Sandy asked.

She had the look that could melt an ice when she touched the pistol.

"Don't panic, babes, it's only for safety," Sosobala said.

"Since when do you carry a gun now, hey?" she asked. "What's got into you these days, it was jail, now guns?"

"Stop stressing," Sosobala said as he gradually changed the subject. "Need to go to the township. I have things to do there; you'll come with, right?"

"Don't want to see you with this again, alright?" Sandy said, pointing at it.

He had nodded, hesitantly. They cruised in the slow lane of the Mangosuthu Highway, and admired the landmarks of Umlazi. A loaded taxi sped past them in the fast lane.

"What's up with these taxi drivers? They drive like maniacs," he said, annoyed.

But then the taxi slewed in front of him to stop and drop-off.

Clank.

The sound of two metal objects collided, tyres screeched, and marked the road surface of the highway with black rubber. Smoke polluted the air. He shook in disbelief trying to erase the image of what he was seeing on the passenger side.

"Sandy."

But his voice had hung in the air.

Tick… tock… tick… tock.

He looked through his cracked windscreen: the loaded taxi had overturned. Bodies were strewn in the middle of the road. And the screams echoed across the little haven of Umlazi. Sandy was unconscious in the passenger seat, as her head tilted to the side with blood oozing onto her face. He rushed out, and opened her passenger door. He slid his hands underneath her and lifted her out of the car onto the sidewalk.

"Sandy, talk to me baby, wake up," Sosobala said.

"Ouch, my head, it hurts," Sandy answered. She ran her fingers over her face, "I'm bleeding."

"You're going to be fine baby, hang-in there," he said.

Within minutes, the highway was abuzz with passers-by, and

ambulances appearing on the horizon. The paramedics rushed to the helpless, still bodies, resuscitating them non-stop.

"Help. She's bleeding," Sosobala said as one paramedic rushed over.

"She's losing blood, we need to take her to the hospital, now," the paramedic, a young muscular guy in a navy-type uniform, said supporting her neck with a brace.

The ambulance whisked her away and disappeared over the horizon. The images of his late father after he thudded on the ground resurfaced as he was whisked away by an ambulance. Guilt and panic compelled him to follow shortly after finding the damage to his car minimal. Sosobala entered the hospital emergency room: an open space with stretchers of moaning, bloodied and feeble individuals. The wall clock had read five-past five. Minutes later, a familiar figure raced through the sliding doors of the emergency room.

"Oh Lord, my child." The familiar figure said. "What happened?"

"It was a car accident, Ma Gumede," Sosobala said, "one minute we're cruising on the highway, the next thing I hear a clank."

"Let's just hope she'll be ok," she said, biting her lips. "I have already informed her father. He'll be here in an hour or so. He took the first flight out of Cape Town."

The wall clock again read six-thirty. A figure with a commanding presence entered the emergency room: He was good looking, and a respectable father figure.

"What happened, and why is my daughter in a hospital like this?" the father asked.

"Calm down, it was an accident, Bill," Ma Gumede said, avoiding eye contact.

"Damn you, Ruth, if only you let her live with me. None of this would've happened," the father said with glaring eyes. "I'm taking her back to Cape Town tomorrow morning."

The exchange of words between the two of them could have caused the walls of the hospital to crack if it had continued.

"This is her friend, the one who was with her when the accident happened," Ma Gumede said, muttering, and pointed at him in a shy way, "Sosobala."

"Don't want to see you near her again, do I make myself clear?" the father said in his face.

"I'm sorry, sir, but it wasn't my fault," Sosobala said.

Sosobala sensed the anger in him and had opted to disappear out of his sight. He got home and stared at his reflection in the bathroom mirror: the guilt was painted over his face. The next day, Sandy's father had indeed taken her away when he came to check-up on her at the hospital. Days later, Sandy called and told him that she was back at varsity. Sosobala navigated his car, worried but happy, until he pulled in at her varsity residence.

"Hey Sandy."

Sandy forced her trademark smile. Both feelings of surprise and relief crept up all at once. She had sustained minor cuts on her face.

"The doctors say my scars will heal after a few weeks," Sandy said.

"Glad to hear that," he said. "I've missed—"

"I have something to tell you," Sandy said, "it's not easy on me. My father is going to take away my financial support if I don't stop seeing you."

"What're you saying?" Sosobala asked, stunned.

"I have worked so hard to get here; I can't afford to throw it all away, not now."

Sandy had just one more year to finish her law degree. The thought of losing her scared him. So he had pursued her relentlessly until they had rekindled their relationship.

* * *

The figure, full of feminine mystique in the WMB hospital, slowly strutted away until she disappeared down the corridors.

"Why did she leave him?" his mind spoke. "Sifiso's death was just a passing storm they could have weathered."

He recalled how petrified she was of him that night. His touches and cuddles had caused her body to develop goose bumps. She was shaking every time he tried to come closer. He felt as if he was the monster in a horror movie—the one who rendered her powerless.

"Soso, how're you?" a voice, weak but audible, said.

Sosobala swallowed, and wiped his face as a familiar voice came from his left side. He turned as if braving the cold weather. He tried to digest the image in front of him. It looked like a rag, feeble like a sick old man. He zoomed in, shocked at the way the green hospital robe hung on the body like wet laundry hung on the line to dry. What could have caused the flesh to melt on him so fast? His chubbiness had evaporated like a deflated ball.

"Madubula," Soso said.

Sosobala failed to hide his shock. He concentrated some more on him: Madubula's eyes spelt sorrow in big bold letters, and had a pitch black complexion with pimples. He also had sores around his mouth. Sosobala shook his head pondering Madubula's bouncy self had been overshadowed by dark eyes that avoided eye contact like a thief caught in action.

"It's good to see you again, alive," Madubula said, "had thought those demons killed you."

Sosobala shied away at the smell of the dragon breath puffing out of Madubula's mouth. Even a sewer drain did not smell that disgusting.

"I'm a survivor. Nothing or nobody can take that away from me," Soso said.

But why did he feel agitated at the sight of him: Was it maybe he was looking forward to his parole review in the coming weeks. Better yet, his release? All that had happened to him began the day he started showing Madubula his soft side. All along his hardcore side had served him well. It had even made demons like Chopper take note of him. But why did he feel such terrible guilt for failing him?

Sosobala sighed.

Was it because he yearned for a character resembling his late childhood friend, Boyi, or was it because Madubula brought the softer and funnier side out of him? The side that was buried the day Boyi died. There was a moment of silence, like an angel had just flown past.

"How're you holding up?" Soso said, trying to hide his shock.

"Better, even though my butthole is damaged. I wear diapers now like a baby," Madubula said. "Filthy bastards."

Madubula dropped tears like a mourning widow. The compassion, the intimate feelings Sosobala felt for him resurfaced, and crushed the anger and the blame he put on him.

"It's going to be okay," Soso said.

"No it won't be, I'm dying," Madubula said, hissing like a viper ready to strike. "The doctors said I have HIV/AIDS."

The hard to swallow words hung in Sosobala's mind like a pauper's bad breath. Madubula's life had been shortened by bastards like Chopper. And also his future had been snatched out of the palms of his hands by his own stupid actions, and a spur of the moment decision to steal his teacher's car.

"Hang in there, you'll get through this," Sosobala said. "I'm here for you."

"Soso, promise me, you'll—" Madubula said, extending his left hand grabbing his own, "—take revenge for me, my friend?"

Sosobala nodded, his eyes misty and his face muscles tightening as he met Madubula's hand half-way, and squeezing it. The hand felt like it was a soft ball. As Madubula's image disappeared down the hospital aisles, his jaws locked like a vice grip. He did not know whether to scream and curse god for his life, or sprang out of bed and search for Chopper and his lieutenants in all the corners of the prison. Squeeze their necks, and watch the oxygen exit their bodies, puff by puff, until they could huff no more.

6

CAUGHT IN-BETWEEN TWO CHOICES

Each day that went by in hospital, Sosobala felt he had dug his hole deeper with Chopper. He had two choices after being released from hospital: to stand up for himself, or to succumb to his tormentor's wrath. The moment in his life when he was thrust to stand up for himself played in his mind. Winter had crept towards a warm spring when the multinational shipping company, Transco, offered him a position in their electrical apprenticeship programme.

"The stipend is modest," Sosobala had whispered to himself, "I have to work hard, make sure I complete the programme in record time."

When he broke the news, his mother was the proudest ever. It was the dawn of a new era as he began his apprenticeship programme in high spirits. The programme had an allocated tutor throughout the three year period... his tutor being Gordon Botha. He was tubby with a pony tail that accentuated his goat face, and had blue eyes that said it all, 'It's my way or the highway.'

Soso's jaws had skidded on the floor when he soon realised that his tutor, Gordon, was abusive, and likely to put him through hell over the next three years of the programme. But he convinced himself that it might turn out not to be too bad. Gordon, an Afrikaans speaking man, was only fluent in his mother-tongue, and anything in English worded differently, other than what was written in model answers, caused his brain to default like a malfunctioning robot—Yabaah... Dabaah.

"Sir, I deserve full marks on this module," Sosobala had pointed out in his first module test.

"I gave you seventy percent, that's good enough for me," Gordon said glaringly. "Get out of here, now."

He nodded sheepishly like a servant told to shut up and eat cow dung. As time went by, Gordon's 'My way or the highway' behaviour became a load that kept on piling up on his shoulders. Sosobala finally decided to dump it on him.

"Sir, I don't know why, but you keep on giving me less marks, module after module," Sosobala said, putting a module on Gordon's desk at tea break.

The office was small and dirty with old files scattered around. Gordon sat on his chair, feet stretched out on the table, in his knee-high socks, boots removed. Sosobala smelt an odour of rotting fish, and flushed with disgust. He wanted to scream, "Put your damn boots on! Your feet stink!"

"Who do you think you are?" Gordon asked as he threw a module at Soso's face.

Sosobala paled, hands and knees shaking with anger, eyes teary. He wanted to wring Gordon's bony neck with his own bare hands.

"You know what? You're not the brainy you think you are," Soso said.

Gordon sprang from his chair like a high jumper, snatched him by his overalls, and pressed him against the wall. Sosobala found himself on tiptoe, like a ballerina. The only thing missing was the ensemble of violinist and pianist. Gordon slapped him, banging his head hard during the incident. His skull rattled like the parade of drum majorettes.

"You're fuckin' hurting me. Let me go," Sosobala said, and tried to break free of his grip.

"Who are you to question me? You're nobody, you hear me?" Gordon said, shaking him as if he wanted to empty all his pockets.

Sosobala blinked once in agony, feeling the balloons of anger and pity equally inflated second after second. He clenched his fists and raised his arm. Like a volcano, he released his fist.

Bam.

"You piece of shit," Gordon said, his face baffled as he took a few steps back.

Sosobala stood in there like a zombie. And then reality kicked in when Gordon's mouth turned as red as beetroot. He had knocked out his tutor's front teeth.

Gordon stormed out of the office, his hands covering his mouth. He rushed behind him and sprinted into the tutor manager's office as Gordon doubled up his pace.

"He hit me," Gordon said as he burst in at the door of Mr. Tanie's office.

"What happened?" Mr. Tanie asked. He lost his cool faster than a steam iron. "You silly boy, how the hell could you hit your superior?"

"I'm sorry, sir," Sosobala said. "Don't know what came over me. Didn't mean to."

"Fire him right now, Tanie," Gordon said. "I want this piece of rubbish out of here *now*."

Huffing and puffing, he explained to Mr. Tanie the events that had led to the incident.

"So you did what, hit your superior?" Mr. Tanie said, pushing his pregnant woman's belly forward, hands behind his back. "Tomorrow you come for your disciplinary hearing."

"But it was a mistake."

"A costly mistake, I might add. You see, my boy, I'll make an example of you."

Anger and hate flickered in Gordon's blue eyes, and a gap in his front teeth showed like an open garage door.

"I want you in my office, nine o'clock sharp, tomorrow morning," Mr. Tanie added, nodding like a yo-yo. "Get out."

Sosobala nodded, his look growing more sheepish.

He exited Mr. Tanie's office with his tail tucked between his legs and escaped to the toilet. He stood in there, arms across his chest, and stared at his reflection in the mirror. His body had been reduced to that of an old crock. He felt anger, pity and sadness all at once. The sight of his mother's joy the day he broke the news of getting a job had resurfaced in his head. He realised he was a broken young man with very little hope for the future. He splashed water on his face…took deep breaths, and then removed his stuff and exited the steel gates of Transco. The following day, he reported for duty and sensed Gordon and Mr. Tanie were thirsty for his blood as soon as he entered his office.

"Sosobaal, you back," Gordon said, "you going to get what's coming to you."

"I'm sorry, Mr. Botha," Sosobala said. "I'm a breadwinner at home, and I have rent to pay."

"Shut up and sit down," Mr. Tanie said, rocking his inclining chair. "You should've thought about that before you put your filthy hands on him." He pointed at Gordon.

His fate had already been sealed: No matter how much he begged for leniency in that office, it was like skating on ice, barefoot. He exited Transco premises, and Gordon gloated like a duck in a pond. As he stepped out of the Transco gates, he felt that the choice he had taken to stand up for himself was honourable yet costly for his future well-being.

* * *

Sosobala's eyes saw through a red haze as he felt the hospital air conditioners blasting a freezing draught while he pulled up a bed sheet.

But then came a time when he had no choice but to succumb to his tormentor's wrath. It was a cool Thursday afternoon blessed with a cloudless indigo sky. He had met with Duke and Bonga, at Duke's. The guilt of Boyi's death was still fresh in his mind. Duke thinking of the future had a proposal for him.

According to Duke, 'It had the potential to triple their earnings', one of Duke's favourite economics terminologies. Sosobala pulled into his driveway and pressed the intercom, "It's me."

The gate slid open. He alighted, and marvelled at the neatly manicured lawn with a garden of bright flowers. He briskly paced towards the front door, and passed Bonga's BMW M3. It was like the skin colour of a snake. And then he took a few long seconds, admiring Duke's machine, like blue skies, under the white awning. A man-made spaceship: the Ford Mustang.

"How have you been?" Duke asked.

Was Duke asking how he was holding up after Boyi's death?

"Carrying on, taking each day as it comes," Soso said. "At least I've got a taxi income, you know. It fuckin' keeps me going."

"A taxi income, come on, Soso, you'd strive for…" Duke said, putting up both hands, meaning ten. "Then you'll see, life will be great."

Duke had burst into laughter, his trademark sinister laughter like a villain in a movie, and ushered him inside the house. The beauty of the house mesmerised him.

"Hey Bonga," Soso said, remembering their last encounter.

Bonga was always dressed in shirts as colourful as daisies, with matching sneakers, and always when he spoke he rubbed his hands anxiously.

"My hustler, how—" Bonga said.

"I've got a proposition for you, CMB," Duke said, looking straight into his eyes.

Duke cut Bonga off because he didn't want Soso to relive the moments of Boyi's death.

"Doing what exactly?" Soso asked, his eyes wandering in every inch of the living room.

"Trucks," Duke said. "Anything you bring would definitely be a winner." His term for a quick seller.

"I have never driven a fuckin' truck in my life, not even in my dreams," Soso said.

"That's where he comes in," Duke said, pointing at Bonga.

"No risks at all," Bonga added. "We only need to hit them at night time or in the wee hours of the morning at the secluded spots."

"One horse and trailer a month with saleable goods. We're

talking big bucks here," Duke said, excitement soaring in his eyes.

"How much?" Soso asked.

"About two hundred grand, tax free," Duke said, giggling.

"If we deliver three horse and trailers per month," Bonga said, "that'd be a cool two hundred grand each."

Duke added, "Before this year is over, you'd have five taxis, debt-free."

"So when do we start?" Soso asked, re-energised.

"Next week, you and Bonga plan your shit," Duke said. "On my side, the buyers are ready."

"So let's meet at the shopping centre on Monday night, say after six?" Bonga said.

"I'll be there," Soso replied.

Sosobala stood up and said his goodbyes. He pulled out of the driveway, his heart left behind when thinking of the interior of the house.

On that drizzly Monday night with a titillating promise of a new dawn, he met with Bonga at the shopping centre's parking lot.

"So you're ready to do this, my hustler?" Bonga asked, jumping in on the passenger seat, and slamming the door. He was caught off-guard. "What happened to your face?"

"Agh, some asshole in Montclair wanted to fuckin' entertain the partygoers at my expense," Soso said. "So I had to be a party-pooper."

"As long as you're okay. Guess what? There's a Volvo horse and trailer we're going to jack tonight." Bonga continued, rubbing his hands anxiously, "It parks at the harbour, say by nine or so."

Sosobala squinted like a cop ready to burst open the secret hideout of a mob.

"That's my hustler," Bonga said. "Now let's go and drive around the city, there's this Beemer." He lit up like wild fire. "It always parks outside the Gables flat every night at eight. We may be lucky, who knows, and score twice."

"Let's deal with the Volvo first," Sosobala said, remembering his last hustle that had caused Boyi's death. "Can't handle another fuckin' drama right now, OK?"

The clock read seven fifty-five. Bonga pulled out his gun underneath his floral shirt.

"This piece, my hustler, even fires under water," Bonga said as he tucked it under his seat.

Within a few minutes, they had exited onto the harbour side of the city. He always admired the city at night. Its tall buildings, with its bright street lights, made it feel like it was daytime. He feasted his eyes on the bustling city dwellers, watching lovers strolling, hand in hand, while some frolicked on the sidewalks. Prostitutes converged on the traffic light corners, flashing a thigh until a car had pulled alongside, causing them to wrestle each other. The winner was picked up by the car.

Bonga pestered him about checking out the Beemer first. Soso drove there just to shut him up, and pulled across the Esplanade road on the exit side of the city harbour. In those few seconds, a BMW M3—like an egg yolk—pulled into a quiet roadside parking.

"What do you think?" Bonga asked. "Do you think I'd go—?"

Bonga quickly opened his passenger door, and pulled out the gun from under his seat.

"What the—? Where are you going?"

Bonga sprinted across the road like a reporter chasing a story. Sosobala scouted the area like a hawk, butterflies in his stomach. The stationary cars parked in parking bays behind him while rows of vehicles travelled in all directions. The reflective windows of the flats across the road contributed to the atmosphere that he felt with heightened consciousness as an anxious watcher. It always felt like this the first time he did a job.

Bonga approached the Beemer and pointed his gun at a Madonna look-alike. She screamed as he tore open the door and pulled her out. He shoved her onto the road and jumped into the driver's seat. The Beemer swayed at the nearby traffic lights, and roared past him to link to the M4 freeway south.

"My car!" the Madonna look-alike screamed.

Sosobala followed Bonga, on the way realising that the Beemer's hijacking had drawn attention on his car. He anxiously fiddled with the stereo until he tuned to a music station that calmed him down. Sosobala pulled in at the shopping centre's parking lot behind him. Bonga ransacked the Beemer for valuables, fiddling with every knob his fingers could find like a kid excited about his new automatic control car toy.

"It's fine here, right? I'll move it after the Volvo," Bonga said as he jumped back in.

"I guess so," Sosobala said, annoyed. "The stunt you pulled back there might put us in the spotlight."

"Agh, relax my hustler," Bonga said, naively. "The harbour side is always bustling. Drama there happens all the time."

* * *

Captain Jones stood in his office, a cigarette on hand as he glanced out of the window, thinking the night was long and quiet.

"A yellow BMW M3 was jacked in the harbour side just a few minutes ago," the assistant said as he barged into the captain's office.

"What, any leads?" the captain asked as he paced back and forth.

"Yes sir," the assistant said. "A black Toyota Conquest was spotted in the area. It could be our guys."

"Bloody CMB gang," the captain said as he put on his jacket and headed for the door, the assistant behind him.

"Where are we going?" the assistant asked.

"We'll patrol the M4 freeway. These bloody guys will come back for more," Captain Jones said, his look intense, "I can feel it."

Sosobala sped out of their neighbourhood and joined the M4 freeway back to the city. Suddenly the blue lights illuminated the dark velvety sky at a distance in the rear-view mirror.

"Shit, there's a fuckin' police car behind us," Sosobala said as the blue lights flashed closer and brighter.

"Keep driving," Bonga said. "Maybe they are rushing somewhere else."

Soso's eyes welled up when the siren started wailing.

"Don't panic. Pull over here," Bonga said, pointing to the yellow lane.

"Did you hide your gun?"

"It's safely hidden. Just relax, will you?" Bonga said.

Two familiar forms alighted on his side mirror and pointed their guns at them. He killed the engine.

"Get out of the vehicle. Out now, hands up," the captain said.

They jumped out, hands up.

"On the ground, now," Jones continued.

The coldness of the tarmac put a chill up Soso's spine as the captain's big figure pressed him down, knee on his back, gun in the right hand, the left frisking him.

"Do you have any bloody weapons in the car?" the captain asked.

Sosobala stole a glance at Bonga, a few inches away from him also being pinned down like a springbok by a lion.

"No, no guns," Sosobala said, his tone unconvincing.

"We'll bloody see about that," Jones said, shifting his weight off his back. "Where are you going?"

"To drop him off at the bus station," Sosobala said, and pointed at Bonga with the tilt of his head.

"Oh, so you think I'm a mampara, sonny?" the captain said. "We'll see who has the last laugh."

"On your knees," the assistant said. "Hands on your heads."

The captain opened all the doors and began searching the cabin, section after section. He performed the exercise twice.

"Hohoho," Jones said. "What do we have here?"

That Father Christmas laughter the captain had just pulled, Sosobala could swear the captain had just hit a jackpot.

"Whose bloody gun is this?" Jones asked.

The captain spat on the ground as he paced closer to him.

"I don't know," Sosobala said with naivety flickering in his eyes. "A friend used my car yesterday. It could belong to him."

"Liar," the captain said with a hard slap that made Sosobala hug the tarmac. "Is mampara written on my forehead, sonny?"

"Noooo, captain," Sosobala mumbled.

The captain's big hands choked the life out of Sosobala, and then released his grip. Bonga deflated like an old tyre... he looked like it too.

"Throw them into the trunk of my car," Jones said to his assistant. "Follow me with their car."

"Where to, sir?" the assistant asked.

"Our usual spot, behind the harbour."

The captain's assistant threw them inside like rubbish, and slammed the trunk, making their ears ring. The silence in the boot was deafening as the roar of the Beemer quietened when it pulled over on a bumpy road after some time.

"Get out," Jones said, and then ordered them to strip naked.

The captain brandished the gun with a devious grin. Their clothes were on the ground in a flash as the captain pulled out a sjambok from underneath his car seat. They were deep inside the harbour. They were a stone's throw away from the sea base where even the boat docks were at a distance. The harbour was quiet with only the ships floating at their berths in still waters. Sosobala realised their screams would be wasted on the calm breeze.

"Captain, maybe we could work something out here," Sosobala said, gingerly as the captain's approach towards them became inevitable.

"I don't negotiate with bloody gangsters," the captain said.

"Aaaahhhh." They screamed in unison as the captain hurtled at them, sjambokking them like the loony that he was.

Sosobala begged mercilessly as the captain used the sjambok like it was a flying broom.

"You scumbags, in this bloody thing," the captain pointed at his ride with a sjambok, "hijacked a yellow BMW M3 tonight. Where is it?"

Sosobala clutched his body, trembling, as he caught a quick look at his conspicuous car, as black as Asian mulberries. If only they had focused on the initial plan, and not the Beemer, for crying out loud. His skin tore apart with every contact the sjambok had made with it. Bonga was more worried about covering his crotch than his body as the captain whipped them with every ounce he possessed.

"It's at the shopping centre's parking lot, in the east of Umlazi," Bonga said.

The captain's devious grin turned to a killer look aimed at Bonga. The captain took a few strides away from them, and to his assistant.

"Phone the Umlazi Captain and ask him to check for it at this shopping centre, in the east," the captain said.

"Right on it, sir," the assistant said.

"If you're lying to me," the captain said as he whipped them some more, "heaven forbid what I'll bloody do to you next."

Damn you, Jones, he sobbed like a kid throwing tantrums, when looking at his flesh marks made by the sjambok.

Damn you, Bonga, his mind continued. *Anything involving you results in bad luck.*

"They have recovered the Beemer, sir," the assistant said.

"Let's go get it."

The captain and his assistant jumped into their car and took off, leaving them smelling the fumes of their exhaust.

7

A MOTHER'S LOVE KNOWS NO BOUNDS

Fear and uncertainty lingered in his mind as he snapped out of it, thinking of one man: Chopper. He tossed and turned all that night as if the hospital bed had ticks nest. Each second that went-by he feared what his fate might choose. The sleep bug finally caught-up with him in the wee hours of the morning.

"Soso," the voice said, softly.

Someone shook his shoulders. He tilted his head to the side, and zoomed in on the figure a mere inch from him.

"How are you feeling?" the voice continued.

"I'm thirsty. Get me water, will you?"

The figure shuffled away and then came back with a plastic cup. It tasted funny, more like the water was not purified, and it needed chlorine.

He read an article, many years before, that one litre of water consumed per day by an individual would total to a kilo of E.coli—the bacteria found in faeces. Which scientist had made that discovery?

"Thanks," Soso said. "How did you get here?"

"Taxi."

"But there are no taxis coming this way," Sosobala said.

"Well, I rode as far as the taxi took me, then walked as far as my feet allowed me until I got here," she said, forcing a smile.

"But, Ma, didn't I tell you to never come to places like this?"

She averted her eyes. His heart ached for her, all bloodshot eyes and slumping shoulders. She had misery painted in her face. Sosobala had not seen her in over three years, and had left her with no source of income after Bonga had betrayed him, and stolen his taxis.

Bonga came into his life at the moment when the CMB had hit a snag with their hustling job. Everything they touched turned into dust. Boyi's and Duke's faces failed to hide their concerns when they hung out at the shopping centre's salon.

"I have a solution to our problem," Boyi said. "Soso, remember the hustler who used to pick me for his sideline jobs, you do, right?"

Sosobala nodded even though the hustler's face was distant to him.

"That dude, I tell you guys, he knows the hidden gems of Durban. Areas where folks wipe their shit with hundred rand notes," Boyi added.

"It sounds like he's a man of action," Duke said. "If you CMB are cool with it, I say let's rope him in. Why not?"

"I have already spoken with him," Boyi continued. "He'll meet us here tonight."

A figure entered the double glass door at the salon. It was seven o'clock. Boyi's eyes and that of the figure locked. Boyi waved like an excited kid.

"Over here," Boyi said, beckoning him. "It's good to see you again."

Bonga was an albino. He was tall, but not too tall, with a blond mop. He was of his age group, maybe a bit older and had a cocky laugh.

"Likewise, my hustler. It's good to see you again," Bonga said.

"This is Duke, our ring leader," Boyi said.

"Come on, who doesn't know Duke around Durban?" Bonga said. "These are our role models."

"And right here is Sosobala."

"Finally we meet," Bonga said, doing a high five. "I have heard a lot about you."

"Bonga," Sosobala said, measuring his gaze as if sizing him up.

"So you're down with being a member of the CMB?" Duke asked.

"I'm the hustler. If there's good money to be made, I'm in," Bonga said.

"Alright then, Boyi will fill you in on how we operate. We're cool?" Duke said.

They nodded in unison.

"Let me bounce, CMB. We'll talk soon," Duke said, sliding away.

"So this is where you CMB hang out?" Bonga said.

Sosobala remembered in passing, seeing Bonga from a distance when he rode a bus on his way to work. Bonga parked his purple Beemer in the parking lot of the shopping centre. The girls in the neighbourhood acted like groupies, always getting excited when they spotted Bonga. Some even acted like stalkers. Sosobala kind of idolised him, although quietly.

* * *

His mother's squeaky voice sounded as he snapped out of it.

"You're my son, Soso, I'll move heaven and earth, just to see you again," she said, pouting.

The last time his mother did exactly that, was when she came to see him in the Umlazi police station's isolation cells. It was when he attended his trial for the murder of Sifiso, even though visitors were chased away. It had been a crisp morning that made him feel like he was having a heart attack. He waited for his attorney before he headed to court for his sentencing. The courts began at nine o'clock, but by no later than eight o'clock he should be on his way there. Eight, ten-past eight, twenty-past, half-past eight, nine o'clock, he paced up and down in his jail cell. Where could the attorney be?

What had gone wrong? He should have been in court already. Sosobala sighed with relief when footsteps and voices sounded, coming towards his cell like a street march.

"Holy moly," Soso said, wide-eyed.

No way in hell.

He maintained his stare at the oncoming voices. It was the captain escorting... His heart pounded in his chest as his cell gate unlocked.

"Come out, you have a visitor," the captain said as he looked to his right.

How the hell on earth did that happen? Fazed, he shuffled out of his cell. He was embarrassed as she jumped on him and gave him a hug and a kiss.

Dammit Ma. He was not in kindergarten anymore, he was a hardcore thug. He snatched a quick look at the captain who had a smug face, and his assistant.

"I thought you're a bloody hard nut to crack," the captain said.

How did his mother manage to pull that off, especially with the captain guarding him like he did not want even a fly to have access to him?

"How are you holding up?" she asked.

"I'm a survivor," Sosobala said, "why are you here?"

"I'm your mother, Soso."

The tears had trickled down her cheeks like paint dripping off a paintbrush. She sighed.

"Things aren't good, my son," she said. "Your friend has taken possession of your taxis since the day of your arrest."

"Chillax, Ma," Soso said, shrugging it off. "Bonga's making sure that nothing goes wrong." He rolled his eyes, "The taxi industry is a cut-throat money-making business, you know."

In his eyes it was justifiable that someone like Bonga would be protecting his interests from some of the greedy taxi owners.

"If you say so, I won't argue," she said, looking away, "you know your friend and the taxi business better than any of us."

The time he got shot the day Boyi died, Bonga had come through for him. While Bonga was the getaway driver, Soso was wounded during the botched micro-loan bank robbery.

"I'm bleeding," Sosobala said, voice fading.

"Hang in there, we're going to the hospital," Bonga said. "Don't die on me now."

"No, no hospital, the police—" Sosobala said. "I'll be arrested if they find me."

"Nonsense," Bonga said. "I know a nurse at Prince Mshiyeni hospital, she'll help us."

Sosobala sank on the rear seat, and tears trickled down his chin, warm and salty. He listened to the whistling exhaust pipes of his car. He felt bad about how he had failed Boyi in that moment of need. Bonga pulled in at the back entrance of the hospital, and sprinted in and came back with a nurse and a stretcher. The pain and guilt were getting worse, minute by minute.

After receiving treatment, Bonga assisted him to the car, and showed true friendship.

"Your friend's very lucky," a nurse—a pretty little thing—said, "the bullet penetrated his right knee and shoulder without causing much damage."

He slumped on the rear seat as Bonga navigated his car until pulling in at his driveway.

"Take the car, will you," Soso said, jaws clenching, "give me a few days to rest."

Bonga came back the following day, and made sure he ran Soso's errands and even his mother's errands too. There was not even the slightest sign that Bonga could betray him. But he had done just that. What a fool he had been.

* * *

Tears ran down her cheeks like the mouth of a river feeding into the sea. She was disappointed with the son Sosobala had turned out to be: evil and dirty, which was what the Christians called people like him.

"How are you keeping?" Soso asked.

"Don't worry about me, son," she said, wiping the tears from her cheeks. "God always finds a way to provide for me."

"Don't do this now," Sosobala said, becoming a bit irritated. "In case you haven't noticed, I'm in a prison hospital. I have bigger things to worry about when I'm out of here."

"Soso, my son, is this the life you've dreamed of. The life that's going to force you to leave this earth before me? This isn't the life your father raised you to live. Where did we go wrong, hey, what became of that young obedient boy?" she said, wiping her running nose, "I love you no matter what, but truth be told, this is too much too handle. I'm old and fragile now. Change your life for the better, if not for you, than do it for me."

Sosobala suppressed his emotions as he felt tears welling up in his eyes. She then left like she was negotiating rough terrains. She vanished down the corridors of the hospital, broken, reminding him of a figure standing under the gallows with the executioner about to pull the lever. Maybe Chopper was the executioner holding his life on a string. A nasty draught sneaked in, like a deadly worm slithering down his spine causing a chill in his heart.

Sosobala stared at the ceiling, his eyes gloomy, pondering... planning... plotting. It made him aware that his days were numbered. If there was a God somewhere, whom his childhood friend, Boyi, never believed in, maybe he had been right all along. He definitely did not exist, or he just did not give a fuck about his well-being, or even that of his mother.

Sosobala created a happy scene in his mind. He was an obedient son married to a beautiful woman—a God fearing child—that was hand-picked by his pastor from amongst the hundreds of such women in her congregation. He lived with his mother, wife, two cute boys and one adorable girl, and a dog named Luke. They lived in a modest three bed-roomed house, enclosed and painted beige in the north of the neighbourhood. And he worked for the local municipality as an office administrator, and his wife, a nurse. He drove an economical car, a Toyota Corolla. And every day, without fail, he dropped his kids off at school and his wife at her workplace: a clinic in the south of the neighbourhood. In the afternoons, he picked them up in that sequence. They had a routine for the weekends too. Every Saturday they visited his wife's family in the east of the neighbourhood, and spend time braaing with them and their relatives. And on Sunday it was church in the morning, and then prayer meetings till the afternoon.

* * *

Sosobala realised he was never born to live a monotonous lifestyle.

8

THE PLAN TO TAKE REVENGE

A day turned into the next when he wondered how Madubula was recuperating.

"Excuse me," Soso said, calling a nurse going past his bed.

She looked young and pretty as he glanced at her with seductive eyes.

"A patient by the name of Madubula, which ward is he in?" Soso asked.

Her look at the mention of Madubula's name said it all: surprised, saddened yet calm.

"Oh shame. You're related to him?" the nurse asked.

"Agh, not exactly, you'd say, he's a friend."

"Oh shame man. Sorry to tell you this," she bit her lip, very appetising as he drooled, "your friend passed away last night."

"How, what happened?" Soso asked.

"The thing is, he refused to take the treatment for HIV, you know, from day one," she said, stepping away from him.

That sounded just like Madubula, always thinking he knew more than others. Chopper's devious grin filled his mind no matter which side of the bed he rolled on. He balled his fists, punching in the air. Madubula's words during their last conversation resurfaced, 'Take revenge for me my friend.'

His mind battled with both the outcomes of the two choices,

neither of which would reward him with a holiday on some exotic beach island where bitches were a dime a dozen. Who was it who'd said that?

He recalled the pledge he took in the centre of the ring, all those years ago, crouching in the chambers with a 26 gang sign up in his face. The gangs' number lore was upheld when he vowed to live or die by it. A soldier who wished to challenge the superior gang member—lieutenants or gang leaders—to a duel... And become the last man standing, would automatically assume that higher ranking of the defeated.

Since he had entered the prison, Chopper had won every duel, bloodied and unrepentant, against those who challenged him. And the only way to redemption was to stand up against the most feared man in prison, shaken by the outcome his fate decided on.

"How're you feeling?" the nurse said, examining him. "You're ready to be released now."

The words 'You're ready to be released now', put butterflies in his stomach. If he went back to the cell with no plan on how to stand up for himself in the kill or be killed world, Chopper would eat him alive.

Chopper would have all the ingredients like barbeque or chicken peri-peri spices, or even garlic and pepper, ready to be marinated in and served raw.

"My ribs, nurse, they're still sore," Soso said long enough for her to get the picture.

"Oh shame. This isn't some hotel, you know," the nurse said, her tone sounding more rebuking than sympathising. "Okay, you'll stay for another day. After that, you hear me, you're out of here."

"Yes ma'am," Sosobala said, nodding like a naughty kid.

Sosobala had to make a knife, small enough to elude the warder's eyes when hidden up his butt-hole. Yet long enough to plunge into a fatal hole. He formulated his plan. He needed a string of cotton, plastic cutlery: at least three pieces. And a wrapper—a plastic cup. The string of cotton would be unravelled from his bed sheets the day of his release. The plastic cutlery would be taken and hidden after every meal, beginning from that day's afternoon meal. And a wrapper, a plastic cup, would be his first task to get hold of.

Sosobala set his plan in motion. He asked for water. The nurse obliged by giving him a full plastic cup. He guzzled it and insisted on dumping it into the bin himself. He hid it under his robe on his way to the toilet. He cut it open with his teeth and flattened it like a paper sheet. He hid it in his crotch on his way back, and stashed it under the bed. During meal times, he hid under his bed the spoons from the plastic cutlery. He pretended to have a running stomach at night as he hid the items: three spoons and the flat plastic cup in his crotch on his way to the toilet. He moaned in the toilet as if dropping a heavy pile as he combined the three spoons, and wrapped them with a flattened plastic cup. He rubbed them against the linoleum, and the friction melted the combination into a bar. He occasionally flushed the toilet; the running water caused much needed noise for him to continue rubbing the bar on the linoleum. He shaped it until he was satisfied with his handicraft. He went back and hid it under his bed. That night, he felt he was a step closer towards his unknown fate when pondering about how his homemade knife came out. He calculated every square inch—in his head—of where Chopper slept in the cell: on the far left hand side, flanked by his four lieutenants. It was going to be a mountainous challenge, but he was ready to stand up for himself and kill or be killed.

Chopper woke up earlier than everybody else in the cell, even before the lights came on. It was a perfect time to jump him, plunge the knife in a fatal point, and slink back to his bed before the steel gates were unlocked. Sosobala sensed an uncomfortable feeling in the pit of his stomach. He dozed off.

"The doctor will do a final examination on you. And you'll be released in the next hour or so, okay?" the nurse said, waking him up. "I'll be back in a jiffy."

Damn, those kissable lips. He dreamt about locking his on them. There were other convicts who spilled the beans about making out with the nurses while in the hospital. His mind ridiculed him as he proposed the subject to the nurse.

"What do you take me for?" the nurse asked as she walked away, "I'm not a slut, I don't screw convicts."

Sosobala began undoing the string from the bed sheets. He rolled it around his pinkie until he was satisfied with the amount. The doctor, a shabby impatient man, did his final examination on him. The doctor then handed the charge sheet to the nurse, and signalled to her with the nod of his finger.

"You're good to go," she said. "The warder will be here shortly to escort you. OK?"

"Need to use the toilet, quickly, you don't mind, do you?" Soso said, anxiety sneaking through his veins, "my stomach." He rubbed it with a frown.

"Oh shame, be snappy, alright?" the nurse said as if implying, 'Really now.'

The nurse was occupied with the doctor, so he gingerly hid his items under his robe and rushed to the toilet. He took out the knife and the string of cotton, and began rolling it from the centre of the knife, tying a knot. A figure eight for an easy pull was the easiest knot when he was a scout at school. The string went all the way back to the blunt side, leaving slack like a tampon. Sosobala stooped, tightening and loosening his sphincter muscle, the exercise Sandy and he read about, a long time ago, in a magazine about engaging in reaming. He felt his butthole ready to expand and grip firmly. Besides, the butthole could retract something bigger and longer than his homemade knife. If women could insert a tampon into their vagina and let it stay in there for hours, it won't be difficult for the butthole to perform such a similar function? He balanced with his left hand on the toilet seat, and lubricated the knife in his right hand with saliva. Then he gingerly pushed it in, bit by bit. His first finger went inside the hole, like a soccer ball into the net. He pulled it out gently, and moaned like the harlot. The slack was long enough to pull the knife out. He measured it in his head, but invisible to the warder's eyes. Sosobala grimaced at the sight of his first finger: it had a brownish coating, like peanut butter. He hated it all those years ago when it smeared onto his fingers after forcing down the peanut buttered slices of bread his mother made him for breakfast. He wiped his finger, dressed up, tightened his butt cheeks and shuffled back to the ward, face muscles taut.

"Hurry up, if you don't want to miss your breakfast," the warder said, his look growing more impatient.

Sosobala minded his steps so that the warder would not suspect anything fishy. The sound of the steel gates unlocked by the warder on their way to the cell... felt like the hooves made by racing horses in his chest. It made him aware that his time was nearer.

9

THE DEMON SURVIVES THE REVENGE ATTACK

Sosobala followed the warder close as they pass the guardhouse of his cell block. He shied away from the guards, thinking: their piercing eyes should not suspect anything about the way he walked.

"Hold on a second," one guard said, coming out of the guardhouse, visibly alert. "Stop right there."

Sosobala's heart turned into ice as the guard with a hawk's eye paced towards them. His butt cheeks sucked in some more. The way the guard looked at him, said it all, he was busted. When a convict was suspected of hiding something up his ass, the warders chained that convict to a cell gate. Put a melamine bowl on the linoleum, and then shoved down your throat the laxatives. If any contraband was discovered, and you mess on the linoleum, the punishment was the beating of a lifetime.

"Where's this man coming from?" the guard asked with a scowl directed at Soso.

"From the hospital," the warder said, "why ask?"

Sosobala's tummy grumbled as he realised the guard would demand a Tauza dance any second. He imagined what would be left of him after the warders' beating… a disfigured face, and his body crippled.

"Just checking," the guard answered. "The cravings are killing me, got a cigarette for me?"

"These things will kill you. You know that, right?" the warder said, taking a loose out, and walking away.

Sosobala's heart beat again as he realised it was a close call. He faked a smile as he gingerly followed the warder until he reached the cell.

"Get in," the warder said, unlocking the steel gate of his cell, and opening it wide.

The nasty draught entering the cell ushered him in. Reality kicked his head upside down as he imagined his last days. His hardcore behaviour all those times before would close in his utmost test to survival. Sosobala tightened his face muscles, chest out, and went easy on his butt cheeks. And he took his first steps inside. It would take at least twenty steps to reach his bed.

He shuffled, aware of every step he took as his feet made contact with the linoleum. The twenty short steps became the longest and the hardest walk of his life. His orange prison uniform itched on his skin like some burning poison had been sprinkled on it. His eyes swung back and forth around every inch of the cell until he reached his bed. He cautiously sat down.

The cell smelt of crotches unwashed in a thousand years as he gasped for air. He sensed an atmosphere of fear and uncertainty when the looks, some hardcore, some downright scared, all melted on him like butter in a hot potato. His hardcore spirit began to crumble, bit by bit, pondering about what was to happen... like a house built on sea sand. He perspired as if a bucket of water was poured over him, his armpits... his crotch... the groove of his butt cheeks... his toes inside his sneakers... burning and sticky. Warm tears floated in his eyelids. He has never felt so afraid in his lifetime like in that moment.

It was only once in a person's life, that that feeling of reaching a point of no return crept into one's mind, eating it like a slow poison. Was it the day of his execution, or the day of redemption?

'Take revenge for me, my friend' those words played over and over again in his mind like a vinyl with scratches. He held a need to retch when his gaze met with that of Chopper standing with a devious grin. Chopper stared at him with intent flickering in his bloodshot eye as if he was a magnet. Sosobala felt all alone like he was in a jungle with the pack of wolves stalking him.

He revisited his plan to take out Chopper in the morning before the roll call. It was too far, as the knife began to irritate his ass. His feet tapped like a tap dancer practicing its dance moves. He silently moaned sensing he could not keep it in any longer. It had to come out one way or the other. It was not by choice but nature demanded it to be so. His sphincter muscle could only suck on it for so long. He caught a quick whiff of his body odour: it was a mixture of an unwashed ass coupled with stinking armpits. He crouched hoping the irritation would go away.

"Fuckin' no." his mind spoke.

He lifted himself up, his orange prison uniform soaking wet. He constricted his butt cheeks on his way to the toilets like a hungry penguin leaving its nest, bounding whilst flapping its wings on its way into the sea. The toilets were situated at the far left end corner of the cell when entering the entrance, just a few feet after the steel gate. He swayed and caught a glimpse of Chopper coming towards him.

"Fuckin' no." his mind begged.

But Chopper was pulled back by a sky-bird. Sosobala thanked his guardian angel as he battled with unzipping his pants until the zip broke. He leapt on the seat like a frog. No more time to waste, as if he was late for a function where he was assigned to be a master of the ceremony. He crouched on the seat while his right hand fingers tried to find the slack of the string. He moaned because the slack had been sucked in.

Do women encounter such problems with their tampons when the string would suddenly disappear into the vagina? It was that last sucked-in he did by the guards' house that caused the string to disappear. Desperation took control of his desire to be free of the knife inside of him. Blood clogged his head, about to shoot out of his pores. He inserted his first finger, directing his mind to locate the string of cotton. He loosened his sphincter muscle just like the exercise, he used when he pushed the knife in. He exhaled, huffing and puffing in rhythm. Sweat trickled down his spine into the groove of his butt cheeks and into the butt-hole, causing more irritation.

"If you don't come out of there, I'm going to be in deep shit," Soso said, spluttering to himself.

He sucked in breath and pushed, moaning and groaning like a pregnant woman about to give birth. He stirred with his first finger.

"Hell yeah baby, you can do it," he whispered to the winds.

His mind cheered for his first finger to achieve the impossible.

"Come on," Soso said, as he mumbled like a man stuck on a rail road, battling to start the ignition of his car while the moving train hurtled nearer.

If Chopper could appear at that eerie moment, drenched in sweat, he would have died of shame: his first finger stuck up his ass. He would have made headline news. Sosobala imagined what the article by a controversial reporter, with an ambiguous headline would have said, 'A Convict Dies—His Finger Prodding His Hole.' Like a woman into labour, he pushed harder, huffing and puffing in rhythm. And then he felt something. It was the string of cotton curled around his first finger. He focused his mind on twisting it some more.

"Hold that position, good job," he said to the winds like an artist was begging his model not to move an inch.

Sosobala pulled the string whilst pushing his sphincter muscle. Some more, he felt the tip of the homemade knife coming out, bit by bit. As he made a final pull, a bomb exploded. If his ass had faced in the direction of the cell, the whole forty plus inmates would have dropped instantly like flies sprayed with an insecticide.

Soso sighed, soaking wet.

His throat felt dry and played with saliva, back and forth, from the mouth to the throat canal. He glanced, displeased, at the knife as he leapt onto the linoleum. It was coated in brown with reddish stains, a distinctive sculpture. He pulled up his pants with his left hand, and then wiped the knife with a tissue. He hid it in his crotch and then shuffled feebly back to his bed like a boxer who had been in the fight of his life, and won by a slight margin. Every step taken closer to his bed, Chopper's glare became more and more piercing to his soul. He revisited his plan again as he sat on his bed. But then froze when he spotted Chopper's lieutenants occupied with ill-treating the sky-birds.

Wait a minute, Chopper was seated, legs and arms folded on his bed, half-naked while a sky-bird massaged his back. Sosobala's heart throbbed. His ears felt itchy...so were his hands and feet, itchy, like he had a rash. Madubula's weak and sad face resurfaced. He crouched, and then sat back down again.

What if? His mind rattled with the thought of seizing the moment. The hooves in his chest stomped harder and meaner. His body temperature skyrocketed faster than catching influenza. Chopper's bed was a few long feet away, about twenty feet or so. Sosobala calculated in his head as he realised the cell was bustling. It won't be a clear slam dunk. He would have to run like a mad man to get to Chopper's bed, and then stab him like lightning before Chopper's lieutenants could be alerted.

Which part of the body was the quickest for a fatal wound, was it the neck or the heart? He stole a peek, numerous times at Chopper's bed, and then at his lieutenants.

'Take revenge for me my friend.'

He crouched, sliding his right hand into his crotch, his fingers searching for the knife.

The time he had been thrust into such a situation played, flick after flick. He had been waiting for the Monday night to meet with Bonga after Duke's proposal of hijacking trucks promised a lot of cash. On that warm Saturday night, he felt positive about the future after the loss of his childhood friend, Boyi. He attended a pool party at Montclair. He took in his reflection in the bedroom mirror dressed in a shirt, as blue as the ocean, with matching casual jeans. He exited the house, but had to go back remembering that he forgot his gun. He had hidden it under the driver's seat before turning the ignition on. He cruised on the winding roads of his neighbourhood, bustling at night as if it was daytime.

Its women converged under the trees on the sidewalks, gossiping, probably about which widow had slept with which married man. And then girls, dressed in their skimpy skirts standing on the street corners, flashed wide smiles to every car that went past. Mobile guys parked on the sidewalks playing music full blast while their girls shook what their mamas gave them. Then penniless boys, oblivious to life responsibilities gathered under the street lights, fantasizing about being laid. And men, converged in the yards, playing some jazz music, and drinking their crazy souls to oblivion. What a vibrant township, as he was mesmerised by it all.

Sosobala cruised along the Mangosuthu Highway, occasionally glancing in the mirrors, seeing all the trees and whatnot—the houses, the steel containers, the motorcades, the streetlights he left behind until he linked with Kenyon Howden, the main road of the suburb. The pool party was packed to the rafters when seeing the parked cars lined up like they were a long shiny snake. The gold moon glinted off the cars' metallic paint.

He found a parking space on the sidewalk, away from the main road, under a street light so bright that you could spot a pin. He jumped out, pressed the immobiliser, and strode to the host's gates, directed by the loud music. Inside the yard, he side-stepped drunkards in the pathways, and lovers in the shade under the trees. He strutted around dancing groups in different circles until reaching the pool area in the back yard. Like a movie star with a thousand movies under his belt. Who was it who'd said that?

Sosobala was immobilised with excitement at the girls in all different forms... every one of them, beautiful and young. Some dressed skimpy while others were only in bright coloured bikinis covered with matching sarongs. It was as if they did not crouch like men when going to the loo. The way the alcohol flowed… everyone had a glass filled with something, or was clutching a bottle of something. It was as if they were at the breweries. He paced around the pool, like a kid in Disney Land. And then he felt a shove and found himself attempting to fly. For a moment, time stood still as he wondered: How far the pool was?

His body sank in water, and he battled to regain his balance like a drowning man trying to paddle out to shore. His heart sank as well as he recalled the cool image he had seen in his bedroom mirror before dashing out. The crowd burst into laughter. Like a livid giant slipping and sliding out of a tiny river, he waded out of the pool. Zooming in on the culprit cackling like a hen. Fury and confusion clouded his mind with a red haze as he hurtled towards the culprit. He jumped him, throwing blows and stomping on him after he had taken a dive. Within seconds, the claws dug into his flesh like a pack of wolves tearing a rabbit to pieces. He was overwhelmed after wrestling, kicking, screaming, punching and biting whatever his teeth came across.

"Stop this shit, now," a voice said, shoving the figures away from him.

Sosobala found a tiny gap to pass through as he sprinted to the gate like a mad man, cursing and swearing. His mind replayed the incident like a video recorder set on rewind as he got closer and closer to the car. He pressed the immobiliser, but then caught his reflection in the driver's window under the street light. His face bled, and his shirt was torn like he had been running through wet thorn bushes.

"Fuckin' dogs, they're going to pay for this," Sosobala said as he opened the door, and lowered his hand under the driver's seat.

He secured his gun and sprinted back to the host's gates like a guided missile heading straight for the target. The laughter of the crowd, the cackling of the culprit, pulled a veil over his eyes. He side-stepped the drunkards, the lovers, the dancing crews, like a football player side-stepping his opponents as he headed for the touchline. He found himself before the culprit, holed up in a corner spot, a distance away from the exit of the house. Sosobala lifted his hand, and aimed like a season shooter. The screams of the party-goers drowned the full blast party music as they scattered in all directions like ticks in a dog's fur.

"How do you like me now, bitch," Soso said.

He was incensed beyond his wildest imagination like a boil ready to be popped. He blinked once, his heart throbbing, and pumped a few rounds at him. He swayed looking around and found those who could not run lay curled on the ground with their hands covering their heads. The culprit fell on the ground, moaning like a masturbating nun, imagining how it would feel like to be ravished under the full gold moonlight. Who was it who'd said that?

Sosobala sprinted out of the yard without a backward glance. He jumped into his car, and sped off, skipping red traffic light after red traffic lights on Kenyon Howden until he joined the Mangosuthu Highway. He had pulled in at his place and stormed into his bedroom, feeling no remorse for his actions. He stared, livid, at his bloodied face in the bathroom mirror, warm and salty tears ran down his cheeks, diverting to his lips. He splattered water on his face, hoping it would erase the memory of that night's events and restore his face again. But as the drops washed away, the scars on his face became fresh and real. He stomped out of the bathroom, and threw himself on the bed, until the sleep bug caught him. As he woke up in the morning, he checked his face and realised that it had all been real.

* * *

'Take revenge for me, my friend', a veil covered his eyes as he pulled the knife out. He clutched the knife lower on his right side; his breath puffing rhythmically in and out. Like a sprinter waiting for the sound of a gun to signal a take-off, his muscles became taut. Blood rushed to his head. His jaw muscles locked like a person attacked by a seizure.

Take revenge for me, my friend.

On your mark, ready, set, go! The gun signal in his mind sounded as he hurtled towards Chopper's bed. Heavy breathing dominated his every move. Sosobala shoved aside the figures obstructing his pathway like a rugby player on the pitch as he sprinted to catch an airborne ball.

Take revenge for me, my friend.

Each stomp his feet made contact with the linoleum, was in tandem with his huffs. He trimmed the seconds in his life, just as he trimmed the distance between him and Chopper. His eyes locked on his target, monitoring its every movement.

Take revenge for me, my friend.

Sosobala sounded a crazed primitive shriek, sickeningly echoing in the hallway as he hurtled towards him, getting closer and closer.

"Look out!"

Dammit. Sosobala lifted his right hand like a renowned swordsman and took aim. The neck or the heart?

"Aahhh," Chopper sounded a shriek. "Moth'fucker."

But then Sosobala found himself wrestling with Chopper on the bed like two bulls in a kraal, their eyes bloodshot, their breathing heavy, each aiming to be the only one left standing. Sosobala lost momentum when many hands dug into his flesh, leaving him overwhelmed. He was on the linoleum, pinned down.

Was he gored in the neck or heart? he wondered as Chopper's supine figure moaned on the bed. Chopper's left cheek was cut open, and a stream of blood flowed down his scrawny neck onto his shoulder, past his chest until it slid down into his waist of his trousers.

"Don't do anything to him, the moth'fucker is mine," Chopper said, demonically.

The words lingered in his mind like cheap perfume, as he realised that death knocked at his doorstep. He had two choices: to open the door and let death snatch his life away, or keep the door shut until some divine intervention took place. It had not worked for him all those years ago. Why would it work now?

"So you want to take me out?" Chopper said, feeling his left cheek, and licking blood off his fingers.

Sosobala wrestled, helpless, trying to break free of the lieutenants' grip. He lifted his eyes, and realised his plan to take out Chopper, stemming from his noble actions to save Madubula from being raped and take revenge for him had failed. And that there were serious consequences he was about to face. He glanced at his homemade knife, a mere inches away from him, and then to the lieutenants—the stocky type—pinning him down. He wished in that moment of need he had magic powers to order the knife to hit a fatal point in Chopper's neck or heart, and then to his lieutenants.

"Moth'fucker," Chopper said, nodding his gigantic head, "I'll give you a chance to make it happen."

Chopper continued with a glare, spitting on the linoleum, "The gang's number lore duel."

Chopper picked up the knife. Sosobala went still when he heard the words 'the gang's number lore duel.' It was not just any duel, it was a barbaric fight performed in the olden days when the old guards fought hard to dethrone one another. There were no time outs, no intrusions allowed from third parties, just a fight till the bitter end. Chopper had described it from one of his many teachings, about the number lore: Both fighters would have their left hands tied to each other's, and then a knife would be placed in the centre of the ring. The fighters would then wrestle to pick up the knife. The one that managed to pick up the knife first, would then use it to his advantage, to plunge the knife into a fatal point. The fight would be to the death, and the last man standing would then pull out the knife from a dead fighter's body, and licked the blood off it in order to ascend to a higher position.

Sosobala never understood the theory behind that, that the blood of the dead fighter, when taken in, transfused more power and wisdom to the living. Also the same knife would be used to inscribe the body of the last man standing with a tattoo of the playing cards that were tattooed on the dead fighter.

"Prepare for the duel," Chopper said with a satanic tone to the uproar of the convicts.

Sosobala's breath was caught in his throat. Fear, anger, and sadness all piled up into one as he accepted his unknown fate.

10

THE FIGHT TO THE DEATH

Sosobala grappled as the lieutenants snapped him up, and shoved him to the chambers. The sky-birds slunk to the front of the cell. They were like a flock of sheep ready to be fed in a barnyard. No matter what, he would never be a sky-bird even if it meant death for him. To be a man with no balls to stand up for himself, a man who allowed others to treat him like a bitch. If told to bend over, he would ask, 'How low?'

Sosobala stood in the centre of the ring as the crouching soldiers, in their uniforms, like the colour of the moon, stared at him with hardcore looks. They belted out the revolutionary songs when thunder struck. He regretted the day he ever challenged Chopper's authority. His feet became numb. Misery was written all over him as Chopper approached the centre of the ring with his slow 'don't fuck with me' intimidating rolling gait. But why at that crucial moment in his life, did the terror of thunder come stomping, and knocking at the door of his heart?

"This is your chance, moth'fucker," Chopper said with hatred in his voice.

The lieutenants tied their left hands—their skins touched—as Sosobala felt electricity, the kind that sent a frightening feeling, causing body spasms. After all, he was tied to the devil's favourite demon, Chopper. Sosobala's heart sank into the lowest levels when the knife was thrown by a lieutenant, more on Chopper's side than his. It was more like duelling in a handicapped fight. He injected his weak and shaken soul with his forgotten hardcore spirit. He never backed down from a fight. He consoled himself. It did not matter who it was.

That distinct moment when Bonga put him to the test flashed in his mind. It had been a beautiful Tuesday, and the sun shone out of an indigo sky. He had just dropped Duke off after their mishap with the BMW M5, and he rushed to the salon to inform the CMB. Hope the CMB believed him. After all, Boyi was his childhood friend, nothing could go wrong. Two familiar figures stood at the front gates of the shopping centre's parking lot. He parked in a hurry and paced towards them.

"Hey, CMB."

They had turned, and Boyi gave him a high five.

Bonga gestured with a nod of his finger.

"I've got bad news," Soso said, "the BMW M5, well, the police—"

Bonga's facial expression seemed as if Soso smelt of shit.

"No ways, what happened?" Boyi interjected.

The BMW M5, a shiny silver glider, jerked on the way to the drop-off point near Isipingo Hills. The fuel was empty. Panic set in as he flicked the headlights signalling Duke. He picked him up and they had rushed to the fuel station. But on their way back the cops were already there, swarming the car like ants on a dead cockroach. Bonga's spiteful grin on his albino face showed that he did not buy his story one bit.

"Bullshit, I want my cut, now," Bonga said.

"Easy Bonga," Boyi said, "didn't you hear him explaining just now?"

Bonga threw a hard slap at him and caused Soso's jaws to rattle. Blood clogged his brain, and he turned pale instantly.

"What are you doing?" Boyi said, darting in front of Bonga.

"I want my cut. Hear me?" Bonga said, following with a gob of spittle into his face.

Sosobala felt disrespected, and reduced to a crock. He approached Bonga, his fists tightly clenched at his sides. Every muscle in his body became taut, and ready for action. Soso lunged at him unannounced, and roughed him up like Bonga had been running through rocky mountains. Boyi jumped in between them, separating them.

"Watch your back," Bonga said with loathing in his voice.

"I'm not fuckin' scared of you," Soso said, fuming like a lizard as he jumped into his car, and drove away.

Duke heard about that incident, and as the CMB gang leader, summoned an urgent meeting at his place.

"What happened at the parking lot yesterday?" Duke asked.

"I can explain," Bonga said.

Bonga's presence, mere inches away from him emitted more heat than he could handle.

"Shut up, you listen to me, my boy, I have been in this game since you were in diapers," Duke said. "You pull such a stunt again, I'll bury you alive."

"It won't happen again," Bonga said, his look sheepish.

Even though Duke managed to water it down, he had been ready to take Bonga to no man's land.

* * *

In that moment, Sosobala began to view the formed ring as his coffin. His hardcore spirit felt drained even more of his strength by the thunder. It was as if the crouching soldiers, with their singing and hard clapping, booed him. His glance met Chopper's, a mere inch away from him. His fear, coupled with sadness and anger slowly became inflated like a balloon. They pulled and shoved, and his mind raced: Whatever happened, he had to prevent Chopper from reaching for the knife first. The skinny bastard was very strong, as Chopper easily swayed him around.

"You're mine, moth'fucker," Chopper said.

Soso's mind suppressed his terror of the thunder. His fright began to turn into guilt for failing Madubula when he was raped. And then it turned into anger for being a man with no balls to stand up for himself, then into hatred for what Chopper had put him through.

Sweat trickled down his armpits, and slithered into the groove of his butt cheeks. He spluttered swear words, more to himself than to Chopper. Chopper's right hand gripped on his neck as if he was turning the handle of a vice a twist at a time. Sosobala bellowed like a dying cow as he punched, kicked and shoved. They found themselves on the linoleum, rolling when Chopper locked his teeth into his flesh.

"Aaaaahhhhh."

Sosobala cried and moaned, like a man his ass whipped, when a chunk of his flesh, the breast, a tender steak, had been bitten off, and chewed by Chopper. Sosobala pulled himself up, while Chopper now had a knife clutched firmly in his right hand. Chopper toyed with him; he now had the upper hand. The thunder struck once, and then twice, sending Sosobala into immobility. He realised the end was drawing nearer. He just had to accept the inevitable.

"Aaaaahhh."

Sosobala screamed as the knife slashed him. It caught him in the stomach. He looked up, his eyes misty, and found Chopper glaring down at him with a satanic grin.

"Fuckin' bastard," Soso said, his tone hopeless.

He knelt on Chopper's feet as he moved his fingers over his stomach. Madubula's face, the last time he came over to his bedside resurfaced: he looked sad and angry. Just like the face of Boyi when he slumped on the ground during their botched micro-loan bank robbery: he looked sad and angry. Also like the face of his father the time he thudded to the ground: he looked sad and angry. Could he afford to be a failure, to be a disappointment in the moment of need?

"I'm the man," Chopper said, glancing around the ring seeing victory was imminent.

The singing and the hard clapping of the crouching soldiers reminded him of the times he was coerced by his mother to attend church when he was a young boy. The worshippers sang and clapped as if the doors of heaven were opening up. If ever there was such a thing. He had been confused at the time. His mother's and other worshippers' faces perspired non-stop. Sosobala never felt the spirit—while others acted like they did—connecting him with the heavenly being.

Sosobala looked at his fingers: there was little blood. The slashing was not that deep after all. But then Chopper pulled him up steadily.

"Remember this face," Chopper pointed at himself with a knife, "on your way to hell, moth'fucker."

Chopper mouthed each word with a satanic voice, and he enjoyed seeing Sosobala in that vulnerable position.

"Fuckin' no," Sosobala said, spluttering.

He sensed it was not the time yet to join Madubula, or his childhood friend Boyi, or even his father for that matter, in death.

"Out now, I need you." His mind shouted at his spirit to burst open the doors where it rested.

"I'm going to enjoy putting you down, moth'fucker. And then, I'll rape you over and over again, and hear you moan just like that sky-bird friend of yours," Chopper said, his laughter satanic.

Sosobala digested each and every word Chopper said. Madubula's moans like a wounded cub resurfaced with Chopper on his behind as if Madubula was some lingerie model Chopper paid to lure into his bed. Sosobala felt the balloon of anger and hatred inflated more and more until it burst, flooding his hardcore spirit with the desire to wreak havoc. His muscles became taut as Chopper opened his mouth and a shriek, satanic scream shot out of him. Chopper lifted his right hand to plunge the knife into him. Sosobala felt his hardcore spirit flowing from head to toe like an electric current cascading through wires to produce energy.

He met Chopper's hand in the air, clutched it, and twisted it. He kicked Chopper in the gut and he tumbled onto the linoleum. Sosobala leaned over his body and forced Chopper's hand to submit to his strength.

"No, moth'fucker," Chopper said as his own hand pressed the knife into his neck.

Sosobala urged his hardcore spirit to have no mercy for his tormentor as he plunged the knife, steadily into his scrawny neck.

"Help," Chopper said, and gave out a gurgling sound. His one eye tried to find his lieutenants.

The gang's number lore stated that anyone who interfered with the duel would be punished by death administered by the other soldiers. Sosobala felt the knife slashing through Chopper's neck muscles. Like a boxer who just landed a right blow on the head of his opponent, but having an urge to pound him some more, Sosobala pushed it deeper, with more vigour that time around.

"Moth'fuc—" Chopper said, bellowing like a dying cave monster.

Chopper's veins ripped, and blood pulsed. His writhing, supine form became lifeless. Sosobala's mind raced. Was he really dead? The man who put fear into the entire prison? He hesitantly leaned over Chopper's body to pull the knife out and lick the blood off it, according to the number lore.

Sosobala forced himself, and pulled it out. And the blood, warm, shot out like a fountain. It painted his face and his clothes in bold red as if he was a sculpture on which a crazy demented artist splattered red paint.

He tried to lick it, but at first the smell of blood clogged his nostrils like he had just inhaled a poisonous gas. And then his lips touched it, and his tongue took in a quick taste of it: a taste and an aroma of half-done grilled meat. Like a wolf licking blood off its dead prey, he let his tongue run wild across the knife.

Sosobala untangled himself and steadily pulled himself up, raising the 26 gang sign, a thumbs-up. He lifted his gaze and swayed around the ring, and realised other soldiers had raised their right fists on their faces with thumbs up. That meant they accepted him according to the number lore as the new 26 gang leader. It was a deep sense of accomplishment just like when the boxing announcer in the ring would shout on the microphone, 'Here's the new heavy weight champion of the world', and the crowd would go haywire with the clapping and the blowing of the whistles.

As the thunder struck again, it was the thunder of applause for his accomplishments in climbing Mount Kilimanjaro: suppressing his terror of it. And standing victorious on top of it: slaying Chopper. And planting a flag to mark his territory: assuming the position as a new 26 gang leader. But as the thunder subsided, he knew it, he felt it, and he sensed it in the pit of his heart that his life in that prison would never be the same again.

"Tell the sky-birds to clean up here, now," Sosobala said to the soldiers, his state feeble.

He had just issued a command, his first of many more to come. He shuffled to the toilet like a hundred year old drunkard with a hangover, and felt the eyes of his cellmates heavy on him. He cleaned himself up, and walked back to his bed. The sky-birds cleaned Chopper's blood with fear and relief. They were so used to seeing dead bodies, and cleaning blood, it was as if they worked in a mortuary.

11

BECOMING A MONSTER

"Breakfast," the warder's voice said as he unlocked the cell gate, and peeped through the hallway.

A middle-aged, dark skinned man was baffled as he blew a whistle and sprinted out. Sosobala counted in his head: one thousand and one, one thousand and two, one thousand and three, one thousand and four... They stood to attention against the wall when Montie and his heavily armed prison guards walked into their cell in that minute.

"Fuck, what happened here?" Montie said, puzzled.

Montie's jaws dropped to the linoleum as he stared at Chopper's lifeless body like discarded waste, in the far end corner of the cell. Soso knew when glancing at the spotlessly cleaned cell that Montie would be coercing the inmates for answers. If there was a shredder to dispose of Chopper's body, not even a sniffer dog could have suspected anything.

"Fuck, who did this, you scumbags?" Montie asked, his sight rotating like a laser.

Montie's look pierced right through him like an ice pick plunged into his eyes. Sosobala's mind gloated: nobody would snitch on him, and he damn well knew he would not be going to solitary. That would spell the end of whoever opened his mouth. The wrath of the soldiers unleashed on a snitch was like the wrath of a lion in a cage unleashed on whatever was stealing its cub. Montie had nothing on him. Nothing.

"Fuck, have it your way, okay?" Montie said. "From now on, no cafeteria or recreation time until you scumbags tell me what the fuck happened here."

His mind ridiculed Montie as he took him in: he had a pulled face, piercing blue eyes like sapphire, and was well-muscled like a German shepherd.

Sosobala spat on the linoleum just like Chopper did when his body was carried out of the cell. He stopped short of singing, "Na Na Na Na Hey Hey-ey Goodbye."

Sosobala assumed his duties associated with being a 26 gang leader. His body accumulated tattoos. He had one on his right arm, the 26 gang sign he had after taking the pledge and earning his stripes. And then the crossed swords on his left arm Chopper insisted on, for showing his rough side. But now, the playing cards: an ace of spades and a diamond of kings inscribed on his shoulders, respectively, for dethroning the gang leader.

He played with the thought of getting another tattoo of the playing cards, maybe, a king of spades. Now that one would demand the killing of the warder or another gang leader. Montie flashed in his mind as he chuckled demonically. Sosobala felt a sense of achievement as the soldiers and lieutenants consulted in him before engaging in any matters. And he enjoyed the perks afforded to a gang leader, of keeping what he desired from the soldier's hustled goods.

As days went by, one of the late Chopper's lieutenants, a buff form with a scar crossing his left bloodshot eye, challenged his authority. Even implied that Sosobala was a Johnny-come-lately in the 26 gang.

"To the fuckin' chambers, now," Sosobala said, summoning the lieutenant.

He felt the need to make an example of him. They stood in the centre of the ring as the crouching soldiers sang and clapped. Sosobala concentrated on the knife in the centre of the ring. He blinked once... he snapped it up; he blinked twice... he plunged it in and out of the lieutenant's neck. The writhing lieutenant slumped onto the linoleum, clutching his neck, and puffing out oxygen through an open wound. Blood spurted like a fountain. With a crazed primitive, satanic scream, Sosobala stabbed him countless times as if with every stab, he wanted the knife to drill through the flesh all the way till it slashed the linoleum. He gouged out his eyes, and shoved them down his throat. He lifted himself up, and raised a 26 gang sign. He found the soldiers' sign rose, another approval of his actions. He pulled the knife out and licked it, and his nostrils welcomed the smell of blood. And his mouth got used to the tangy taste. Like a zombie, he stared at the linoleum: it was not so shiny anymore. He shouted for the sky-birds to clean up. He liked it shiny, very shiny, just like his first day in prison when he glanced at his moving shadow on the linoleum. It was very shiny. He chuckled when his body accumulated some more tattoos.

"My goodness, no," Montie said the next morning during a roll call, his face red and eyebrows twitching. "Fuck this, its lockdown."

The lockdown was the time when the prison cells were ransacked for any contraband. The convicts' privileges to go to the cafeteria, or to have visitors, or have recreation time, were rescinded. It had happened before, numerous times, Sosobala knew it would be a thing of the past in the next coming week or so.

The way the soldiers and the sky-birds avoided eye contact when engaging him, they had fear written on their faces, spelt in big bold letters. Something more perverse and demonic had found a dwelling inside him.

Monster.

The time when the monster in him brewed like a volcano that had not erupted in a thousand years, resurfaced. It was when he fatally shot the beefy man during the christening of his first taxi. And shortly after that, the monster in him had been awoken, ready and taut. It played in his mind, scene after scene.

The gold moon and the stars illuminated the dark velvety sky on that Friday evening. His gang, the CMB, had gone to the affluent suburbs of Durban to hustle. They scored a winner, Duke's term for paying merchandise, did a drop-off and headed to the shopping centre, their smiles wider than a ruler.

"The sound system in my taxi is the bomb," Soso said. "No fuckin' taxi in Umlazi, I tell you guys, can beat it."

"No ways. I won't waste thousands of my moolah, for what, a sound system?" Boyi said.

"That's how money is made," Bonga said. "If your taxi doesn't beat the loudest, my hustler, it won't attract commuters."

Boyi shook his head. Sosobala pulled in at the usual parking lot.

"My fuckin' taxi, guys—" Soso said as he leapt out. "My sound system is gone, all gone."

Sosobala circled his reddish taxi like an ant circling a dead worm.

"Who did this shit?" Boyi asked.

"I bet you it's those junkies who smoke this shit, whoonga," Bonga said, rubbing his hands anxiously. "I know where to find them."

The guns were nearby, and Soso was boiling hot: it was about to get chaotic in the neighbourhood. Bonga's directions ended in a backyard shack of a red-brick four roomed house in the east of Umlazi. They jumped out with guns in hand, and slipped through to the back, busting open the shack door. Three junkies relaxed inside, puffing the drug through the mouth of a broken glass bottle. They looked skinny, and young, about fourteen years or so.

"Where's my sound system, you fuckin' junkies?" Soso said, with disdain.

Before the junkies could say one syllable, they lunged at them like lions tearing at a helpless prey. Sosobala peeped under the bed secured on bricks, and found his stereo.

"Let's fuckin' take them away," Soso said, his eyebrows twitching.

"Where to?" Boyi asked.

"Behind the shopping centre," Bonga said.

There was an open field behind the shopping centre, where they used to play soccer a long time before. Within a flash, they pulled in at the open field.

"Out you fuckin' bastards," Soso said. "Where is my sound system?"

They shoved the junkies on the ground as they knelt in a row, their faces already disfigured with fear. Soso's heart beat faster, so was his palms itchy.

"Sorry CMB, it's a mistake, have—" the junkies said, their tones pleading.

What Sosobala felt on that night was more pure and demonic, in control, knowing he held the lives of the pleading junkies in the palm of his hand.

"Let's finish them off," Bonga said.

Bonga uttered his last syllable, as Sosobala took in a fresh breeze of Lucifer's breath. It brushed tenderly against him, letting him know, coaching him, and giving him the assurance that he was now going to be ONE with him. He blinked once as the gunshot crashed. In slow motion, the junkie's body in front of him slumped on the ground. His eyes locked with that of his fellow CMB as he felt like he graduated summa cum laude, and he loved every minute of it. As he heard and obliged at Lucifer's voice in his ears to pump a fusillade of bullets at them, Sosobala accepted that from henceforth something more sadistic had been awoken inside him. They jumped into the car without a backward glance, leaving the junkies' lifeless bodies on the ground, covered in blood. Days later, the gossipers at the salon mentioned that even the police in the area had been happy about the junkies' death after they eluded them for quite some time, after terrorising the neighbourhood.

Days went by smoothly but his nights turned sweaty as he was haunted by the beefy man and the junkies. He had gone to Duke to allay his fears.

"Go to a sangoma, Soso, and get cleansed. The dead don't sleep, my friend," Duke said to him.

The next freezing morning he painted the tarmac with his tyres until he exited from the main road onto the narrow gravel path, about the half-a-kilometre away, with fields of sugar cane on either side. Dust lingered in the air as he drove uphill until he reached the isolated horseshoe-shaped homestead. He pulled in at its wooden gates, and was directed by an initiate to a hut, dingy and dimly lit. Ndosi, the sangoma, lit the incense and threw the bones, and cleared his throat.

"Ho ho, I see blood on your hands," Ndosi said with a hoarse voice. "The ancestors are very upset."

Ndosi shook his head, a feather protruding from his silver Afro, and summoned an initiate.

"Ho ho, find a white goat, a pregnant one in the cattle kraal," Ndosi said. "Bring me its foetus. Mix its blood with the cleansing muti in a large bowl. Hurry up now."

The initiate came back into the hut, placed the large bowl next to Ndosi's pet. Sosobala had never felt comfortable near a sprightly python.

"Ho ho, take-off your clothes. Hop over the pet, into the bowl."

He cringed but did as per orders.

"Guardians of the universe, cleanse the boy of the blood on his hands. Give him a new start in life just like a foetus," Ndosi said, summoning the ancestors. "Go now; take the bowl mixture to the kraal. Bury it together with the white goat. Don't look back, and come back here."

He nodded, did as per instructions and came back into the hut, shaken.

"Use this muti for seven days." Ndosi pointed at the 2-litre container with a yellow concoction. "Induce vomit in the mornings, and bathe with it at night to revive the spirit of your ancestors," Ndosi said.

* * *

Time went by when again he felt the monster in him had been emancipated after the shooting of a bandit at the pool party in Montclair, shortly followed by Sifiso. The sweaty nights again had recurred. And he had taken a decision to go back to the sangoma's homestead.

"Ho ho, that look in your face, means you're troubled, again,"

Ndosi said.

"My lion tooth necklace broke, need to know what it means, Makhosi," Soso said, addressing him with a praise name for the sangoma.

He then showed him the broken necklace.

Ndosi lit the incense, the light smoke permeated in the hut, and shook the bag made of goat skin, and threw the bones. Ndosi frowned, and snuffled his snuff on the floor, sneezing aloud.

"Ho ho, this isn't good, not good at all," Ndosi said, combing his beard. "I have to speak directly with your ancestors."

Ndosi extracted a small bottle out of his shabby cargo pants, and guzzled the potion in it, and began speaking in different tones.

"Guardians of the universe, the boy's constantly doing wrong, be lenient on him," Ndosi said, staring at the bones on the floor.

Stealthily, Ndosi picked them up, and shook the bag again. This time he threw them with vigour.

"Why take away the lion tooth necklace, it's the boy's protection?" Ndosi insisted, concentrating on the bones as he picked them up, shook the bag and threw them again.

Ndosi got irritated as he communicated in different voices with the bones; he gestured as if there were three to four more people in the hut.

"He's just a boy, he's still growing up. He needs your guidance. Without you, he's nothing," Ndosi said to the bones, showing signs of growing frustration. "You can't disown him now."

By the look of things, Ndosi was not backing down to whoever he was engaging with. Ndosi had the look of a man about to go to war with his detractors.

"I am Cele from the Ndosi clan with powers to make a tornado. I was bestowed with these powers under Lake Jozini by my forefathers who also gave me the authority to make sleet. I graduated with a medal of honour," Ndosi said, gesturing like he was a choir conductor.

It was as if Ndosi had explained to the invisibles about which degree he was conferred with when he graduated to be a sangoma.

Naming the institution as Lake Jozini, one of the biggest lakes in the world, and under whose professor—who knows what—he studied.

"I plead with you, let me help the boy," Ndosi said to the invisibles, looking drained.

"What do they say?" Soso asked, growing impatient.

"Ho ho, your ancestors are difficult spirits," Ndosi said, rolling his eyes. "They say you're on your own."

"On my own?" Soso cursed and swore at the invisibles.

"Mind your language. You don't talk like that in here, Sosobala," Ndosi said.

Sosobala had crawled out of the hut, and threw away his lion tooth necklace on his way out.

"Ho ho, what you've done today, I'm afraid, your fate has chosen a painful death," Ndosi said, saddened.

Sosobala sneered at him, and jumped into his car, and raced it onto the narrow gravel road, dust lingering in the air like a thick misty fog until he linked onto the main tarmac road.

12

PAROLE DENIED

Sosobala became distracted when Montie and the heavily armed guards stomped into the cell.

"Sosobala NoZulu," Montie said across the hallway, "come, and crouch over here." He pointed to the front of the cell.

He digested Montie's orders as he lay on his bed like a deer half-digesting its cud.

"Fuck. Get here, now," Montie said, his tone intimidating. "Don't make me repeat that, okay?"

The words 'Get here, now' hung in his mind like the smell of a drunkard's vomit. His father's words ringed back in a flesh, calling him when he was in his bedroom, doing his schoolwork.

"Soso, get here, now," his father said in a military tone.

He nodded like an obedient child, treading carefully so as not to get on his wrong side.

Sosobala shuffled, his look glaring, for having been disturbed in his 'me' time. He reached Montie encircled by the prison guards, and then crouched.

"Today's your parole review, okay?" Montie said, staring down at him.

Sosobala had no high hopes of being granted a parole. Montie as the rehabilitation officer would certainly be testifying about him. Montie had loathing in his eyes, as he took a quick look at him. If ever he was hanging over a cliff on a string, and Montie was there. Between pulling him up and cutting it loose, he believed Montie would pick the latter.

How time flew, it was like yesterday when he first entered the steel gates of the Westville Medium B Prison. How its constipated warders looked, still looked menacing each time he made eye contact with them. And how he heard another convict who looked like prison was his home away from home, in the van as it pulled in at the prison gates.

"Your lives are about to change for the worst. Some of you will be somebody's bitches before nightfall." The convict said, giggling, "kiss the smell of pussy goodbye."

Wonder what that convict would have said if he saw him now? He huffed oxygen, warm and smelly, as the guard pulled him up and searched him, and then shoved him out of the cell. Their footsteps sounded noisily along the corridors like tubes, steel gate after steel gate, opening and closing. Sosobala smelt fear and uncertainty as the prison guards sandwiched him. The way their eyes were intense, it was as if they were waiting for him to sneeze, and then pounce on him with their stun guns and batons.

"Get in," Montie said, opening the door to a secluded office.

The office set up had three tables formed in a U-shape. Each table accommodated two people, but only five seats were occupied by the parole review board members: four men, and one woman, in dark suits. Their eyes were intense with pens in their fingers, and notebooks on the top of the tables. And they were seated shoulder to shoulder. Directly opposite the U-shaped table was a chair, isolated. Montie shoved him with hands the size of a bull skull, and directed him into the isolated chair. Montie took a vacant seat on the side table, adjacent to him.

"We may begin," Montie said, his blue eyes as intense as the rest.

Sosobala crouched on the chair looking at the setup: the looks and the atmosphere in the room. It all came back flooding him during his trial date for the murder of Sifiso. It played like he was staring at a projector, and the movie was screening. He had been locked at the Umlazi Magistrate's Court underground cells awaiting with eagerness for his name to be called.

"Sosobala NoZulu," the officer of the court had shouted.

He emerged from the underground cells and climbed up the stairway into the courtroom. His eyes found his attorney. He remembered how he came to be acquainted with his attorney. It had been raining cats and dogs on that night. The sky seemed darker than usual as he lay coiled on the foam mattress with the aroma of dog urine, in an isolation cell. Footsteps came towards his cell. The sound of the footsteps grew louder and nearer, and then stopped. Someone cleared his throat.

"Wake up," the feisty voice said. "Come here."

Sosobala aimed his look at the cell gate, not recognising the voice. But it sounded like one of those rare voices with the impact of a high pressure jetting system. He slowly lifted himself holding his breath, and then shuffled towards the cell bars, showing visible signs of pain.

"You're Sosobala, right?" the deep voice asked, the speaker holding the cell bars with one hand.

While trying to understand the man's reasons for enquiring, he nodded hesitantly. The speaker was of average height; had loose hair hanging at shoulder height, and looked directly at him with clear eyes.

Sosobala figured out whom he resembled: Danny Crane of Boston Legal, an American TV series about big shot lawyers that would acquit a mass murderer using their wit.

"Who are you?" Soso asked, his tone shy as he leaned against the bars.

"I'm Billy Thornton, your attorney. I'll be representing you in your trial."

"But I never—" Soso said, his mind racing fast.

"Don't worry about that," the attorney said. "For now, try and get some rest. We have challenging days ahead of us."

"Who hired you?" Soso asked.

The likeable attorney grinned with a cockiness that could bring the world to its knees. Who was it who'd said that? And he paused for a while longer, milking as much anxiety out of Sosobala as possible.

"Duke," Thornton said with a firm stare.

Sosobala listened to the attorney's steps receding until he could hear them no more.

On the day of the trial, at the public gallery: his mother was there, as was Duke and Sifiso's mother, a strong black woman, who threw a disgusted glance at him coupled with sadness.

"All rise," a straight faced officer of the court said.

The judge entered the courtroom. Her upper lip was thicker than a lower lip, and she had small green eyes.

"Be seated," she said.

The various officers of the court shuffled papers until a prosecutor with long straight hair addressed the judge, enumerating the charges levelled against Sosobala.

"Your Honour, the accused has been charged with first-degree murder, under schedule 6," the Indian prosecutor said as she shot him a venomous look.

Sosobala became agitated: The witch did not know him.

"How do you plead?" the Judge asked.

"Not guilty," Soso said, in a not-so-convincing voice while aiming his gaze at his attorney.

"Will the state present its case," the Judge said. "Are witnesses here to testify? Call them now."

"Yes, your Honour. I'd like to call Captain Warren Jones to take the stand," the prosecutor said, her tone growing in confidence.

The courtroom door opened, and a fuzzy draught sneaked in. It ushered the high spirited captain, who had skidded past the public gallery to leap into the witness box. The captain's soldier's haircut brought out his flapping ears like an aero plane wings. The captain struck a pose that affirmed his passion for fighting crime. His big figure caused his body to bulge out of his shabby coat.

"Raise your right hand, and take the oath," the officer of the court said, holding a bible on his hands.

"I swear to tell the truth, nothing but the whole truth. So help me God," the captain said, placing his left hand on the Bible with his right hand raised in the air.

"Please, state your name and your occupation, sir," the prosecutor said.

"Warren Jones, Captain of the Durban Serious Crimes and Prevention Unit," the captain stated.

"Please tell us a bit about you and your involvement in this case, Captain."

"Well, I've been a bloody—" Jones cleared his throat, gesturing with an 'excuse the language' hand, "member of the SAPS for thirty years. And I've been a captain of my unit for the past ten years. I've had a conviction rate of ninety five percent, the remaining five percent being that the alleged accused died."

The prosecutor nodded in a way as if a doll with a broken neck.

"I'm the leading investigating officer in this case, the murder of Sifiso Mkhize. My team and I have worked tirelessly in compiling a tight case against the accused," the captain said. "The deceased was gunned down in broad daylight by the alleged accused in the parking lot of the Executive Hotel."

"Please go on, sir," the prosecutor said.

"The evidence is in fact overwhelming. It puts the accused on that day at the Executive Hotel gunning down the deceased."

"Objection," Thornton said, hunched in his chair. "Until the court has proven its case, the captain should refrain from giving his own concocted verdict."

"Overruled," the judge said. "Go on please, Captain."

"The accused's girlfriend was allegedly raped on the day of the murder of the deceased. And a video footage of the alleged accused in the hotel lobby, together with the girlfriend and the other suspect is available here, if the court pleases."

"Your honour, we present the court with evidence A," the prosecutor said, leaping towards the judge's bench to place a small package on it.

Before the trial began, Thornton told Sosobala not to be concerned too much about the video footage. It showed what the mind wanted the eye to see.

"Is the man who murdered Sifiso Mkhize in cold blood, in broad daylight, here in court today, Captain?" the prosecutor said with verve. "Please point at him."

The retch nearly came out at the repeated mention of Sifiso's name.

"Yes, he's seated right there," the captain pointed at him with confidence in his eyes, "Sosobala NoZulu."

"Thank you, Captain. No further questions," the prosecutor said as if smelling the taste of victory.

Thornton sprang from his chair as if it was toast and began his questioning. Sosobala sat itching in the seat not knowing what to expect from him.

"Captain, I'll like to commend you for being the dedicated crime buster," Thornton said with a straight face. "The country certainly needs more man like you."

He had been confused as to why his attorney would commend the loony captain on his work.

"What are you fuckin' doing, that's the enemy?" Soso's mind had blown off the rooftop.

"But surely, Captain, you must have recovered a murder weapon. However I do believe, you only saw my client strolling in the hotel lobby with his sweetheart, and his friend, as per your video footage. But not as you assumed, captain, in the parking lot where the so-called murder took place," Thornton said, his presence commanding.

The captain fiddled with his tie, red as fire, as the attorney continued.

"How long have you'd encounters with my client, Captain?"

"For a while now," the captain said, clearing his throat.

"And how'd you describe your encounters, pleasant, unpleasant?"

"Unpleasant. You bloody listen to me," Jones crouched, scowling. "I have an unwavering commitment to the SAPS. Sosobaal should be kept behind bars. He has no conscience, and gangsters like him subscribe to the motto: kill or be killed. You hear me?"

Holy shit, the captain had lost his cool demeanour.

"So Captain, guys like my client, Sosobala, disgust you. They'd be kept behind bars, right?" Thornton said while chancing a gaze at the prosecutor, who tucked her hair behind her not-so-small ears. "You'd do anything to remove them off the streets. Correct?"

"It's my duty to fight crime, and make the city of Durban a safer place," the captain said. "Yes, that means putting away guys like him."

"Is there someone right here in this court room who'd testify that he saw my client, Sosobala NoZulu, murdering the deceased?" Thornton said while aiming his look at the captain, then the judge, and then the prosecutor.

Sosobala knew that people from his neighbourhood would not dare risks their lives to come forward, and testify.

"All the evidence points to him," the captain said, his revolting look directed at him. "Unfortunately the woman in the video footage and the other suspect couldn't be traced."

"So Captain, you do admit that you don't have a witness that'd finger my client in your witch-hunt?" Thornton said with his eyes firmly directed at the judge, then the prosecutor, "do you captain?" He paused. "No further questions."

The captain paused for a while longer with a distraught look, then shook his head.

"I'd like the honourable judge, if the court pleases, to grant me more time to bring these key witnesses to the court," the captain said, his tone pleading like that of a dying man.

"You're wasting the court's precious time, Captain, and most importantly my client's freedom is being prejudiced by your inflated ego," Thornton said as he paced back and forth in front of his table. "I'd like the honourable judge to throw this case out of court, and set my client free."

The atmosphere in the court room became intense as the captain glanced sheepishly at the prosecutor.

"I'd like the matter to be postponed for a week in order to allow the dedicated captain more time to add to his evidence," the prosecutor said, crouching with a defeated tone.

"Not a chance. I'll go through the evidence presented before me. Understand, this matter will be finalised tomorrow. Court's adjourned," the judge said.

He shook Thornton's hand with a smile that implied, 'Great job buddy.' He was whisked away back to the cells in the police station. Just one more day, he gloated when realising that Thornton thrashed the captain on the witness box. The next morning announced itself with a clear blue sky as he sat in the courtroom. Sosobala monitored the judge's lips, second by second.

"After going through the evidence presented before me," the judge said, not mincing her words. She read out the sentence.

"What, ten years?" Sosobala said in the courtroom realising the judge screwed Thornton, moreover him. Eligible for a parole in the third year was not so bad after all.

* * *

He came back to his senses when he heard his name being mentioned by the parole review board member.

"Montie, as a rehabilitation officer, please state your objections, if any, in granting Sosobala NoZulu parole," a female parole review board member said.

"I've been a warder for over thirty years. And have seen hardcore convicts in my tenure, come and go. Some left prison as changed men, some died in prison through gang violence or being subdued by the warders," Montie said, and coughed a bit. "But I have never encountered a demon like Sosobaal."

"What?" Sosobala said, choking. "What about the late Chopper," he repulsed, "was he an angel?"

"Please, Mr. NoZulu, you'll get your chance to speak," one of the parole review board members said.

"As I was saying before I was so rudely interrupted, this convict has been nothing but trouble since the first day he entered this prison. But of late, he has been a monster in the making. Now you board members know a convict who has assumed the position of a gang leader is like a God to these so-called soldiers. Or at least that's what their crazed hypnotic number lore states."

Sosobala stared at him with that, 'I don't believe you have just rubbished me so disgustingly look.'

"Fuck, a young boy was raped a mere month ago, and Sosobala failed to reveal who the culprits were. I suspect he was one of the rapists. Maybe he choked when it was his turn. Putting him into solitary, I'm afraid was like fuelling him. Guess what he did afterwards, he went into the cafeteria, and left another convict bloodied on the floor."

"So what you're implying, Montie, is that he'd not be rehabilitated under one of our programmes?" another board member asked.

"I'm afraid not," Montie continued, "what I have told you is just the tip of the iceberg."

"Okay, go on then."

"After the warders subdued him, he goes to hospital for a week, and when he comes out, guess what he does, he kills the gang leader of the 26s. While that causes an uproar in here, in a mere week," Montie twitched his eye brows, "he takes out another convict in the most sick way I have ever, ever seen in my thirty odd years as a warder. Fuck, this convict's a monster, and I'll urge the members of the board to consider moving him to another prison. Maybe the Kokstad Prison."

So he had rubbished him, and moreover he wanted to have him shifted to Kokstad prison, where prisoners were locked down twenty-four-seven in isolated cells. He glared at Montie as he continued.

"What you have here is the new gang leader of the 26s. The reason even now there's a total lockdown in here, it's all thanks to him. Now I've got a family I go to everyday after I knock-off here, and the feeling I've been getting recently when I come to work," Montie frowned as he shook his head, "is of fear, and uncertainty as to whether I'll be going home in one piece or as a corpse. Fuck, this convict doesn't deserve a parole, not now or in the near future. Trust me."

The parole review board members scribbled something on their notebooks, and then began asking him questions.

"Do you have anything to say for yourself, Mister NoZulu?" a member asked with an intense look.

Anger welled up inside him when he looked at them in their formal wear and formal attitudes, and formal dialogues. They knew nothing about his life, or the pain he had felt since the day he entered the prison and took the pledge of the gang's number lore: to live or die by it.

"I've got nothing to say. You people know jack about my life in here. How it is to live in fear, not knowing if tomorrow will be your last. To be pushed around like you just a vomit. You don't know, do you?" Soso said, raising his voice in disgust. "Look around you, this is prison. It's a dog-eat-dog world. Shove that fuckin' parole up your asses."

"Well, you have said enough," the member said, rebuking him.

They continued to scribble down something, and then tore out the pages and circulated them around, to one another.

"Sosobala NoZulu, you have been denied parole. You'll be locked in here until your rehabilitation officer is fully convinced of your ability to change and act in a humane manner, and to go out there, as a decent member of society again."

"Let's go," Montie said, pushing his chair back and stared at him with satisfaction in his eyes.

He stood up harshly, swore and cursed, and then exited the room. As he shuffled back to his cell, Montie's figure, a mere inch away, boiled his blood faster than a steam kettle.

13

DEATH OF AN OLD FOE

Sosobala lay on his bed on that night, and Montie's words, rubbishing him in front of the parole review board replayed like a tape recorder on rewind. Where was Montie when he tried to help Madubula from being raped, knowing very well that his actions could jeopardise his parole? And what did Montie do instead... he threw him into solitary. If he had revealed the culprits, his life would have been finished right on the spot. For crying out loud, where was Montie when he was nearly sliced like a slab of tenderised meat by the late Chopper after he was released from solitary?

Like a naughty kid fidgeting with the buttons on a remote control, he continued: Where was Montie when the buff lieutenant provoked him at the cafeteria while he ended up being taken to pieces by the guards for standing up for himself?

Did Montie see Madubula's weak and sick body, eaten by HIV/AIDS as he shamefully begged him to take revenge for him? Where the hell was Montie when the late Chopper spewed those words about putting him down, and then raping him over and over again during the duel? Where the bloody hell was Montie when the buff lieutenant challenged his authority to the point of no return until he had to make an example of him?

Montie could judge him all he wanted but the fact of the matter was, Montie was on the other side of the fence. He could not fully comprehend the pain and the suffering that he went through. Sosobala created a hard shell around him where no one would ever get in.

No one.

Sosobala slept with one eye open when in the midst of it, he dreamt. His late father, good looking and solemn, was seated, relaxed, in a serene garden filled with all kinds of blossoming flowers, and ripe fruit trees. The father was encircled by men and women, young and old, in white bright clothes, dancing and ululating. Just a short distance away, were sprightly herds, fatted, and whatnots, feeding on knee-high green grass. A short distance away from the herds ran a stream with shades of whiteness flowing quietly under the banks. His mother, looking radiant, appeared across the stream in a white gown waving to get his father's attention. But she was too far away, and the father's back was turned. Then the stream cascaded over a cliff: a colossal dark brown frowning structure that seemed like it had been there for a thousand years. Beyond that cliff was an open land, dark and red, where sounds of shrieks reverberated under a dark gloomy cloud. Boyi, looked thin, dirty and miserable, was amongst the wriggling and imploding figures sounding a shriek of his own. A short distance away was a burning heap of fire in a cavern where Chopper, with fire blazing on top of his head, bursting into a satanic laughter, stood at the entrance of it. He shoved the screaming figures into the flames. Next to Chopper, was a buff lieutenant, blind, shoving his own victims into the heap of fire. Inside the burning pile were the faces of Bonga, his former gang member who betrayed him; the beefy man, the one he shot at during the christening of his first taxi; the three junkies who had broken into his taxi; the bandit who pushed him into a pool in a party in Montclair. And Sifiso, the one who raped Sandy. All shrieked as they were consumed by the burning flames. But then he–Soso–suddenly appeared into the heap of fire. Somehow the burning flames did nothing to him…

"Roll call," the warder said as the cell gate unlocked.

Sosobala sprang high as the sweat cascaded down every part of his body, warm and sticky like a slithering hungry worm. His heart throbbed and heavy breathing dominated much of his thoughts as he stood attention next to his bed. A familiar figure, Montie, guarded by a column of heavily armed guards, approached the centre of the hall.

"Listen up, you convicts," Montie said, "Fuck, the ban is lifted, so your privileges are back on."

Montie moved closer to him. Sosobala knew without a doubt that Montie despised the ground he walked on.

"Fuck, should just one incident, just one, happen in the near future," Montie said with a stern tone, speaking to his face. "So help me God, none of you scumbags will ever see the light beyond these prison walls again. Ever."

Montie's eyes meant every word of it. Soso roared silently knowing that when another chance came, there was no defying the monster inside him. Montie's figure slithered out of the cell.

Sosobala crouched on the spot trying to make sense of the dream. His father seated in a serene garden must have been the ancestral sacred place. And the women and men dancing and ululating must have been the ancestors. The open land, dark and red, where Boyi was making a shrieking sound was probably a place for bad souls like him waiting to be judged before being sent to hell. And the cavern must have been the real hell where all those who served the devil with distinction before death, like Chopper, and the buff lieutenant, would continue with his work. And the heap of fire with the dissolving faces of all those he disposed of, must have meant that, they themselves had done bad deeds and now their souls were burning in hell. His mother on the other hand, in a white gown, waving as if trying to get his father's attention across the stream, and him appearing into the heap of fire, but the burning flames doing nothing to him, confused him as to what it meant.

Soso sighed.

As the week progressed, he felt it in his heart, he sensed it in the way he walked, and in the way he gave orders that the prison had become his playground.

"Sosobala NoZulu, report to the visitors' room," the intercom sounded repeatedly.

Sosobala rolled his eyes, wondering who it could be. His mother again. He became agitated. But he had made it loud and clear to her to never visit him in prison again. He shuffled out of the cell when the warder unlocked the door, and called him out. He entered the steel gate of the visitors' room, and realised who was behind the visitor's booth. His cheeks lifted like a kid offered ice cream as he took a seat.

"It's been a long time," he said through an intercom.

"Indeed, it has been," the visitor said.

The visitor looked relaxed behind the glass booth glittering in gold.

"Glad to see you again, Duke," he said, sizing him up. "So what brings you here, after like what, fuckin' three years?"

"Good news, old friend. Better yet, great news for you," Duke said. "Your friend died a week ago."

The exact words Duke said when he came to visit him a few months after being imprisoned, not even a syllable missing. The idea of being in prison had not sunk in as yet, and that in prison to have regular visits was a sign of a good life in the outside. The intercom had summoned him for his first visitor.

"How're you holding up?" Duke asked.

"Look around you. I'm in a fuckin' prison, but slowly learning the ropes," he said. "Thought you were my mother."

"No man, it's me. If I was you, I wouldn't want my mother subjected to the kind of treatment that the female warders give to female visitors in here."

"What's that?" Soso asked.

"The way they conduct body searches, I tell you, beyond degrading," Duke said.

"In what way?"

"Hm, these bastards insert fingers in a vagina when conducting body searches, can you believe that shit?" Duke said, wide-eyed. "Trust me, it's better you keep your mother far away from here."

"You know, when I tell her to not come here, she thinks I'm being a fuckin' jerk," Soso said, remembering her last visit. "Try telling her that."

"I will when I go past to drop off the sale money for your Beemer."

The time he went to buy the Beemer with Duke had flashed in his mind. They pulled in at the gates of the dealer's yard in Pinetown, west of Durban.

"Is that the car?" he asked, pointing at it.

"You like it?"

"Fuckin' love it."

His eyes feasted on a BMW 325is, white as an ice, with all the desired features. That would be Ricky; he renamed the car on the spot. After the deal had been concluded, he pulled out of the yard, a proud man. It was like he had big balls the size of his new acquisition.

"That's a beast that one, take it easy on the road, CMB," Duke said over the whistling engine.

"See you in the township," he said, hooting and exiting the yard.

He sunk into the sports seat until he pulled in at his mother's. He left his mother speechless at the beauty of his new machine. It was Sandy's time to get acquainted with Ricky. He pulled in at the parking of her varsity residence. Ricky became a feast for the eyes of everyone who had come past him. He fondled with Sandy's door a couple of times. She opened with a beguiling flickering in her brown eyes. He took her by the hand as they walked along the corridors until reaching the parking. He then pressed the immobiliser; Ricky cockily unlocked.

She fiddled with every button her fingers could find like a child presented with a new toy. She sank in as her butt cheeks massaged the sports seat. Her face showed that she loved every minute of Ricky's whistles, and the Samba dances Ricky performed on the streets. He dropped her off, and headed to the shopping centre's parking lot. Sosobala had come back to his senses again when Duke giggled.

"It's a German made machine."

"I'll definitely miss Ricky," he said, with a 'So long' gesture.

"Don't fret, CMB, when you out of here, you'd still find your way back to riches."

"Maybe," he said, his voice saddened.

"Hang in there, we have all been through this, and we have survived," Duke said, clearing his throat. "The great news is—"

He wondered what could be so great because he was in prison.

"Your friend, who died a week ago," Duke said, "it's that two-timing B-O-N-G-A."

He felt a sense of relief and shock, even though his taxis were gone.

* * *

Sosobala snapped out of it, feeling anxious.

"Which friend you mean, now?" he asked, listening attentively.

"Captain Jones," Duke said, giggling. "Yes, I said it."

Sosobala crouched in his seat at the sound of Duke's words, gold on the front teeth of the bald-headed man flashed. Very shiny, the gold teeth and the bald-head, just like the linoleum.

"What's this, so you're a joker now, Duke?" he asked, trying to digest his words like an antelope chewing the cud.

"Nope, I mean it, the bastard died of a heart attack last week."

Sosobala took a seat again, feeling mixed emotions.

"Fuckin' bastard," Sosobala said in one mouthful. "How do you know this?"

"Come on, hey, you'd know me by now."

The first time he met with the captain was a chilly night as he cruised along the Mangosuthu Highway with Boyi. They listened to their favourite old school jams on their way to a night party at Sandy's varsity. The blue lights flashed in the rear-view mirror.

"There's a police car behind us," he said, a worried frown on his forehead laid bare.

Boyi turned, stone-faced.

"Pull over, right there," Boyi said, pointing at a bus terminal in a distance.

His stomach churned as the faint sound of the siren grew louder and nearer. Blood in his head pulsed, his heart pounded faster than usual. For a good reason though, there was a small leather handbag hidden under the passenger seat. His rear-view mirror showed the police car at an arm's length, flicking its headlights. He pulled over like Boyi had suggested, and turned the ignition off. He adjusted the rear-view mirror to get a clear snapshot. Two white figures, one tall and one stumpy, in the police car alighted from the unmarked BMW3-series, as red as a tomato. The cops approached as the reflection on the side mirrors showed guns pointed at them.

"Out of the car, hands on your bloody heads, now," the tall figure said in a feisty Afrikaans accent.

They got out of the car in unison, hands on their heads. His conspicuous car glowed under the streetlights. His mind had lingered at the two cops, trying to make sense which movie stars they resembled, but with no luck. He came back to his senses when they were pressed against the side panel, and subjected to a brutal search.

"Driver's license?" The tall figure asked.

"It's in the cubby-hole," he said, chest pounding.

The stumpy figure opened the cubbyhole, wiggled his hands in, and came out with a driver's license card. The tall figure had taken it, scrutinised it and then put it in the back pocket of his blue jeans.

"Whose bloody car is this?" The tall figure asked, casting his glance over it.

"It's mine," he said, chancing a gaze at him.

They opened the bonnet, checked the engine and the tags of the car. The tall figure pulled out a two-way radio hung on his waist, and radioed the control.

"Control, need to check the status of the vehicle, over," the tall figure said.

"Go ahead, over."

"November Delta five-five-two four-zero-nine, over," he said the number plate of the car.

"Black Toyota Conquest RSI, year model – nineteen ninety five.

Status, negative, over."

The tall figure had nodded with suspicion and then closed the bonnet.

"Where you two clowns headed to at this time of the night?" he asked, screwing up his face.

'Clowns' Sosobala felt struck by the word with a force that stole his breath.

"You bloody boys better not cause any mischief in my city or else you'll be sorry. Get out of here," the tall figure said, with an appalled look.

"My license. Please," Sosobala said.

"Oh!" he took it out of his back pocket and threw it in his face, then walked away.

Sosobala grabbed it, pissed-off, but kept his cool with a forced smile. They could not afford for them to start searching the cabin. Relief took-over when he started the ignition of his car and drove away.

"Who's that?" he asked. "He looks like a bad-ass."

"That's Captain Jones of the Durban Serious Crimes and Prevention Unit," Boyi said, his look frightened. "He's the meanest cop ever, lots of gangsters are either in jail or six feet underground. Thanks to him and his unit."

Boyi related some of the unpleasant past stories about the captain. The butterflies in his stomach, and the blood throbbing in his brain subsided as soon as they finally reached their destination.

"I hope I don't cross paths with him anytime soon," he said, feeling a bit worried.

"For your sake, I hope so too, my friend," Boyi said.

* * *

Duke tapped the glass booth realising Sosobala was miles away.

"Remember the time we were saved from the lion's jaws?" Duke asked.

Sosobala lifted the corner of his eyebrow like a suspicious school teacher remembering.

It was three-forty in the afternoon when he pulled into Duke's driveway.

"Good timing, CMB," Duke said.

"What's up? And where's Boyi and Bonga?"

"Don't know. They brought the BMW M5 this morning, but my buyers made an appointment for four o'clock this afternoon."

"Good for them," he said, faking a smile.

"Now I can't find them. You know what? Can't wait any longer," Duke said. "I'll drive your car. You follow me with the Beemer to the drop-off point."

"I'm getting a fuckin' cut for doing this, right?"

"Damn right," Duke said.

Duke coolly pressed the remote control and the double garage door tilted open. A shiny BMW M5, silver as the grey hairs, in mint condition appeared. His mind played with the thought of Duke's Ford Mustang going head-to-head with it on the road. He pulled out of the driveway, and followed Duke, driving it like it was his most prized possession.

The BMW M5 acted stubborn on the road as he floored the accelerator. It was only a few kilometres before the drop-off point. He cursed and swore at the wind as he found the petrol light flashing amber at the digital dashboard.

"Dammit, the fuckin' tank's empty," he hit the steering wheel as the BMW jerked non-stop.

He flicked the headlights to Duke driving just ahead. Duke made a quick U-turn, and pulled over on the sidewalk. The area was prone to being patrolled by the police.

"What's wrong now?" Duke asked.

"The fuel tank, it's empty," he said, panicking. "Must I leave it here?"

"Yes, jump in quickly," Duke said, "let's go buy it at the fuel station."

Within a few minutes they were driving back to the BMW.

"I don't believe this," Duke said, staring out of the windscreen.

The men in blue with their guns out loitered around the BMW

M5 like vultures on a dead carcass.

"Damn!" he said, thinking 'there goes my cut.'

"Don't look, don't look," Duke said.

Duke watched the police with the corner of his eye as they drove past the abandoned BMW.

"Did you see who that is, did you?" Duke asked.

He swung his head with haste to view the action through the rear windscreen, to satisfy his curiosity and noticed a red BMW.

"Was that—?"

"Damn right, Captain Jones."

Duke sighed.

"We're the luckiest bastards on this planet earth, I tell you," Duke said. "Our ancestors must be really watching over us."

The time read four-thirty, and he pressed the air conditioner to maximum, and felt his sweat break out in tiny particles.

"Today we've been saved from the lion's jaws," Duke said. "I'll tell you what, the entire week, I'll be indoors."

* * *

Sosobala came back to his senses. The captain who had barked the loudest was taken out by a silent killer.

"So wish Boyi was still alive to fuckin' gloat at his funeral," he said.

"I went. Had to satisfy my curiosity," Duke said, smiling. "Remember the time he gloated during Boyi's shooting?"

Sosobala dwelled on his words slowly. Boyi's shooting incident happened on a cool Friday afternoon. He drove to the shopping centre to meet up with the CMB. He had walked towards the front gates when he was bumped by two familiar figures. He tried to regain his balance, stunned, but couldn't.

"Something bad has just happened," Duke said.

"What?"

"It's Boyi," Duke stammered. "He's shot on the Mangosuthu Highway, near the stadium."

"What, how do you fuckin' know this?"

"Don't ask me how, just come with us," Duke said, pulling him along.

They jumped into his car and made their way to the scene.

"What happened?" he asked.

"We jacked a Benz, an S500 last night. A real stunner. I said to Boyi, 'Let's park it in Duke's garage,' right, cause the buyers will collect it this afternoon at five. Guess what, he laughed at me, saying he'd bring it around that time," Bonga said.

Soso searched for time on the dashboard: four-fifty.

"Boyi was cruising on the highway when he was blocked by an unmarked red BMW 3 series," Duke added.

It must have been Captain Jones, recalling the last time's night search at the Mangosuthu Highway's bus terminal.

"You know how stupid Boyi can be at times, he must've sped-off," Duke continued, "we don't know if he's alive or what?"

The Mangosuthu Highway was unbearable to navigate at peak hour. Sosobala spotted the blue and red lights illuminating the indigo sky. The highway's two lanes had narrowed to a single lane when they had approached the scene.

"It doesn't look good," Duke said, hands on his head.

The chubby figure was on the tarmac, still and prostrate, with the paramedics kneeling on his side, and the S500 Benz at a short distance away, riddled with bullets.

"That's not—"

It could not be him, he reassured himself looking confused at the motionless figure. His insides tore. There was a possibility that he might be… A trickle of tears ran down his chin, still willing that the inevitable reality would turn out differently. He had even recognised the motionless guy's shirt, pink as a snapdragon flower, and sneakers, as blue as ink. It dawned on him: Boyi was the guy wetting the tarmac in a pool of blood.

"Oh shit, it's him," he said. "He's fuckin—"

"Be strong, CMB," Duke said. "Pull over on the sidewalk so we can take a closer look."

A policeman pushed away bystanders as he got closer to the

scene.

"Let them see how you end up if you're a bloody criminal. You end up like this no-good piece of shit, gangster," Captain Jones said, gloating like a duck in a pond.

Sosobala stared at the captain as he frowned and scowled, thinking of the motionless form, and his hands on his cheeks.

"Wake up, dude," he said incredulously, but his voice had lingered in the air like smoke.

The captain had a proud look on his face like he had just made love to his wife over the moon. Boyi looked frail being lifted on a stretcher into an ambulance.

"There's nothing we can do for him right now," Duke said, "we better go and tell his family."

Sosobala's body shook in disbelief, and tried to start the ignition of the car, but his hands and feet had given up on him. He felt nauseated, upset and sad... all in a bucket of emotions.

"How do I fuckin' stop this horrible pain I'm feeling right now?" he had whispered more to himself than to anyone else.

Boyi, at just twenty one years of age, it was disheartening to think he would not make it. But after two weeks in the hospital, and a court appearance for car hijacking that he posted bail, he was his old bouncy self again.

* * *

"So the bastard's really dead?" Sosobala said, feeling a sense of anger and relief.

"Damn right, he is," Duke said.

It all came back flooding his mind like a racing car driver circling the race track over and over again. The time the captain pounced on them at the shopping centre's parking lot as he strolled with Sandy and Boyi, which had turned out to be a wrongful arrest. The time he had endured his first torture from him at the secluded offices; the time Jones took him and Bonga to a secluded open field at the harbour, and sjambokked them for hijacking a BMW M3. The time he had pounced on him at his place for the murder of Sifiso, and how he had tortured him until he felt half-dead.

Sosobala hated the way the captain pronounced his name 'Sosobaal', in that staunch Afrikaans accent as if he—the captain—was wiping his ass in the toilet. His mind ridiculed him: if he had the captain's home phone number, he would have given his family a courtesy call.

Krrrrrrr… Krrrrrr.

The ring of the irritating tone of the phone in a quiet room would have sounded, and then answered.

"Hello, is Warren there?" he would have asked with a smirk.

Maybe there would have been a sudden pause on the phone as if the receiver had choked on his words.

"Who's this," a woman, the wife's soft voice would have asked, "is this some kind of a sick joke?"

"It's Sosobala, his old buddy, missy," he would say in an excited tone.

"Who, Sosobaal, the gangster," she would say, "what do you want, asshole?"

Arrogant and a bitch, just like her dead husband.

"Is he really fuckin' dead?" he would have asked. "I hated him, you know."

"Well, who gives a fuck, asshole," she would have said. "Yes he's gone, and he died peacefully."

"Hallelujah," he would have screamed, squeezing the handset, overwhelmed as he laughed like a villain. "I'd have loved to fuckin' choke him to death myself, the bastard."

She would have shrieked behind the phone. He would have trotted like a polished horse pulling a golden wagon, and bang the handset in her ear.

'The Loony' was indeed, gone.

14

THE PLOT TO TAKEOVER THE PRISON

"Apart from the captain's death," Sosobala asked, "what's the real reason you're here?"

"Straight to the point, that's what I've always liked about you, Soso," Duke said.

Duke's square face with his plastered nose, exhaled and then smiled. The time Duke had that exact expression was after he asked him to sell his car, Toyota Conquest, RSI. He had been taking a shower on that morning as he discovered his two taxis were yielding profits for him. He wanted to treat himself with a new ride. He knew just the man to talk to. He jumped out of the shower, towelled himself dry, sprayed his woody scented cologne, and put on his casual wear. The scent of the cologne trailed him everywhere like a mystique. He took the car papers and dashed out of the house, pressed the immobiliser, walked around his car a bit, admiring it.

Maybe for the last time.

He held the steering wheel with one hand whilst the other hand had shown out of the window. A cool breeze had encircled the cabin blowing against his face, and offering him a promise that not all was gloomy on that scorching morning. He felt like a true captain of a ship—in control and alert—till he pulled in at Duke's. His eyes could never get enough of Duke's house.

"You've got the look of a man on a mission," Duke said, appearing and shuffling towards the gate with a slow 'I am the coolest cat on the planet' rolling gait.

"What's on your mind?"

"Need to get rid of this baby," he said, pointing at it.

"So you'll consider anything in the region of what, thirties?"

"Maybe," he said, nodding.

"Well, I'll try," Duke said. "My acquaintance might be looking for something, small and reliable."

He agreed on the deal.

Duke added, "I'll drop you off at the salon; you just give me one hour. Okay?"

Duke's slender built sprinted in and out of the house. Soso jumped in his baby for a last ride until they pulled in at the shopping centre's parking lot.

"One hour," Duke said, reversing out of the parking.

He waited at the salon anxiety killing him slowly, minute after minute, glancing at the double glass doors. The wall clock read eleven-thirty. It was one hour and thirty minutes, and Duke had still not returned. But then a familiar figure entered the salon with an A4 size white envelope. He chuckled.

"Thirty grand, it's all there, not a cent missing," Duke said, flashing his gold teeth.

Duke exhaled and then smiled. It had the potential to keep an explosive secret that could reduce the world to ashes. Who was it who'd said that?

* * *

He came back to his senses when Duke whispered the word that stole his breath, "Drugs."

Drugs in prison were like cheese in a rat house.

"Listen now, if we push drugs, in here, oh what a killing we'd make. You can count on that, CMB," Duke said, his eyes intent. "Just think about it."

Duke invoked their gang name, CMB—Cash Money Brothers. It had been born during that time of trying to sell drugs. The summer heat during that time had made the dolphins play out in the sun as they had met at the salon, as usual.

"I'm leaving for Cape Town this weekend boys," Duke said. "It's a week's holiday."

Sosobala had never set foot outside of Durban, and he had never even fancied being a traveller. Duke resented Sifiso, and always mentioned in passing that Sifiso was not cut from the same cloth as them. Sifiso's well-off family background disqualified him from being a gangster.

The afternoon clouds heralded the welcome cool breeze when Duke's week long holiday ended; his first stop was at the salon.

"Guys, I'm back," Duke said, gleefully.

They—Sosobala, Boyi, and Sifiso—all rushed to greet him as soon as he stepped in at the salon like kids seeing Father Christmas. They went out to the parking lot opposite the shopping centre's front gates. Duke had the weirdest smile of them all. The beautiful landmarks of Cape Town had hypnotised him.

"What goodies did you bring for us?" Boyi asked.

"Come and see."

Duke popped the trunk of his beast, the Ford Mustang, wide open. Two big suitcases lay next to each other as if hugging. Duke grinned. They hoped it was clothes or something as Duke slowly unzipped them. Soso's jaws almost fell on the ground as the contents lay bare in front of his eyes. There was no way this could be it, taken aback, rolling his eyes like reading a comic book. Duke busted into a sinister laughter seeing their puzzled faces. Sosobala gasped, his breath caught in his chest. Questions raced through his mind on how on earth Duke had pulled that off? Indeed, he was the duke of the underworld.

"Guys, I've got an offer for you," Duke said, winking and then closing the trunk as he swayed to face them. "Each suitcase has ten one-kilograms of snow. Real pure snow. Each kilogram goes for two hundred and fifty thousand grand, wholesale price."

"Hmm!" Soso nodded, paralysed with excitement.

"Do you know what it means, hey? That these suitcases in there," he pointed at the trunk, his tone measured, "carry merchandise worth a cool five million bucks."

"Now, that's what I fuckin' call a lot of ching ching," Sosobala said, his mind thanking his lucky stars.

Soso revisited his memory box, butterflies in his stomach. It was a viable option for the future with huge immediate and tangible rewards.

"So, you're on board or what?" Duke asked, staring at them as if trying to read their minds.

"I'm in," Boyi said, taking high fives.

"Oh yeah," Sosobala said.

"Now the deal is, for every kilogram sold, I'll take one hundred and fifty grand. You split one hundred grand amongst yourselves," Duke said, stone-faced.

"Hey, count me in, too," Sifiso said.

"Not you, mommy's boy," Duke said.

Sifiso frowned, and faked a smile all at once, his face deflated like an old tyre.

"We'll make real dough with this, boys," Duke said, thrilled, "hope you're ready to hustle in the big league?"

The promise of a new and better life was on the cards. Money makes the world go round. It takes even the pauper and turns him into sir.

On that warm evening, the twinkle little stars illuminated the velvety dark sky, as they hung out at the salon. They listened to classic songs by Colour Me Badd, a US-based RnB group. He wondered: did it still exist?

"Guys, from now on, I'll be called, Nino Brown," Duke said, cackling.

The Colour Me Badd track playing at that time was the soundtrack of a movie: The New Jack City where Nino Brown was the 'larger than life' drug dealer.

"And you guys, CMB—Cash Money Brothers."

They said aloud, "C-M-B".

"So what's next, Nino?" Sosobala asked.

"I'll set up an appointment with a dealer, and let you, CMB, know before the end of the week," Duke said, with the proud look of a man witnessing his son's graduation.

The end of the week had not gone fast enough as he counted the clock down. Finally the day announced itself as he went to the salon to meet with them. Sifiso was also there too.

"The appointment is confirmed for tonight, eight o'clock at the parking lot, CMB," Duke said. "He's taking the whole stock in one go."

"That's great news," Sosobala said, chuffed.

"Money money money, living just for the money in the New Jack City," Boyi sang.

"You're the man, Nino," Sifiso said, forcing a smile.

All shops close at six, so eight was the perfect time as the parking lot would be empty.

"This is it, no more being small time hustlers, CMB," Duke said, pulling him and Boyi aside.

Sifiso stormed out of the salon, scorning. The time now read six-thirty. The euphoria in the atmosphere compared to that of a lottery win as Soso already felt the millions rubbing his itchy palms.

"This is our first big deal of many to come," Duke said. "The stock's in the boot, what could go wrong?"

They waited in the parking lot. A Mazda sedan, white as the snow, with tinted windows kept on driving past. His sense of danger had not been aroused. Sometimes the parking lot became a lovers' den at night. One minute before eight, Soso peeped at the Mustang's dashboard clock; the buyer had still not arrived.

"There's the car lights approaching," Duke said. "It's the dealer's car."

A BMW Z4, as captivating as a black jaguar, parked directly opposite them, and its driver's door opened. A stumpy Indian man in a colourful coat alighted as if he owned the world. They jumped out with faces beaming with happiness, Duke in his black leather overcoat, shuffling towards the dealer.

"How're you, old friend?" Duke said, right arm outstretched

"The full moon is out, the air is fresh," the dealer said, poetically, "I couldn't be better."

"Guys, bring the cases," Duke said.

They popped the trunk open and brought out the suitcases. They placed them on the ground. But then loud sirens wailed in their direction. The blue lights illuminated the velvety dark sky.

"Dammit, it's the police. Let's split," the dealer said as he sprinted to his car and sped-off.

"What's fuckin' going on here?" Soso said, in disbelief.

Duke grabbed one case and threw it in the boot while Boyi followed with the other case.

"Come on, for Christ's sake," Duke said to him, slinking behind the steering wheel.

Sosobala seemed frozen as the dealer's car vanished over the horizon. The voice that called for him lingered in the air like a thick mist. It was too risky to jump into the car as he took off using his hooves as if the devil was after him. The police dog hurtled at him, causing him to hit the ground, a short distance away from the scene.

"Get this fuckin' dog off me." Soso kicked and screamed.

He rolled on the ground as the dog tore his clothing into shreds as if he had been running through the forest.

"Help," he said, pleading like a dying man on the guillotine.

"So, you need help, Mr. Drug Dealer?" the policemen said, until after a while, put a leash on the dog.

Like a bag of cement he was thrown into the back of the van, and he thudded. He saw in a haze of agony where the dog's paws and canines had dug deep into his flesh. He screamed like a wet baby, bashing into all corners of the back with the van being driven at high speed. Finally, the back door unlocked.

"Come out, Mr. Drug Dealer," the creased face policeman said.

Sosobala was at the Umlazi police station when he was dragged out in a huff. The whistles blew as he passed the charge office. The police were ecstatic about the huge drug bust they had just made. A familiar figure stood behind the counter at the charge office but Sosobala looked down on his way into the cells. He smelt an odour of dead rats as he flew into the dimly lit cell. What could have happened to Duke and Boyi?

"Your friends, in a Mustang, were just caught on the Mangosuthu Highway," the creased face policeman said, gloating, "but the Z4, gone, poof."

Creased face talked as if he was auditioning for a stage play or something. Sosobala stopped short of screaming, 'Shut up you fuckin' looser.'

"They'll be detained in Montclair," creased face added, "tomorrow you're going to shit yourself."

A nasty draught sneaked in through meshed windows and bars as he tried to sleep on the foam mattress. He lay there saddened, pondering that his chances of hustling in the big league were thrown out of the window. He attended to his wounds and fell asleep.

The next morning, the news of their arrest spread like wildfire in the neighbourhood. The sound of the keys rattling in the lock on the cell gate woke him up abruptly. A scary looking man entered the cell, and stopped a few feet away from him, tapping his left foot.

"I'm the IO of this case, alright. So level with me here, where did you get such a huge consignment of drugs?" the Investigating Officer, in shabby clothes, asked.

"Don't know, I wasn't involved," he said.

"So it's a wrongful arrest, hm?"

"The thing is, I was strolling around my neighbourhood when I was taken in," Soso said.

"You're sure about that?"

Neither guys had sold him out as an accomplice the way the investigating officer interrogated him.

For certain Duke would pull a few strings: that was Umlazi, the police officers were hungry just like every other hustler on the township streets. At the end of the week, they reunited with his fellow CMB at the Umlazi Magistrate's Court.

"The bail is set at five thousand rands, each," the magistrate, with booze face said, winking at Duke's lawyer.

Did he just do that, he marvelled?

"Thank you, your worship," Duke's lawyer, an up-and-coming suit man said, winking back.

Duke took care of the bail monies, and they exited the court room in style. On that windy weekend, they gathered at the salon trying to piece together the events that led to their arrest but it became fruitless.

"The filthy rat who tipped the police, is dead, you hear me?" Duke said, livid.

"Whoever it is, we'll find him, and sort him out," Boyi added.

"I'm with you guys," Sifiso said, displaying shock.

But Sifiso's uneasiness showed that he knew more than what meets the eye. Finding the filthy rat should be the least of their worries, finding ways to recover that consignment was an issue they had to look into. The next morning he headed to the salon, and Boyi was there.

"Where's Nino today?" he asked.

"He's gone to pick up 'the beast,'" Boyi said. "He's meeting with his lawyer at the police station as we speak."

Duke pulled in at the salon. The wall clock… the short stick was on twelve and the long stick was on six. Soso's late father had taught him as a kid how to master the art of reading an analogue clock. The short stick always told the hour, and the long stick always told the minutes. He had mastered the art of telling time at just four years old.

"CMB," Duke said, "the stock has pulled a Houdini at the police station."

"What?" Soso asked, stunned.

It was the survival of the fittest in the Umlazi hustling world; the cops were bigger hustlers than the gangsters.

"Fuckin' bastards," Soso added. "They'll be rolling in big bucks one of the days."

"It's that scar-faced investigating officer," Boyi said.

"What will we do with him?" Soso asked.

Boyi had the look of an indecisive man, and Duke had blood-shot eyes but was content with finding out the facts first.

"They're all blood suckers anyway," Duke added, raising his arms.

"How long it'd take to hustle another one?" Soso asked.

"Well, we need the dough for this one first before my supplier could release anything again," Duke said, his look visibly worried.

* * *

Sosobala snapped out of it when Duke demanded his response.

"What say you, CMB?"

"What're you proposing?" Soso asked, intrigued. "Now you're talking. My supplier is eager," Duke said, "to supply you, through my prison connections, with whatever stock you'll need. The more we push, the bigger the dough. Got that, right?"

Sosobala nodded like a kid in a classroom taught how to write and spell his name for the first time.

"See now, its success will depend on how you keep an eye on it," Duke added, "vigorous selling, one way."

"There's one fuckin' problem," Soso said, lowering his voice. "Half of the entire drug trafficking in here is controlled by the 28 gang leader, a ruthless man, he is."

"We'd negotiate with him to push our stuff, right?"

"We can't, you see Nino, the man's fuckin' greedy and shrewd. A real bastard."

Sosobala stared at him like he was an artist examining the contours of his sculpture.

"Something will come up, you know what," Soso said, drooling, "it's time the 26s' run things in here."

"Now that's the Soso I know, a go-getter," Duke said, pressing his buttons.

The 28 gang leader did not leave his cell block, no matter who or what, summoned him. It would be impossible to organise a hit on him, let alone come within an arm's length of him. It would be like taking a knife and going into a lions' den hoping to plunge it into its lion king. But his food was brought from the outside, everyday without fail. Sometimes delivered by the food outlets, or sometimes collected by warders on duty.

"Got it," Soso said, his face lighting up, "I'll need you to fuckin' do something though."

"Sure, anything, just name it," Duke said.

"To do this shit, clean, with no fuckin' comebacks," he said as he leaned closer to the glass booth. "Poison."

"Come again," Duke said, trying to make sense of his word. "You'll need what?"

"Keep your fuckin' voice down," Soso said, shushing him. "Rat poison, don't you know, it's an instant killer?"

Sosobala whispered his plans to him through the intercom on how to take out the 28 gang leader, which he believed would have no comebacks. Duke was to pay or threaten someone's life, whatever worked, his prison connections, a warder, to put rat poison in the 28 gang leader's food when it was being delivered.

"You know, I've got just the man. He owes me big time, and he'll do it without thinking twice," Duke said. "Consider it done."

Sosobala felt it in the pit of his stomach that after the 28 gang leader was out of the way, he would order his soldiers to pursue a vigorous selling strategy. Just like in sales and marketing books, where they push for vigorous sales and marketing strategies like knocking on consumer's doors or pestering them with phone calls, and then bombarding them with the available products. Who was it who'd introduced that?

Sosobala would run that drug operation with an iron fist, making sure that not even a gram of the stuff would go missing. His maths teacher came to mind, the nerd with no social life. Sosobala had listened attentively at the time, being taught about numeracy.

"If Joe has ten apples; he keeps one for himself, and cuts the rest into four pieces each; he then divides the pieces amongst his nine classmates. How many pieces does each classmate have?" the teacher asked.

"Four... four," he said, thinking that that was the only part of maths that made sense to him.

"It's a deal," they said in unison.

They said their goodbyes and Duke promised to get his part of the job taken care of the soonest. Sosobala shuffled with a slow intimidating rolling gait, thinking that should anything go wrong with their plans to take out the 28 gang leader, there would be a blood-bath in prison. As the day slowly turned into the next, then the next, he waited for news of the success of his plan. He had confidence in Duke to fulfil his end of the bargain.

"Roll call," the warder said as he entered the cell encircled by heavily armed guards.

Soso's eyes flickered open, and his mind raced in disdain. His heart became darker just by looking at Montie who loathed the ground he walked on, and vice versa.

"Fuck, listen up, the 28 gang leader died last night. So until we know what happened, no cafeteria, or recreation time, or even visits this week. Okay?" Montie said, his tone growing more suspicious.

Sosobala stopped himself from screaming, 'Hallelujah' after hearing those words. Montie's form evaporated like steam from a boiled kettle as he summoned his soldiers to the chambers. He briefed them on the new developments, the drug trafficking, and the vigorous selling strategy he wanted them to 'breathe, eat, sleep and shit.'

In the middle of that night the cell gate opened. Footsteps marched in cautiously inside, and then a soft voice called out his name in the darkness. Sosobala woke up, and hurried to the front entrance. It was the warder, Duke's connection, playing delivery boy.

"Duke sends his regards," the warder said, as he handed over a package to him.

The train had been set in motion, as the soldiers began to push his agenda to the 'T'. His cell became a hive of activities as the carry-bag, using sheets, transported the drugs and money, day and night. And his lieutenants guarded the trade-offs under his watchful eye, like sniffer dogs. Like Nino Brown in the movie, New Jack City: ambitious, dangerous, and monstrous.

"The world's mine, all mine," Nino Brown had shouted, while the movie Scarface starring Al Pacino played in the background, on the projector.

Finally the prison was his to rule.

"The prison is mine, all mine," his mind shouted, its tone, satanic.

15

A YOUNG CONVICT ENTERS THE PRISON

Sosobala ran the drug operation, implementing tight controls, day in and day out. The drug trade that once again has promised him a new and better life, not on the outside but in the prison. The very same drug trade born out of a toxic meeting between two old friends that culminated in the death of the 28 gang leader. Duke kept the supply of snow flowing in like a stream feeding into the sea. In the midst of that, the steel gate of the cell was unlocked. The warder walked in followed by a youngster with slouching shoulders.

"There's an empty bed," the warder said, grimacing.

He pointed with a baton at the bed frame on the right side, a few feet away from the entrance.

Was prison a Big Brother house—a reality TV show—where contestants were provided with free food and booze to keep them entertained? Well think again, Bozo (couldn't figure out who it was that said that). Prison was another kind of a retreat, alright. Nothing was for free, and everything came at a hefty price.

The youngster had a light complexion, of average height, and was squint. Sosobala snapped his fingers as he tried to connect a face with a name the youngster's image resembled. He clicked his fingers some more as he delved deeper into thoughts. Just like Sandy's ex, Monde, the bully. He flushed in disgust.

A long time ago Monde's actions left a void inside him for failing to settle the score between the two of them. During that period he had left Transco, the time when he pursued Sandy until he won her heart. On a cool Wednesday afternoon he dreamt in the living room about how he could not wait to visit Sandy at her student residence that coming Saturday. A hard knock sounded on the front door.

"Who is it?" he said, shuffling towards the door with a 'do not disturb' rolling gait.

A harsh draught swept in as he opened the door wide. Three figures with 9mm pistols hung at their waists, and a pimped BMW 3 series, whitened everywhere, parked outside. Threat flickered in their dead eyes as if they were cannibals, and he was a succulent steak just waiting to be devoured without condiments.

"You're Sosobala, right?" one of the guys asked, his voice squeaky.

As far as he was concerned, he did not owe anybody anything.

"Yes," he said, his glance growing more concerned.

He took in the front man forthwith: he had a light complexion, and had a feminine built with an average height; was squint.

"Wait outside," the squint man said to the other men ushering himself inside, and shut the door.

Sosobala pointed to the couch, and offered him a seat. The squint man hesitantly took the seat as if it was going to set him on fire.

"You don't know me, do you? I'm Monde from the north. I work at the Umlazi police station," the squint man said cockily, looking straight at him as if weighing him up.

Sosobala tried to act brave and listen.

"I'm here, OK, cause of my woman."

"Sorry, your what?" Soso asked incredulously.

Monde stood up as if his behind, a big one, had a worm slithering into its grove.

"You think I am a fool, hey, do you?" Monde said. His temper flared with a touch of a button.

"What's going on here, hey?" Soso asked, his mind buried underneath an avalanche of fear.

"I'd you checked out." Monde rubbed his chin. "I know that

you're messing with my woman. You see, maybe you're just having a bit of fun with her." Monde continued, his tone intense, "You better stay away from her. You got that?"

Sosobala tried to make sense of everything. The man was a cop and sometime ago, he read an article about how some cops were capable of acting senselessly in the heat of the moment.

"You're the one standing between me and Sandy," Monde said, jaws clenching, "I won't lose her, not to you, or anybody else, OK?"

Sandy's name stole his breath as if he had been kicked at the groin. Monde's hands moved along his waist, and caused his heart to skip a beat.

"I hear you man," he said, nodding sheepishly.

Monde opened the door, and then slammed it on his way out.

"Guys let's go. I'm done here," Monde said.

Their Beemer's engine roared as Soso listened behind the door until it roared no more. It was the survival of the fittest in the female jungle. That evening, he felt let down, reckoning whether there had been a serious breach of trust on Sandy's part.

On that hot Saturday midday, the indigo sky turned cloudy, accompanied by a cool breeze that helped lower temperatures to comfortable levels. He anxiously boarded a taxi to varsity since his car honked like a goose that morning. As he jumped out of the taxi at the bus terminal on Francois Road, he strode towards the front gates of the university, his heart pounding. The students swarmed the area like ants collecting food for the winter. The university was one of the oldest of South Africa's prides and joy. A familiar figure appeared in the distance as he paced towards the entrance gates of the student residence, Mabes. It was her alright… her beauty had thrown his doubts out of the window. He paced briskly towards her and embraced her. She wore a blouse, as white as a rose petal, matching her loose shorts, worn with wedges.

"How're you, my love?" she asked.

"Never been better," he said.

They entered her fifteen square metres or so room, and the vanilla scent lingered in the air like smoke. He played it cool, and made himself comfortable on the bed.

But then a knock rapped on the door.

"Who is it?" Sandy asked.

"It's me, open up," a man's voice said. "Open the door, Sandy."

That distinct stranger's voice rang in his mind, recognising it straight away.

"No ways in hell. It couldn't be, was it—?" he said, voice clipping. "Am I being followed?"

Sandy shuffled to the door. Sosobala could not believe what was about to happen.

"Open up," the voice said with a bang at the door, "Sandy?"

"It's Monde," Sandy said, her voice strangled with anxiety. "What must I do?"

The air in the small room instantly permeated with fear. Sosobala lifted himself up and shielded her away from the door. He touched the door knob, his stomach grumbling, and opened the door wide.

"Monde," he said, forcing a smile.

He doubted whether Monde's eyes were looking at him, or Sandy.

"Sosobala, what're you doing here?" Monde said in his squeaky voice.

"You followed me?" he asked, feeling his hands, his feet, moist. "That's it, you're fuckin' crazy."

Sosobala froze, and turned, seemingly in slow motion to find Sandy's reaction. But then Monde's punch caught him off-guard: a solid right hook. It was not feminine at all like Monde's physique. Soso's prostrate figure lay dazed on the floor, like a boxer waiting for the referee to finish a ten count.

"Leave him alone, what're you doing, you crazy fool?" Sandy said.

His nose oozed blood, and dyed his white shirt like a tap that had just been opened. Like a toddler learning to crawl, he reached the corner of the room, trying to make sense of what had just happened. Sandy darted in front of Monde, but he shoved her aside like a tree branch discarding a leaf. Monde hurtled towards him with a crazed primitive shrill. Monde stomped on him like a rammer, and sandwiched him with the floor. And knelt over his still body, choking the life out of him. Sosobala counted the seconds before the last ounce of his breath wheezed out.

"You're making a fool out of me, hey?" Monde said, and then turned towards her, "Sandy you've made me a laughing stock, you know that, to my family and my friends?"

"Stop this madness, Monde," Sandy said, her face the picture of fear.

"I gave you everything, what more was I supposed to do, Sandy, hmm?

Monde enjoyed watching her squirm, helpless. In that eerie moment, Soso found a few seconds breather, and dashed out of the room like an arrow shot by a hunting bow.

"Don't leave, Soso, come back. Let's talk about this," Sandy said as she chased after him, her wedges connecting with the ground as if high jumping.

"Let him go," Monde said, following on her heels. "I love you, Sandy, OK, see what you made me do?"

Sosobala sprinted to the taxi rank and jumped into an empty taxi like a mad man.

"Driver, go," he said, his tone trembling.

"The load is three-fifty," the driver said, fiddling with his car radio.

"OK, fuckin' get out of here, will you?" Soso said, knowing very well the taxi load was one-fifty.

The driver extended his arm to collect his cash, counted it as if counting beans in a bag. And then pulled out of the rank, his smile wide, dropping him off at the taxi rank in the CBD. It was clear of any sign of Monde.

Ever since, that incident was stored in the back of his mind. A big void had been left unfilled, the need to let Monde have a taste of his own medicine.

* * *

Soso's curiosity got the better of him as he shuffled towards the youngster. Déjà vu: The same curiosity that the discarded Chopper showed when a new inmate entered the cell.

"What's your fuckin' name, youngster?" he asked, frowning.

"Sipho, but call me Si," the youngster said, acting cockily.

"I'm Sosobala," he said. "Let me see your prison card."

The youngster reached for his back pocket, and drew out the card. His wide face looked like it had been sketched with a blunt pencil.

"How you ended up in here, youngster?" Soso asked.

"Agh man, it was my ex," the youngster said. "I caught the bitch, red-handed. I gave it to her, and the dude, some muscle man, jumped me. So I poked him."

"You don't have a brother from the north of Umlazi, hey?" Soso asked, wanting to confirm his suspicions.

"Not that I know of," the youngster said. "I'm from KwaMashu."

He snatched away his card, and shook his head realising the youngster got five years for attempted murder, and assault with intent to do grievous bodily harm.

"This is prison, not your daddy's fuckin' backyard," Soso said, his look stern, "stick to your chores, alright?"

He tossed back his card and turned away to retreat to his bed.

"Thanks, Soso," the youngster said.

Sosobala seemed frozen in place, thinking, did that cocky prick just called him, Soso?

His late father, his late childhood friend, Boyi, Duke, the late Madubula, Sandy, and his mother, were the very rare ones in his lifetime who had shortened his name with verve. How dare the youngster try to put himself in that category? Sosobala turned and gave him a monster look. He shuffled away and retreated to his bedside as guilt resurfaced.

But why? He had finally managed to suppress the terror of thunder that had caused him to fail the ones he loved in their moment of need. And he had taken revenge on the men responsible for the rape of Madubula, and had achieved dominance as the 26 gang leader, but why? He did not need any new Madubula in his life to soften him up. His hardcore attitude had worked well for him ever since he had been elevated to supremacy in the 26 gang.

As the days went by, the youngster behaved naively and cockily by chain smoking with the gang members. That was what got Madubula into a whole lot of trouble in the first place, that had caused him to be thrust to the point of no return. Stupid youngster.

"Sipho, come over here," Soso said during one recreation period, screwing up his face.

"What's up?" the youngster said, sniffing.

"Fuckin' listen to me, and listen well you little shit," Soso said, his tone menacing, "didn't I tell you, this wasn't your daddy's fuckin' backyard, stick to your chores?"

The youngster in his casual wear shrank like burnt rubber, and smelt like it too.

"I don't ever want to see you, ever, fuckin' chain smoking with my soldiers." Sosobala pointed at him.

"You hear me, or even talking with them?" he said in disdain, "fuckin' get out of my sight, fool."

The youngster retreated in shame to his corner. Sosobala could not afford to go through another Madubula rape incident.

As a six year old, Soso's father rebuked him too when he befriended an older boy, about thirteen years or so, who lived on his own in one of the shacks. His father had been livid after hearing the rumours that the older boy smoked and drank alcohol. His older friend had the freedom to do as he pleased. Even had a girlfriend, a midget, although older than him. Soso's older friend described juicy details of their sex escapades.

At that age, Sosobala had been disgusted by the thought of a girl's private part. One day Sosobala came home late, just after the sun had gone down, and his clothes smelt of cigarette smoke. His father had been in the sitting room watching TV when he tried to sneak to the bedroom.

"Soso, come over here," his father said repeatedly, "you going to tell me where you're coming from, my boy?"

"Ahh, from my friend's place, father," he said, realising the stench of cigarette was lingering in the sitting room like a cheap perfume.

His livid father sprang out of the couch, and then pressed him down on the coffee table and belted his behind until it was black and blue.

"I want you home, every day, by no later than four o'clock. Come rain or shine," his father said, brandishing his leather belt in his face. "No more hanging out with that older friend of yours. He's bad news."

He did not understand at the time why his father had forbidden him from keeping a company of such a cool friend. Weeks later when his older friend had been fatally stabbed in a tavern during a brawl involving the midget, he instantly turned into a good and obedient kid again.

* * *

Sosobala snapped out of it when they were ordered back to their cells for head counts, and locking in. He realised that the youngster also did not understand his reasons for being hard on him.

16

PROFOUND WORDS OF A KILLER

As weeks went by, the youngster toed the line. The line if cocky Madubula had toed very long ago, he would still be alive. And he, on the other hand, would have been granted his parole.

The sky-birds laundered for the soldiers, and so Sipho chose to do Soso's dirty laundry as if the clothes had been laundered and neatly folded in a launderette. The youngster even scoured his favourite sneakers, and removed dark marks that had been there since the first days Sosobala entered the prison. The late Madubula liked to clean his sneakers for him even though dark marks never vanished. The monster look he gave to the youngster began to turn into a compassionate look. Why was that? What happened to the hard shell he had built around him? It was beginning to show some signs of cracking.

After Madubula's death, he had promised himself that he would never allow anybody to come close to his heart again. It was compassion that people like Madubula waltz into his life and caused him to spend a gruesome and dark week in solitary. The compassion that caused him to be Chopper's number one enemy. That same compassion that put him to the hospital, beaten by the warders after a provocation in the cafeteria... Like a squinting drunkard Sosobala tried to come to terms with the recent developments.

It was that compassion that caused him to take revenge for Madubula's sake in order to find redemption. The same compassion that put him and Chopper in a barbaric duel. The same compassion that had elevated him to be the 26 gang leader. God knows, the same compassion that had eventually led him to discipline a lieutenant in a monstrous way. His heart felt heavy as if a giant had taken a sledgehammer, and had begun to pound at the surface surrounding his hard shell.

That same compassion for Madubula that had denied him a parole due to statements made by Montie, a man who, over the years, had loathed the ground he walked on.

His body felt like it was buried in the earth's bowels. The hard shell Sosobala had built around him, and which had served him well in the past now showed signs of cracking. It began to soften him up.

But why?

The drug trade and his well-being both required him to be a monster in order to survive prison life.

Sosobala tilted his head trying to sleep. And the profound words of Sgola Dube—the brother of the beefy man he shot during the christening of his first taxi—he had uttered to Duke, about what prison was capable of doing to any man, dominated his mind. It all played as if a movie director had just shouted 'Roll the tape.'

On that night of slaying the beefy man, Sosobala had difficulty sleeping. The beefy man's bloodied image haunted him. Sosobala counted, 'Sheep one… sheep two… sheep ten… sheep twel—' and the dream had slowly begun...

Duke, with an Afro, stood in a tranquil way behind the gates of his house when Bonga with a ginger mop, had pulled into the driveway and hurried towards him.

"Have you heard," Bonga said, "Sosobala?"

"What about him?" Duke asked, calmly.

"He scored big time, pocketing a cool ten mill after robbing a bank. Incredible, right?"

Duke seemed speechless.

"With that kind of dough, I'd have a Rolls Royce, swear to God, Duke," Bonga said.

"So he's finally reached the top as a kingmaker," Duke said.

"Guess what," Bonga said, "Soso's throwing a house warming party tonight at eight at the Zimbali golf estate. The who's who of Durban will be there."

Time made them aware the party was about to start.

"It's almost seven-thirty, we better get going," Bonga said.

They had pulled in at the estate, as beautiful as the Mediterranean Villas, into a long driveway.

"Seems like no expenses were spared on this party," Duke said.

"Damn right. There's Boyi, dancing with a group of skimpily clad chicks," Bonga said. "Hey Boyi."

Boyi turned but seemingly in slow motion. His face was snow white.

"It's been a long time, guys," Boyi said.

"Where's Soso, the big man?" Bonga asked.

"Probably, inside the house, frolicking with some floozy or something," Boyi said.

"Let me go inside the house and look for him. Nino, I'll be back in a jiffy," Bonga said as he walked away.

"Cool, will be checking the place out," Duke said, mesmerised.

Bonga strode into the house, admiring the beauty of the house.

"Hey Soso," Bonga said, waving.

Sosobala turned coolly in a designer suit, white as a daisy petal, with shiny pointy shoes, and glittered in gold, even wearing a gold crown.

"You look like a million bucks," Bonga said.

"I feel like a million bucks," Soso replied. "Life is great, no regrets whatsoever. Come, let's drink a fuckin' toast to Lé Good Life."

They toasted as the sound of two glasses clinking created a tinkling rhythm.

"Come see here, those four guys." Soso pointed across at them. "They fuckin' look suspicious," he said, his tone worried. "Yeah, the ones in blue jeans and black windbreakers. Just look at them, they're gate crashers."

"How come?" Bonga asked.

"Come on, fuckin' look around you. People in here are in designer wear, but they, they're aliens on earth, my man," Soso said.

"I can't see them clearly," Bonga said. "Let's move a little closer to get a good look at them."

Sosobala tailed Bonga closely until they found an angle where they had a good visual of the four strangers.

"See that one?" Soso said, gesturing with a tilt of his head.

His mind raced to infinity to put a name to the face.

"I think it's Sgola Dube, his out of prison?"

"You mean, the brother of the guy you shot, no ways, that night of the christening of your taxi?"

"Holy shit, they're carrying guns. The heat is on," Sosobala said.

"Quick, let's go get Boyi and Duke," Bonga said, and pulled him.

"It's too late, they have already spotted me," Soso answered.

"Payback's a bitch, Sosobala," a stranger's voice shouted.

"No, run Sosobala, run," Bonga said. "They're shooting at us."

Sosobala froze as Boyi sprinted towards him while the party goers shrieked. They dispersed on their heels as if Count Dracula had appeared to suck on their blood. A volley of bullets were sprayed, and penetrated through windows, walls, flesh, and the ground.

"Let's split, these assholes are dead," the voice said.

The shrieks reverberated across the hills in the north of Durban. Police sirens wailed, and the blue lights and the ambulances' red lights lashed in the sky.

"My Goodness, what do we have here? Very few survived, heavy body-count, captain," a police officer said.

"Bloody animals, this is a massacre," Captain Jones said. "I'll be damned."

"What's wrong, sir?" asked the police officer.

"See those three dead guys." The captain pointed at them respectively. "This one with blood soaked on his white suit, next to a gold crown, is bloody Sosobaal," the captain said, gesturing, "the albino in a colourful shirt and matching sneakers, yeah, that one in a pool of blood, and that chubby one with a snow white face, were the CMB gang."

"So you knew them, sir?"

"Yeah. They're bloody suspects on a number of hijackings and murder cases. What goes around comes around," the captain said as he leaned over to Sosobala, and felt the gunshot wound on his forehead.

* * *

...Sosobala's eyes had flickered open as a mosquito bit his forehead. He had crushed it and sprang out of bed drenched in sweat. His fingers ran wild as he felt every inch of his body, especially his forehead that had a gunshot wound in the dream. He caressed his lion tooth necklace, and recalled the sangoma's words. He realised he had a very nasty premonition that was about to become a reality, somehow. The pedestal clock had read six forty-five. On that chilly Sunday morning with the sun hiding behind the clouds, he jumped into his yesterday's clothes and took off like a vampire hiding from sunlight, and was at Duke's house in a flash.

"Hey, CMB," Duke said. "What's eating you up?"

"How well do you know the Dube gang?"

"Well, Sgola and I go way back before he was flushed down the toilet with a life sentence," Duke added. "He's just been released, after twenty years in the slammer."

"I had a horrible dream," Soso said, his gaze notably worried. "Can you fix this thing with the Dube gang, right, right?"

"Maybe, but you see, Sgola was a heartless bastard. Killing a human being to him, well, it was just like squashing a mosquito," Duke said. "OK, let's go to KwaMashu right now."

They navigated out of Umlazi, with the beast roaring around each and every sharp bend they manoeuvred until they pulled in at the driveway of an enclosed red brick two-roomed house.

"Stay here, and be invisible, OK?" Duke said as he alighted.

Duke shuffled towards a figure crouching under the tree. Sosobala stayed behind, invisible, but his ears upright like that of an alert dog. The crouching figure had a skinny body that could pick fruits off the branches with ease. And the creases on his face gave away his age.

"It's been a long time, old friend," Duke said.

"Indeed, old friend, indeed," Sgola said, flashing a cautious smile.

Sosobala zoomed in on Sgola and concentrated, and saw a man with flesh melted on bones.

"I heard you're back," Duke said.

"It's been two weeks, three days and six hours," Sgola said. "And now I'm in a period of mourning."

"My condolences for your loss," Duke said. "It's the reason why I'm here. You and I go way back, when we were the lords of the cliques."

"I thought as much, your reason for coming here," Sgola said, nodding. "How times have changed. Youngsters these days seek popularity more than respect."

"It seems so," Duke said.

"So level with me, old friend," Sgola said, measuring him.

"The guy, who took out your brother, is my protégé," Duke said. "I'm willing to compensate you, just as we, the lords of the cliques, did in the past."

"Oh those days are behind me," Sgola said. "Prison tames even the wildest beast of them all."

"I don't get you?" Duke said, confused.

"I mean, I don't base my life on that anymore, an eye for an eye," Sgola said, "I found Jesus Christ in prison. He changed me for the better. Your protégé will not perish on this earth by my own doing, old friend. But my late brother's gang want revenge."

Sgola sighed.

"I hope I did enough to talk them out of it."

"Such profound words," Duke said. "I am humbled, old friend. Thank you."

"Come visit me again when you find time," Sgola said. "Would love to tell you more about how Jesus saved my life in prison. God decides on everybody's fate, so He shall your protégé."

"Will do, old friend," Duke said, giving him a handshake.

Duke pulled out with a hoot. Sgola waved goodbye with the look of a man who had done it all, and was left with nothing to show for it. That very rare wave that probably Sgola used when he was saying 'So long' to the prison life even knowing exactly that nothing awaited him on the outside except a glimmer of hope that all the years he had lost would somehow be regained, or his deeds forgotten and forgiven.

17

THE BEARER OF BAD NEWS

The sound of Montie's stomping boots entered the cell, as he said, "Roll call."

His prison guards encircled him, and looked like mean spiders.

"Fuck, as from now, the cafeteria and visitors' privileges are back on," he added.

The course of death for the 28 gang leader was unknown, or better yet, inconclusive. It meant Sosobala was in the clear... nothing or no one would stand in his way now of owning the prison. Not even a dedicated warder such as Montie, who wanted to make prison a safe haven for all. As time went on, Duke's connection, a warder, began to have cold feet. Sosobala summoned Duke for an urgent meeting.

"Your connection is becoming trouble. Sort him out," Sosobala said. "Or I'll feel the heat."

"I hear you. The bastard fears losing his job over this now. He's even hinting about spilling the beans on how the 28 gang leader died if we don't cut him loose," Duke said, his tone worried.

"If that's the case, you better do it quickly on the outside cause right now, my hands are tied," Sosobala said.

Sosobala felt the warder had to go, one way or the other, and find another delivery boy.

"I'll get right on it," Duke said.

* * *

"Sosobala NoZulu, report to the visitor's room," the intercom said, repeatedly.

So soon Duke was back to discuss their mission of a drug operation. His smile incriminated him as he hurried to the visitor's room. He would demand an urgent supply of more stock after their initial delivery boy disappeared.

The steel gates of the visitor's room opened wide. The sun pierced through the small barred prison windows. It was a rare sight if you had never set foot away from the cell blocks. His geography teacher, a very seductive woman, all those years ago, taught them about the sun rising in the east each morning, and then making its journey across the orbit of the earth, and then setting in the west. The cell blocks were neither in the east nor the west since the sun had never risen or set that side on any given day. The visitor's booth became nearer, and his vision became clearer. Sosobala wiped his eyes numerous times as if to wipe away dust that had settled in on his eyelids. The figure in a suit, as beige as the prison walls, sat behind the thick glass of the visitor's booth.

Sosobala whispered to the wind, screwing up his face, "I don't fuckin' believe this".

He tried to open his mouth, but his saliva turned into foam. His heart raced faster like he was having a heart attack. His eyes and nose became wet and itchy as he took a seat. Was he daydreaming or the person seated behind the glass booth was real?

"It's good to see you again," a voice said, consumed with emotions.

"It's been a long time," Soso said, his eyes glued to the figure, "how've you been?"

"Good, life has been good to me," a voice continued. "I've never thought I'll ever see you again."

"Neither did I," Soso said, trying to keep a straight face.

"So you've been here, how long now?"

"Three years, three months and twenty three days," Soso said, startled by the presence of the figure, mere inches away from him.

Every word that came out of the figure's mouth, was like a guitar string plucked by an amateur, sounding an irritable note. Was it really her seated right in front of him, or her ghost? His heart became buried by an avalanche of pain. The words she had last said were like a blade plunged into his heart and twisted, inch after inch, and pulled out as blood gushed out like a fountain. Their last conversation played like a tape recorder set on repeat mode. She had phoned him.

"I'm off to Cape Town next week for a scholarship programme. I've got to get away from all this madness, Soso," she said. "It's best this way, you do understand, don't you?"

Sosobala had stopped himself from screaming, "No, don't fuckin' leave me. Please stay, I love you. I can't live without you".

He had dropped the phone, and his gut had shrunk, too stunned to move. He died a thousand deaths and still been reincarnated with a broken heart. His mind accepted her hasty decision to relocate, but his heart could not let her go, hoping one day their paths would cross again. A trickle of tears slithered down his cheeks, warm and sticky, as he realised their paths might never cross again. But now their paths have crossed again.

A distinct sacrifice he had made for her played in his mind. It had been pouring, the autumn rain that carried with it all the coldness and promise of winter. Sandy became sick, and was admitted to the hospital. He rushed to be at her bedside. Her mother held her tiny hand, praying non-stop at her bedside.

"How's she?" he asked, his look sad.

"Soso, it's worse than the doctors anticipated," her mother said, holding back tears.

"What happened to her?" he asked, caressing an unconscious Sandy's forehead.

"The doctors said its appendicitis," the mother said, "she'll need an urgent operation, or else, it'd burst, and kill her."

Panic had unsettled his nerves after hearing the words, 'it'd burst and kill her.'

"The doctors said the operation is thirty grand," she continued, hands on her head, "to tell you the truth, I don't have that kind of money."

Sandy's mother was an older version of her, and had the facial features of a beautiful black woman. His mind worked overtime, pondering, his savings were to buy another taxi but Sandy's life was irreplaceable. It crippled him to see her suffer like that. He put the taxi buy on hold, calculating he could always make more money.

"It's going to be okay," Soso said, "I'll sort it out."

"God bless you, my son," she said, taken aback. "I'll go tell the doctors."

He dashed out of the hospital, his thoughts racing with his breathing as he jumped into his car and floored the accelerator pedal on his way to Umlazi. The images of a fragile Sandy flashed in his head: her tender touches, her silk skin, and her vanilla scent... Priceless. He got to his place and found the CMB waiting for him in the driveway.

"What's up?" he asked, anxiously.

"It's after six-thirty now, we've been waiting for you," Boyi said, his tone growing more irritated by the second.

"It's getting late, that SL 55 AMG Benz in La Lucia Mall leaves at seven," Bonga said. "If we hurry now, we might catch the owner at the door step."

"Sorry, CMB," he said. "Not tonight, I have something fuckin' urgent to take care of, okay?"

"Come on, what's he saying now?" Bonga asked, throwing a look at Boyi. "If we don't go now, it's going to be a long wait before we trace it again."

"I just can't," he said, becoming annoyed.

"If you say so," Boyi said, in shock. "It's no use, Bonga, let's bounce."

Nothing else mattered at that moment as he sprinted into the house, except Sandy. He went to his secret hiding place, underneath the couch, and then dashed out with the speed of lightning. He got back to the hospital with crisp hundred rand notes.

"You're a life saver," Ma Gumede said. "The doctors should be done in an hour."

"I couldn't let her suffer like this," Soso said.

He went home feeling emotionally drained that Sandy was in so much pain after the operation, but had been relieved though that she would recover well.

* * *

Sandy's petite form had not changed much. The heart shaped face with voluptuous lips, and a cute nose. But underneath that beauty lay a pitbull that showed its true colours when Sandy was provoked. The incident played in his mind like a horse race. Sosobala had been wooed by long legs standing on the bus stop at KwaMnyandu Station. He hit the emergency breaks and then stopped next to her. The car nearly burnt the tyres. He killed the engine and lowered the passenger window, crippled with envy.

"Hello sunshine," Soso said, "need a ride?"

She turned in slow motion: a true African woman blessed with a pear shaped body. She was a few inches taller than him.

She asked as she hopped in, "Do you always pick up strangers?"

"As long as they pay for the ride," Soso said, giggling. "Care to tell me your name?"

"I'm Tladi," she said, pouting, "from Woodlands."

"I'm Sosobala," he said, "but you can call me Soso."

He acted like a school kid with a crush on a popular cheerleader.

"What brings you to my neighbourhood?" Soso said, trying to keep his cool.

"My grandmother, she stays just across the station," she said. "You can drop me off at the Pavilion Mall. You don't mind, do you?"

"It's cool by me. Better yet, how about I take you out for lunch. Afterwards we'll go for a two o'clock movie. I want to get to know you better."

"If you're not a serial killer, it's fine by me," Tladi said, excited.

He navigated the car like a ship's master sailing across the rough seas with a fragile cargo until they pulled in at the mall parking lot. They entered the mall, and strolled into the top level elevators. He pressed G and felt the exhilaration as if his bladder was becoming weak as the elevator shot down. How would it feel like to have sex whilst the elevator shot down swiftly? He chuckled.

"Don't want to be killed, but is there a woman in your life, hm, a girlfriend or a wife?" Tladi asked.

"Not quite. Me and my girlfriend, well let's just say, we're having fuckin' problems these days," he said, his look stern. "And you, any one special?"

"No, I've been single for the past two years," Tladi said.

A very well-mannered girl that didn't rush into anything. He grinned: What Sandy doesn't know won't kill her. The mall corridors were bustling when he imagined a voice calling out his name. Not alarmed, he carried on with Tladi away from the voice.

"Sosobala." The voice was more aggressive and nearer.

That sounded like a woman's voice. Who could it be? Smiling from ear to ear, he sneaked a backward glance to satisfy his curiosity.

"Holy shit," he whispered more to himself than to her.

"Soso," the woman's voice continued, "stop right there, you hear me?"

She had eyes that could pierce through the concrete walls. It was his worst nightmare coming down the escalators, a few feet away from them. She hurried towards them.

"Hey," Soso said, like his mouth had swallowed hot potatoes, "what're you doing here?"

"What am I doing here, hm," the woman asked, "who's the floozy?"

His heart turned into ice, and his pulse ceased to beat. Tladi took a few strides back when a livid Sandy confronted him, standing right in his face.

"Soso, you're going to tell me, or not?" Sandy said, heating faster than a toaster.

Sandy tried to contain the tears that were streaming down her face, messing up her make-up.

"Mmm…" Soso said, voice clipping.

They became the centre of attraction as other shoppers looked on. Tladi had a worried look wondering about how the whole incident was going to turn out. Sandy, a petite built, startled him when she charged towards Tladi like a hungry pitbull. They wrestled, and pulled each other's clothes and hair, screaming all the while.

"Dammit. Fuckin' stop this, both of you," Soso said as he darted in between them. "Sandy."

The mall security guards, the big and no-nonsense guys in their black uniforms and batons briskly advanced, and then coerced them outside the mall. Sandy attempted another go at Tladi but Soso contained her, and pulled her into the parking bay next to the car. Tladi made herself an invisible woman. Sandy fumed like a lizard waiting to strike a butterfly. It was like pouring water over a duck, as he tried to calm her down and reason with her.

"I'm sorry," Soso said.

"Sorry for what, I caught you, or for being a pathetic cheat?"

"Please get in the car, I'll take you back to varsity," Soso said, his look sheepish.

"No, what for?"

Her grim expression toned down after some time as she jumped in. Sosobala drove out of the mall, anxious, until he pulled up outside her student residence.

"I don't ever want to see you again," she said, alighting and banging the door on her way out.

Weeks went by as he pursued her with vigour, wanting her back until she succumbed to his charm. Besides, she was the only woman for him. Their reunion was sealed on the warm north beach sands. Her eyes sparkled at night like the rare gems only found in caves a thousand miles underneath the earth's surface: Who was it who'd said that?

They sat and stared at the breaking white waves, pounding at the pier. At that very moment, he knew nothing else had mattered in the whole of the universe except the two of them.

"I'll love you till eternity, Soso," Sandy confessed, her look sincere.

* * *

Sosobala suppressed the anger and sadness welling up inside him. Sandy had torn his heart into shreds, and stomped on it until the arteries and veins enabling it to love again had been obliterated.

"So how long have you been back," Sosobala asked.

"It's been a month," Sandy said, staring straight into his eyes like she was searching his soul.

"From Cape Town, you mean," Sosobala said with a 'who gives a crap' look. "When're you going back?"

"Not any time soon, maybe for a visit once in a year," she said. "Cape Town was great while it lasted, but the weather is shit."

"So what brings you here?" Soso asked, not blinking an eye.

"What do you think, it's my hobby to visit prisons?" Sandy asked.

"Just asking, no need for fuckin' hostility," Sosobala said, caught off-guard. "Tell me, did the female warders do a body search on you?"

"Hell no, I told their superiors, if they dare touch me, I'd sue their asses. After I'm done with them, they'd be scrubbing floors in my house," Sandy said cockily. "Do you think I'll let some woman shove her fingers up my v-jay?"

"Yeah, it's how they do bodily searches in here to women visitors," Sosobala said.

Had such a thing happened to his mother when she visited him in the prison hospital? He shook his head trying to suppress those thoughts. Sandy began to weep as she put her palm on the thick glass booth.

"I've got something to tell you, it's bad news, Soso," she said. "It's about your mother."

"What is it Sandy?" Sosobala asked, anxiety killing him. "Fuckin' say it."

Something was eating her inside as she tried to open her mouth, but choked a few times.

"She suffered a stroke, a few days ago," she said, swallowing over and over, "she didn't make it."

The words 'She didn't make it' hung in his mind like steam from a coal train. He hid his emotions like a deadly virus that ate one's body with verve and endurance. The last time she came to visit him in the prison hospital, she looked old and fragile.

"How did it happen?" Soso asked.

"I was with her the day it happened," Sandy said. "A day before I'd brought her a special gift. She was over the moon, even urged me to visit you, to give you the news. I told her I'll think about it."

"Sandy, what happened to my mother," he agitatedly asked, caring less about a special gift.

"Well, on that day I passed by the house, she was in the kitchen, cooking, as we chatted, she just dropped on the floor."

The giant, once again, went at it with a sledgehammer, pounding his hard shell. And every blow that connected caused more cracks in it like an earthquake capable of cracking wide open the earth from a thousand miles away.

"I'm sorry about everything," Sandy said, a trickle of tears streaming down her chin like a cascade.

Monster.

"When is the funeral?" Sosobala asked, his face disturbed.

"This coming weekend. Her congregation has arranged everything," Sandy said.

Monster.

"The prison authorities, could they release you, to attend her funeral?" Sandy asked.

"I don't think so," Sosobala said as he shook his head, "but I'll try and see what they say."

Something ate him alive inside that would never stop even if he pledged with gold and silver. He gasped for air for a while as he attempted to exhale but it became difficult. His failures in life flashed before him, too stunned to respond. But his mother, a woman who had never asked for her husband to be taken away so soon, and for her son to choose the life of crime. All she ever wanted was happiness that was overtaken by misery on that night she accompanied her moaning husband to the hospital. The misery that had found a home in her gloomy eyes until her last days, like the blowing easterly winds slinking to the seas.

"I'm sorry for leaving you. I really am. You see, after my tragic rape, I became overwhelmed. And then Sifiso's death, it destroyed me," Sandy continued, having hiccups, "I had to get away from you, I'd to. You'd turned into something more sadistic like..."

Monster.

Sosobala sighed like a writhing monster retreating into its cage, hoping to catch its breath after a gruesome fight. Sandy tried to utter some syllable but choked on it while her lips pouted. She stood up and left without saying a goodbye.

"Sandy, come back here," he said, his tone hopeless.

Her petite form disappeared as if into the surface of the prison walls. What was it that she wanted to say, he wondered, irritable. What else could be more important than his mother's death?

18

THE MONSTER IS WEAKENED

He walked back to the cell, his feet stomped with every contact they made on the linoleum. His body felt depleted as he struggled like he was running on sea sand. Sosobala was disturbed, confused, heartbroken, and angry... all emotions locked in a box. He went past the guardhouse. The armed guards had a smirk on their faces as if they knew. It was as if they were making fun of his mother's death. As he entered the cell, the eyes of his cellmates pierced through him like arrows shot from a hunting bow, as if chanting his failures once again. It felt like the powers at be chastised him for all the bad choices he had made in his life. Sosobala retreated to his bed, the only place he found solace, roaring inside like a bruised and battered sea monster. He pleaded with the prison officials to let him attend the funeral. Sadness and anger welled up inside him when his request was denied.

That night, Sosobala wondered: Did his mother die a peaceful or painful death... what special gift made his mother be over the moon…what was it that Sandy wanted to tell him... would she ever come visit him again after leaving like that... when would his failures all end? But the cell was dark and silent, with no voice to answer his questions except the snores of the fellow inmates.

His dream about his mother in a white gown across the stream, waving to try and get his father's attention, in that heartbreaking moment, made sense. He dozed-off having felt he did not have it in him to go on living. In the morning, after the roll call, the youngster paced towards him while other sky-birds did their daily chores of cleaning the cell and whatnot. The youngster had something in his hand. As the youngster's steps got louder and nearer, his stomach grumbled wildly... his danger senses aroused.

"I thought you might like these," the youngster said as he extended his right hand.

The youngster's palm slowly opened like a blooming flower. Warm tears floated in Soso's eyes, and his saliva turned into foam. His heart throbbed like a mountain biker manoeuvring over uneven terrain... his breathing in tandem with his cycling.

"No," Soso said.

Like a wounded bull realising it only had an ounce of breathe left in it before it succumbed to death, he broke-down remembering the content on the youngster's palm. It was his mother's favourite biscuits. She loved to have them with coffee in the mornings just before breakfast. The giant again slammed the sledge-hammer, this time around with full force, causing the hard shell to crack wide open like an earthquake violently ripping the earth apart.

"Aaahhhhh."

Sosobala roared openly causing the prison walls to shake... causing the warders' hearts to shudder... causing the convicts' souls to shiver... most importantly causing his heart, the very same one he had guarded so intensely to be flooded with pain. It was the pain that only came once in a human being's life. His emotions welled up like an inflated tyre. Like a kid watching his mother leaving him behind with unfamiliar faces on his first day of school, he screamed, "Ma."

He slumped on the linoleum, very shiny... very cold, feeling drained and flooded by unimaginable emotions.

"Change your life for the better my son, if not for you, than do it for me."

It had been her last words when she had visited him in the hospital. The youngster's and other cell mates' eyes roasted him like he was a chicken in a heated oven as he pulled himself up. His look became more sheepish by the minute.

"What're you fuckin' assholes looking at?" Sosobala said, trying to hide his discomfort. "Don't you have things to do?"

It was obvious, the whole cell had witnessed his breakdown. The monster in him had been burnt down like a wooden house with just ashes left in the aftermath.

19

THE PLOT TO TAKEOVER PRISON BACKFIRES

"Sosobala NoZulu, report to the visitor's room," the intercom sounded, repeatedly.

He shoved the youngster aside as he shuffled to the cell gate. The warder opened and escorted him to the visitor's room. On the way, he kept on thinking, maybe Sandy was back to tell him what she had choked on previously.

"Duke," Sosobala said, disappointed but not surprised as he took a seat.

"CMB," Duke said, showing signs of uneasiness.

"We need to talk."

"What's up, everything in order on your side?" Sosobala asked.

"Hhuh, things were going according to plan, until recently," Duke said, leaning over to the glass booth, his face troubled. "I couldn't finish the job on our delivery boy. He got away."

"What? You failed to do just this one simple thing," Sosobala said. "How come?"

"I sent my best guy to do the job quietly," Duke said. "That warder has muti, I tell you. My hitman has never missed before till now."

His respect for Duke flew out of the window fast when calculating the consequences of his miss.

"My hitman was a few feet away from him, just a few," Duke

said, incredulously. "Don't know what happened, the gun misfired. And the bastard managed to flee."

If ever there was a time he had felt like choking the life out of Duke, it was in that very moment.

"It gets worse though, the prison authorities have concluded their investigation on the death of the 28 gang leader," Duke said, his eyes deceiving him.

"Have they?" Sosobala asked, his look far from being impressed.

"It doesn't look good," Duke continued, "our delivery boy, well, he was found and during the interrogation, he confessed to everything."

"To fuckin' what exactly?" Soso asked, frowning and scorning.

"I'm afraid the whole thing. You, and me, involved in poisoning the 28 gang leader. And running the drug operation inside here," Duke said, visibly fretting. "They can't link us though; it's only his word they're relying on."

"Fuckin' moron. Don't you know," Sosobala said, as he felt anger and disappointment at the pit of his stomach, "his word is enough in here for the 28 gang to fuckin' declare war."

"What're you going to do about this," Duke asked, feeling emasculated. "What about our drug trade?"

"You're fuckin' kidding me, forget it. You see, as from today, the prison officials will shut down everything," Soso said, pulling his bristly hair. "And when the 28s hear about this, they'll be gunning for blood, this very week." He nodded warily.

"Can we fix this?" Duke asked.

"In here," Soso said, squinting, "you fuckin' know, only the spilling of blood fixes things. Nothing else."

Duke said his goodbyes in a huff, as Sosobala pictured the aftermath of his actions. The prison corridors would soon reek of blood. It would be like watching a speeding train with no breaks hurtling towards helpless victims trapped on the railroad tracks. He briskly paced back to his cell remembering his first year in prison. The clash between the 26s and 28s gang had made headline news across the country, with even the army deployed as extra guards.

He entered the cell, and retreated to his bedside digesting the after-effects of Duke's hit and miss. The cell gate unlocked and Montie busted in like a mad man running naked on the highway.

"Fuck, what've you done?" Montie asked, grimacing. "Why did you've to poison the 28 gang leader? For what, your greedy ambitions?"

Montie's neatly trimmed red beard trembled as if a kid was playing with it, pulling his cheeks up and down. His face turned different colours like a chameleon.

"The blood spilled in here is on your hands, do you hear me?" Montie said, glaringly. "Fuck, I hope you pay dearly for this."

Sosobala looked away, sheepishly. His suspicions were confirmed that the 28 gang had already found out about him poisoning their gang leader. The 28s were housed in cell blocks across their building. Montie exited the cell, and Soso quickly summoned his soldiers to the chambers.

"War is brewing, my soldiers," Sosobala said, trying to convince them but more like himself. "The 28s think we're just going to roll over and let them walk over us. This is our fuckin' territory. The 26 gang rule." He raised a 26 gang sign, and a thumbs-up.

The soldiers' roars thundered as they began to sing and clap the revolutionary songs. They were ready to defend the honour of their 26s' number lore even if it meant death for them. The soldiers were like robots, you just had to say the word or press the go-button, and they would run through fire without any hesitation or objection or complaint. The fire that he had started and for sure the hastily winds were going to blow it towards him.

"Anytime from now, I don't have to fuckin' tell you, you know. The warders are coming to ransack the place," Sosobala said. "I want everything, knives, and drugs, stashed."

The only way the soldiers stashed the knives or drugs, during lockdowns was to use condoms. Fill them up with drugs or knives... seal them... lubricate them with saliva or water, and then shove them up their butt-holes. Some would stash as much as four bags inside their bodies for a week. Their stomachs would be bloated like they were pregnant. The soldiers drank Epsom salts when the time came for the contents to be taken out. They would assist one another in being the goalies, and push it all out in the toilets. And the whole cell would reek of a sewer plant for the whole week during those exercises.

Sosobala briefed his soldiers, and retreated to his bed. His eyes locked with that of the youngster: he looked scared. It was that same look Madubula had when he locked eyes with him after Montie had found dagga stashed under his bed. It was the petrified look of a fragile rabbit when cornered by a hungry predator. He realised that when the gang war happens, people like the youngster would be ambushed like sitting ducks.

If the 27s—the assassins of prison—entered the fray, not even an insect would be spared from bloodshed. The 27s were like racing horses, they charged forward with knives, stabbing just about anything in their pathway. He realised that the sky-birds and the prison staff would pay the price for his greedy ambitions.

In the wee hours of the morning he tossed and turned, calculating the consequences of his actions to find the solution. The cell gate unlocked abruptly. His heart almost skipped a beat, not knowing whether it was the warders, or the 28s deciding to ambush them earlier. The sweat trickled down his torso like a worm slithering into its hole. He stealthily pulled himself up, and concentrated at the entrance of the cell. The sounds of the boots stomped in like the gumboot dancers stomping in rhythm.

"Everyone, against the wall, now," a voice shouted as the lights came on.

The voice was that of an Afrikaans speaking man.

Heavily armed prison guards, covered in bullet proof vests, surrounded every inch of the cell. Montie, with the nod of his finger directed them to search the cell. They ransacked every inch of it, only recovering what the soldiers had not been able to stomach any more.

"Fuck," Montie said as he paced closer to him, "where are you hiding them, you scumbag. Where?"

Montie was looking for drugs and knives. If only Montie took his time and monitored his soldiers' movements, he would easily spot the bloated ones. Just like a bloated snake, its movements would be exhausted and slow.

"Fuck, the blood of all these people," Montie said, rotating his finger, "will be in your hands."

Montie ordered his squad to exit the cell. The words 'The blood of all these people will be in your hands', hung in his mind like a pauper's dirty laundry.

Was he beginning to believe Montie's insinuations? Why would their blood be on his hands? They chose their destiny... the soldiers had taken a pledge to live or die by the 26 gang's number lore. And as for the sky-birds, they ended up in prison because of their own transgressions. They were transgressors just like any other prisoner. As for the warders and prison staff, they took up posts in the prison knowing very well the danger of working in such a place.

Sosobala pounded himself with unanswered questions... yet deep down inside, the answer was staring him in the face. His conscience slunk into the pit of his heart weighing like a heavy anchor.

Hours turned into a day, and then the next, as the entire prison smelt of fear and uncertainty. The warders doubled-up their security on every part of the prison. The warders might be caretakers of the prison guarding the convicts. But just like in the zoo, the animals knew sacred information about the zoo better than their caretakers.

Through his spies, the 28s had acquired the assistance of the 27s, by promising them half of the drug trade. They were planning an attack on the 26s the following day. Everything had been planned to the tee.

When the warders entered the 28 gang's cells for a roll call, they would ambush them, and take away the master key. They would then proceed to the guardhouses on all the floors, taking out anyone or anything they came across. They would go, steel gate after steel gate, hurtling through the corridors as they made their way to the cell blocks of the 26s, directly opposite their building. They would dispose of the guards in their guardhouses. And then they would enter the cells, and massacre anything their eyes fell on until they got to Sosobala. They would then behead him and parade the prison with his head.

Sosobala shuddered in the depths of his heart when realising the 28s plan was a doable stunt. It had been done before by the 26s. And there was no way the 28s could not have the same results the 26 gang had achieved three years ago, of entering the other cell blocks and killing a gang leader.

That night at the chambers became longer and darker. He stood in the middle of the ring while his crouching soldiers encircled him. He monitored each and every one of them—their eyes, their facial expressions, and their body language—as they sang and clapped in rhythm. They were like a school choir battling for the number one spot in a competition. He threw his eyes across the hall and found the sky-birds. They had crept into the front of the cell like sheep waiting to be sheared. Their eyes stared at him, piercingly, as if they were acid poured over his body, brutally melting his hair and his skin surface, and then eating with vigour into his skeleton until only black ashes remained on the shiny linoleum. Who was it who'd said that?

Sosobala shifted his eyes back, and focused on the crouching soldiers. When the 28s entered their cell blocks, he would have no guts or have the will to issue a directive to attack and defend his greedy ambitions.

Or the honour of the number lore for that matter. His order to the soldiers to stay alert and be ready made him aware that the monster in him was dead and buried. He found his words hollow as the soldiers dispersed to assume their respective positions. He sat on his bed, head bowed, and with every minute that went by, like Montie had insinuated: the blood of all these people would be in his hands.

His hands trembled as he read them as if they were a book. They were tainted with the blood of the beefy man during the christening of his taxi... the blood of the junkies who had broken into his taxi. The blood of the culprit in the pool party... the blood of Sifiso who had raped Sandy... the blood of Chopper who had raped Madubula... and the blood of Chopper's lieutenant who had challenged his authority. And then there was the blood—the souls of his father... of his childhood friend, Boyi... of Madubula... and lately, his mother.

He felt that all those souls were not at peace with him. They screamed, and shouted at him to take responsibility for his actions. If the 28s, sworn to massacre anything in their way to get to him, got their way, then a lot more souls would be barking on his conscience.

'Change your ways for the better, my son. If not for you, than do it for me', he recited those words from his late mother like a learner reciting a poem.

When would it all end?

"What's going on, Soso?" the voice, consumed with emotions, asked.

Sosobala lifted his head, but then put on a brave face realising it was the youngster, a short distance away from him. Sosobala did not take kindly to people who disturbed his 'me' time.

"What do you want?" Soso asked, his tone forced.

"It's true, isn't it?" the youngster continued.

"Fuckin' speak up," Soso said, feeling agitated.

"You poisoned the 28 gang leader, didn't you, now they want revenge?" the youngster said with a gurgling tone.

Sosobala nodded in shame as he stared at the youngster with the eyes that spelt 'I am sorry, I have failed once again.' The youngster's eyes welled up with tears.

"I'm afraid," the youngster said, "I don't want to die, not like this anyway."

Tears ran down on the youngster's cheeks. It was the look his father had when he thudded on the ground, that 'I don't want to die... not like this anyway' look. The same look his childhood friend, Boyi, had when he slumped on the ground as he called to him during the botched micro-loan bank robbery... The same look Madubula had when his body writhed after being raped. It was the look that only assailed an individual's heart once in a lifetime.

"It's going to be OK," Sosobala said, extending his right hand to hold his. "I'll fix this."

Some form of electricity cascaded when the youngster clutched his hand. It was the same form of electricity he had felt when his father clutched his hand, when his mother clutched his hand, when Boyi clutched his hand, when Sandy clutched his hand—an intimacy that made him feel like he was needed, he was loved, he was understood.

"It will all end soon," Soso said, reassuringly.

His conscience spoke in alien languages, but he understood each and every expression of those words. He had finally found an answer to his question, 'When would it all end?'

"Go to your fuckin' bed, now," Sosobala said. "It's going to be a long day."

The youngster released his hand, and that form of electricity released as well, making him aware that all those who had been intimate with him were gone... he was all alone. The youngster turned and shuffled away with a slow frightened gait.

Sosobala realised that what was about to happen was his way of taking responsibility for his failures. He glanced around the hallway like a man glancing around his repossessed house for the last time, about to go under the hammer.

His eyes closed for a moment as he began to dream: He was standing outside a room and a steel gate opened. It was an open dark room with wriggling shadows. He peeped inside, and heard voices speaking in alien languages. He became afraid when the shadows pulled him in. He lowered his eyes and realised there was no ground for his feet to stand on. He then aimed his gaze upward, and realised there was no roof either. The room was like a long tube.

"Where am I?" his unconscious state asked.

Nobody answered him, although the voices kept on rambling. The shadows came towards him. They looked angry and afraid, all at once. The steel gate locked behind him. Why or who locked it? He shuffled towards the shadows. The closer he got, the more visible the shadows became, and the more the voices started to make sense. The shining light appeared, and hurtled towards him. It stopped at an arms' length from him. He extended his hand wanting to touch it. But the shadows attacked him, and ripped his body apart.

His eyes opened, not understanding what the dream meant. His heart throbbed, and his body perspired like he was in a steam room. The sweat ran into every part of his body.

When would it all end?

It would end soon.

20

AN ULTIMATE SACRIFICE

The sound of the keys jiggled in the lock of the cell gate, and it opened. He froze, remembering the plan formulated by the 28s to ambush the warders as they came to do a roll call, and take away the master key and begin their attack until they got to him. His heart sank, pondering... it was about to end. The time it took for the cell lights to come on, and the sound of the footsteps stomping inside the cell became the longest seconds of his life. He sprang up high... his muscles taut, ready to end it all: the guilt, the failure, the loneliness, the misery, and the uncertainty. Sweat poured through his pores like a hundred metres sprinter. The words recited in his mind, 'On your mark... get set... ready...'

"Roll call," a familiar warder's voice said.

It was Montie, in a foul mood as usual, and his squad that looked like they munched roaches for breakfast. They stood attention next to their beds as the counting of heads began. Montie's glare found him as he clutched his jaws. It became evident that there was a thin line between the warders and the convicts when Montie reached him. The way Montie acted sneeringly around him, made it vivid to Sosobala that they will never, in any way, be cordial to one another.

Not even in another lifetime.

"Convicts, as you were," Montie said, and then ordered his squad to exit the cell.

Sosobala held back the need to confront Montie about what was about to happen in the prison. Montie had little, or no sympathy at all for what was labelled as his mess. Montie had his own idea on how to curb violence in the prison, while he had a different way mapped in his mind to stop the bloodshed.

As their boots stomped towards the cell gate, the siren wailed non-stop like a new born baby hungry for milk. When that happened in prison, it only meant one thing, that danger was imminent. The moment of truth dawned on Sosobala that it would all end soon. His heart rate skipped a beat, and blood rushed to his head, nearly bursting out of his every body part. His hands and feet became moist and shaky.

Danger.

"Fuck, what's going on, over?" Montie said, pulling out a two-way radio through his waistband.

"Convicts in B-blocks, the 28s and 27s," the voice behind the two-way radio said, panicking. "They're out, over."

"Confirm your status, over?" Montie said, looking confused.

"North, in gate 1, over," the voice said.

"Seal the entry and exit points, over," Montie said, alarmed.

Montie spoke on the two-way radio as if trying to get inside it.

"Montie," Sosobala called out his name.

Montie became surprised, seeing the voice that called out his name, about twenty feet or so, came from none other than him. Sosobala paced towards him with a 'need to talk with you urgently' gait.

"What do you want?" Montie said. His eyes grew more intent. "Fuck, I've got a crisis on my hands here. Your mess."

Sosobala moved closer until he was mere inches away from him but the prison guards restrained him.

"Let me fuckin' help you," Sosobala said as he was shoved back. "I can stop this shit."

Montie frowned like a squatting man. And then he glanced at the two-way radio, and then back at him.

"Let him go, now," Montie said in a feisty tone, tapping his left foot.

The boots were very shiny as always, just like the linoleum.

"You know it, the 28s are out for revenge," Sosobala said, his spirit broken. "Let me go out there."

"For Fuck's sake. Are you mad?" Montie said. "You think you can fix this just like that?"

Montie thought Sosobala wanted to go out there, with his gang, and fight the 28s and 27s gang till the bitter end.

"Fuck, no gang wars in my prison. Hear me?" Montie said, sizing him up, "I won't allow it."

"Come in," the voice behind the two-way radio said, "they've gone past gate 1, over."

"Seal the blocks, I repeat, seal all the blocks, over," Montie said, his hand swallowing the two-way radio.

Montie turned from red to pinkish in mere seconds as the siren kept on wailing in a rhythm.

Danger.

"Fuckin' listen to me," Sosobala said, "there'll be carnage here soon. You don't want that, do you?"

Montie paused, irritable for a while.

"Montie, they've gone past gate 2," the voice behind the two-way radio said, "officers down, over."

"Double-up security in all the strategic points. Do it, now," Montie said, agitatedly. "How many officers down, over?"

"Two, over."

Danger.

"It's me they're after, let me fuckin' go out there, alone," Sosobala said, tears trickling down his cheeks, warm and salty. "Let me take responsibility for my actions, will you?"

Montie had a sudden change of heart as soon as he heard those words.

"What're you going to do, hey," Montie said, closing the gap between them, "fuck, beg them to stop this madness, in return for what?"

Sosobala bowed his head like a disgraced soldier who had been dismissed from the army. He lifted his gaze again and found Montie's eyes staring intently at him as if counting every strand of hair on his head.

"Fuck, you really want to do this," Montie asked, "hand over yourself to the 28s, just like that?"

"Let me stop the bloodshed," Sosobala said, his tone hopeless. "Let me redeem myself, OK?"

Montie shook his head and looked away, and then turned to him again, tapping his left and then the right foot, hands on his hips.

Danger.

"They're in gate 3," the voice said, hysterically, "officers down, I repeat, officers down, over."

"How many officers down, over?" Montie said, choking on his words.

"Six down, over."

"God Dammit," Montie said, roaring like a wounded Ox. "Fuck, prepare to use live ammunition, over."

"How many more must die?" Sosobala said, gesturing, "It's me they fuckin' want. Me."

Danger.

Sosobala swayed back, and found the eyes of his soldiers staring at him with contempt. These fools, they wanted to go out there and fight, for whose sake exactly? And then he found the eyes of the youngster staring at him with sincerity. The sky-birds would be slaughtered like sitting ducks. It had to be stopped. He turned back and focused on Montie: he had an uneasy and unconvinced look.

"They're contained at gate 3," the voice said, "but not for long, over."

With each second that went by, Sosobala made it known to Montie that it was a second too late if he did not let him go out there.

"Fuck, I don't know how you're going to do this," Montie said, lowering his face, "but it's your call."

He took off his bullet proof vest in a hurry, and wanted to fit it on Sosobala.

"That won't be necessary," Soso said, shying away from it.

"OK, let's do this," Montie said, as they escorted him out of the cell. "Fuck, you're really going to do this?"

Sosobala nodded, his stomach heavy, so was his heart. This was the only way for him to take responsibility for his past failures, even if it meant cutting his own life short. Besides, he had nothing to live for.

When would it all end?

Sosobala constructed a brave face, exhaled deeply, jaws clutched, butt cheeks in, shoulders out... like a boxer in a fight of his life. He dug deep as he felt his feet wobbly like jelly.

"Soso," the youngster called to him, "don't—"

Sosobala turned but his made-up mind blocked the last syllables by the youngster. He took his first steps, his prison uniform soaking wet, encircled by Montie and his squad. The footsteps made by the sound of the boots felt like horses' hooves pounding on his chest. And the sound of the key grating in the locks of steel gate after steel gate, felt like a razor blade lacerating his skin, causing the blood to throb mercilessly.

It would all end soon.

"We're retreating, over," the voice said behind the two-way radio.

Montie shouted back in the two-way radio, "Restrain them. Fuck, don't let them through gate 3, over."

"We can't hold them any longer, if they get through here," the voice behind the two-way radio said, "that'd be it for us, over."

After gate 3, the corridors split to other parts of the prison, like the cafeteria, the hospital, the social worker's offices, and other prison officials' offices. And anyone or anything would be in harm's way. They had only one steel gate to go through before they appeared at gate 3.

The mental flashes of his late father and mother... of his late childhood friend, Boyi... of the late Madubula appeared... sad and angry. His feet became numb, his body under the orange prison uniform, itching. His hands became moist, his armpits sticky, and smelly. Fear and sadness engulfed him.

When would it all end?

His father's words that he heard as a child resurfaced, 'A good man lives with integrity, hard work, and always takes responsibility for his actions.'

His mother's words replayed in his mind, 'Change your life for the better, my son. If not for you, then do it for me.'

He roared silently like a lion pierced by thorns in its paws, who could step no further. His shuffles became shorter and weaker as the sound of the key rattled in the steel gate lock. He swayed, and his eyes locked with those of Montie looking pale and drained.

"We've hated each other's guts ever since you came here," Montie said. "Fuck, what you're doing now, is the bravest thing anybody has done in my thirty odd years in here."

Montie's words slowly ate him alive inside. He forced a smile, held his breath, and turned to face the steel gate, which had just opened wide.

"We can't hold them any longer," the voice behind the two-way radio said, frenziedly. "This is it, we're retreating, over."

The words 'we're retreating, over' triggered his conscience as he began to take daring steps through the gate. He visualised the long, tube like, corridor leading to gate 3.

"OK. Retreat to gate 4, over," Montie said, his hand squashing the two-way radio.

"They've gone through gate 3," the voice said breathing heavily, "they're on our tail, over."

The roar behind the two-way radio sounded as the mob, the 28s and 27s, hurtled behind the prison guards like demented men.

"Please, do me this one last favour," Soso said, his voice hopeless, "tell Sandy Gumede, she's the love of my life. I'm sorry for everything. I hope in the next life I'll come back as a better man for her. A man she and my mother could be proud of."

"Sandy Gumede," Montie said the name repeatedly, "I promise, I'll do it."

When would it all end?

"May God have mercy on your soul," Montie said, patting him on the back. Those words caused his body to shudder, his spirit to crush. He dug much deeper, and began to increase his steps, which were brave to a human eye yet painful to his soul. The feebly looking prison guards sprinted past him, as the corridor surface trembled. The crazed primitive shrieks came his way.

When would it all end?

Sosobala found himself standing before the mob. Their eyes looked angry and thirsty for blood. Fear, sadness and willingness all piled up at once. He looked behind him, and found Montie staring compassionately at him from afar. The corridor, like a long tube, only allowed for three to four people to walk side by side. He turned back to face the mob again; their body language showed they had a certain degree of fear for the man in front of them. That was Sosobala NoZulu, the man who had disposed of Chopper, the most feared 26 gang leader in prison... the man who had, in a barbaric way, killed a lieutenant and gouged out his eyes, and shoved them down his throat... the man who had meticulously orchestrated the poisoning of their gang leader... the monstrous Sosobala.

In a timeless bubble, he wondered: Who would perform his reunion with the ancestors? That time shortly after his father's burial resurfaced. His mother had made efforts to have his late father's reunion with the ancestors performed in a befitting manner.

"It's being true to your African roots," Soso's father had said to him as a youngster.

It played out, intensely, flick after flick. The woven white clouds had welcomed the smoky perfume lingering in the air. As a seven year old, he sat next to his mother in a crowded taxi filled with the odour of bad breath and spoiled cabbage, enroute to the west side of his neighbourhood.

"Driver, how about you turn up the volume," an elated commuter said, "I get goose bumps when I listen to Brenda Fassie's hit song, 'Too Late for Mama.'"

Sosobala caught a glimpse of his reflection in the window. A blanket of sadness overshadowed his brown eyes. How was his family to survive after his father, their breadwinner, was gone? After jumping out of the taxi, they strode with his mother the half-a-kilometre distance to their modest home.

"Son, it's time we consult a sangoma, to find out if your father was reunited with the ancestors," she said.

"Anyone comes to mind, Ma?" he asked.

"People heaped praise upon Ndosi in Umbumbulu," she said, her smile filled with hope and love.

Before the sun could rise, before the cock could crow three times, on that crisp Tuesday morning that had gradually warmed... they had boarded a taxi to Umbumbulu.

"Excuse me, do you know Ndosi, the sangoma?" his mother asked inside a packed taxi.

"Sure," the taxi driver, a loud-mouth, said. "I'll drop you off at his homestead."

Dust lingered in the air as the taxi exited from the main road onto the narrow gravel path with sugar cane growing on either side. An isolated horseshoe shaped homestead sat uphill, about the half-a-kilometre away. They jumped out of the taxi to the sound of the beating home-made drums at the gate, echoing across the homestead. Inside the yard, were men and women of all ages—the initiates—in their red attire smeared with red soil all over their bodies. They wore colourful beads in their head-gear, wrists and ankles, as they performed the ritual dances.

"You're here to see Ndosi, right?" an initiate asked, opening the wooden gate, ushering them to one of the huts.

"Yes," the mother said as they followed closely behind. "He's here, right?"

"Certainly. Please, shoes-off before entering the sacred place," the initiate said, his tone respectful. "The consulting fee—to throw the bones—is one hundred rand."

"OK," she said, breathing a sigh of relief as they entered the shoddy plastered hut.

They sat on the woven traditional mat. And his eyes widened as the reptile skins hung on the trusses of the hut, and different muti strewn about the hut.

"It smells bad in this dimly, and dingy place," his mind said as he tried to gasp for air.

His mother's wristwatch read six-thirty. The singing and dancing stopped. The elephant footsteps accompanied by heavy breathing drew closer to the hut.

"Ho ho, I've been expecting you. I'd a vision of a woman and a boy standing at the wooden gates of my homestead. It means your ancestors wish you well," the man said, crawling into the hut.

The sangoma's belly could stock food for the village, while his grizzled Afro, was definitely in contempt of cleanliness. Sosobala was gripped with fear when noticing something else that was nearer.

"Ho ho, please, don't be alarmed," Ndosi said with a hoarse voice as he sat across them, legs stretched.

He carried a goat skin bag and a decorated tufted beast-tail.

"What can I do you for?" Ndosi asked, caressing his pet draped over his shoulders like a medal of honour, and lit the incense.

The long bloated pet was sprightly too. Ndosi had then snuffled the snuff, the ancestors' favourite tobacco as he reminded them. His nostrils could gobble the oxygen for the entire village, as Ndosi sneezed aloud and then spat.

"We want to know, if my husband was reunited with the NoZulu ancestors?" his mother said.

"Ho ho, come and spit in the bag, my child," Ndosi, in shabby brown pants, and a vest said, staring out of bloodshot eyes.

His mother took out a hundred rand note, and placed it at a short distance from Ndosi's feet without uttering a single word. She spat in the bag and assumed her sitting position again, wide-eyed.

"Guardians of the universe, I summon you, to share light on the matter," Ndosi said, jiggling the goat skin bag.

Ndosi threw the bones, and they scattered near his feet.

"Ho ho, the ancestors want to know where's the father's offering to them for a clear passage to the gates of their sacred place. They say you're living according to the western ways now. They want to remind you, wherever you're, your ancestors' blood will forever cascade in your veins. Don't ever forget that," Ndosi said, snuffling and sneezing loudly.

Ndosi then cleared his throat.

"What do they want?" she asked.

"Ho ho, an old buck," Ndosi said in a measured tone.

One of his father's many teachings was that the ancestors' demands were always the family's first priority no matter how much it would cost.

"How much would a buck ceremony be?" his mother asked.

"One thousand rand," Ndosi said.

His mother dropped it next to Ndosi's feet. Ndosi summoned his initiate with instructions on which buck to take out of a nearby cattle kraal, and put it at the back of his van.

"What's going to happen now?" his mother asked.

"We'll go to your late husband's grave. I'll sacrifice the buck and sprinkle its blood on the grave. Then I'll set it alight, and summon the NoZulu ancestors to come and feast," Ndosi said hoarsely. "We'll then walk away without a backward glance. Your late husband would've by then been reunited with his forefathers."

Shuffles came back to the hut quickly.

"I've got an old buck," an initiate said, entering the hut.

"Ho ho, good, we can leave now," Ndosi said.

Ndosi slit the buck's throat at the cemetery, and sprinkled its blood on every inch of the grave. Ndosi laid the buck on top of the grave, anointed it with oil, and then set it on fire. The flames hungrily devoured the buck's skin as the white smoke soared into the sky. Ndosi danced around the grave like a demented man, summoning the NoZulu ancestry to converge at the grave, and feast on the offering. Sosobala went home with a glimmer of hope that his late father had been reunited with the NoZulu ancestors.

It was that commitment his mother had showed to his family, which had made it possible in his dream for his father to be seated, relaxed, in a serene garden, filled with all kinds of blossoming flowers and ripe fruit trees, and encircled by men and women, young and old, in white bright clothes, dancing and ululating.

* * *

A veil came over his eyes as he assumed a Jesus on a cross stance. The crazed primitive screams sounded again as the mob hurtled towards him. Like lions attacking a fragile prey, they pounced on him, stabbing him with no mercy. He bellowed like a wounded sea monster, realising the inevitable.

When would it all end?

It would end soon.

If he could just go back to the happy and carefree days as a youngster who loved to play soccer. Those memories all played out: it had been a spring month. The air smelt fresh and the people were sprightly too. He had imagined himself one day becoming a soccer star, and playing professional football overseas. And he jumped at the first chance to join a new soccer club that trained on a dusty man-made soccer field, which years later the Umlazi shopping centre had been built on. Boyi, his childhood friend, opted not to join. His chubbiness discredited him. The soccer club was owned by Mr. Dimba, a short tempered man with a girly voice.

The humid midday breeze brushed against his face after another long training session. The sweaty and stinky players gathered for a pep talk from the coach. His teammates, with dirty worn-out white soccer jerseys and duct-taped soccer boots, panted non-stop. Being made captain of the team had solidified his commitment to Umlazi Bombers. It had been his first recognition of honour by his superiors. He had been a striker at heart, a left footer who had the eye to spot the net from miles away. But the team coach, Lucky, a bald-headed man with dark skin and uneven ears, instead positioned him as a defender. But he was not about to let his ego get in the way of his love for soccer. He held his head high up.

The Umlazi Soccer League fixtures began. He woke up at six on that cool Saturday morning in high spirits ready for their first game to be held at the King Zwelithini Stadium. The clear indigo sky welcomed the flitting and singing birds going haywire in the spring trees. He beamed with excitement, naïve and cocky at the time, to be showcasing his dribbling skills, better than anybody alive. His objective for that day had been to dribble and score superb goals, and pick-up a win. But it was not to be.

For starters, the smooth-cut green playground had all of a sudden appeared three times bigger than what they were used to training at. The goal posts were wide, but because of the distance to get to them, they looked smaller. Also, their opponents were tall with strong muscle definition in their yellow tops and black shorts. A local newspaper front page had showed that team with a headline 'Trophies of Impressive Young Lions.' Nevertheless, team morale picked up as the club owner passed around new sponsored soccer kits. They wore white shorts and green tops with their jersey numbers written in bold white at the back, and new pairs of soccer boots. Whistles had echoed from his teammates.

"This is more like it," he said, admiring his jersey number seven: his lucky number.

Smartly dressed in their new jerseys, they looked like professional soccer stars, all smiles. The coach gave them the last minute talk on what to do and how to tackle the game. Then the referee made a toss. They won it to kick-start the game.

"Pree."

The whistle blew at eleven-thirty as his team began making their touches, passing the ball around whilst warming up. But it had been short lived as the opponents snatched the ball away from them. And then made a few passes to a loud cheer, accompanied with blowing whistles from the opponent's supporters.

"Pree."

The referee blew the whistle, and ordered the ball to be placed on the centre. So soon, he became a bit baffled. But their nightmare had just begun. In no time the score was already three–nil down. As captain, he tried to boost the morale of the team, trying to keep them calm. But he also could not believe what he was preaching. The situation went from bad to worse as the rival team ran like they had supercharged batteries connected to their long legs. By half-time, the score board read five-nil.

What an embarrassment, his neatly tucked-in jersey portrayed him like the leading goal scorer of the league season. In the changing rooms, some of his teammates looked like they had just finished running the Comrades Marathon. The second-half began. His team tried its best, but they were like dying soldiers who were being slaughtered like sheep in a slaughter house... their fate already sealed.

Six… seven: the goal scores were highlighted on the score board.

"These guys are lame ducks," an opposition midfielder said.

If only he could get the ball to land on his feet. Just as he made the wish, at that moment, the ball landed at his feet. He calculated in his mind: it would be a minute or so before stoppage time.

"Run, dribble, kick the ball," the coach said to his young soldier with admiration.

His eyes intensified as he hurtled from the quarter back, dribbling the midfielders, then their defenders. He ran like a mad man to deliver that last kick of a dying horse. Because of the size of the football ground, he ran endlessly until he kicked the ball with the last breath of a brave warrior. The ball had been discharged from his left foot at a massive speed, but reached the goalie at tortoise pace. The goalie had not even exerted a muscle as he picked it up and kicked it back to his players.

"Pree."

The score board had read... seven-nil. His team dragged their sweaty behinds back to the changing rooms as if they were dragging bags of cement.

Their bodies felt like it had been crushed by a bulldozer. There was silence in the changing rooms, the players not speaking to one another. They were mortified about their defeat after the rigorous training the coach had put them through, more like soldiers training for a World War. Worst, he sucked in football. He exited the stadium with his head bowed in shame, and signalled for a taxi to his neighbourhood.

* * *

His guilt for the death of his father... the death of his childhood friend, Boyi... the death of Madubula... the death of his mother... the loss of Sandy, evaporated like steam in a boiling kettle. He held in his last ounce of breath, finally taking responsibility for having failed them. Like a captain of a sinking ship who failed to safeguard the lives of all those on-board... he straightened his white uniform and a cap, hit a salute as the ship went under. He let go of his last gasp of breath as he slumped on the linoleum.

Very shiny... very cold.

It all ended.

Epilogue

After what transpired the previous week, Montie wanted nothing to do with the convicts. If he had a choice, between being a warder or a farmer, he would choose the latter. The memories were still raw in his mind: the cells... the corridors... the smell of blood... the crazed primitive screams of the convicts, and Sosobala's bravery. His handling of the situation was criticised, and he was summoned to a disciplinary hearing. It was going to be a mountainous task to exonerate him. Even his most trusted colleagues distanced themselves from him.

He entered an open office that had three tables formed in a U-shape. Each table accommodated two disciplinary committee members: four men, and two women, wearing the official prison uniform. Their looks were stern with pens in their fingers, notebooks on the top of the tables, and a tape recorder. And they were seated shoulder to shoulder. Directly opposite the U-shaped table was a chair, isolated. Montie was directed into the isolated chair with a nod of a finger.

The prison commissioner blamed him for not placing Sosobala in solitary after the findings on the death of the 28 gang leader.

"The investigation into the death of the 28 gang leader fingered Sosobala NoZulu, right?" the prison commissioner asked.

"Not quite, sir," Montie said, "the warder who was involved confessed to everything. But when it was time to put it in writing, he just vanished without a trace."

"But what action did you take against Sosobala NoZulu?" the prison commissioner continued, annoyed.

"Things happened so fast, sir," Montie said. "I misinterpreted the unfolding events. I wanted to follow the proper procedures and have mister Sosobala NoZulu charged, criminally, for the murder of the 28 gang leader."

"You've been a warder for over thirty years, right?" one disciplinary committee member asked.

"Yes ma'am, thirty years, nine months, and thirteen days," Montie said.

"In that thirty odd years, how could you've misinterpreted what was right in front of you, a monster?" a disciplinary committee member added. "Did your feelings towards this man cloud your judgment?"

"Fuck, I guess I was overwhelmed, ma'am," Montie said, his look feeble. "I have never encountered such a convict in my thirty odd years. Never."

The disciplinary committee members scribbled something on their notebooks, and then continued:

"The record books showed that not even once have you transgressed."

"Yes ma'am, not even once," Montie said, his eyes puffy.

"So how did you lose sight, all this time, of a monster right under your nose?" the prison commissioner grilled him.

Montie explained to the disciplinary committee the years he spent with Sosobala. How he had evolved from just being another convict, to a heartless 26 gang leader. And that he believed Sosobala was a monster until the time he did the unthinkable. Sosobala offered himself as a sacrifice to save thousands in the prison.

"If ever I was thrust into the same situation again, I'll still do it the same," Montie said. "Maybe the second time around, I'd be more empathetic on the man."

"If a warder cannot separate emotions other than being objective in here, I guess it's time for you to exit." The prison commissioner pointed to the door.

Montie's cheeks slumped as he was lost for words.

"Please step outside sir, will call you back when we've deliberated on the matter," another disciplinary committee member said.

Montie breathe a sigh of relief as the disciplinary committee was lenient on him. Instead of being given an exit package, Montie was issued with a written warning. And he was demoted to work on the front desk, registering the daily visitors. His mind felt at ease when occupied by different faces with different personalities, entering past the front desk oblivious of what the inside of prison was capable of doing to a man's soul.

They came through the small steel gate just a few feet away from the main aluminium gates, all with a common purpose to see their loved ones in jail. He perceived the front desk to be like his sanctuary: a big room with a wooden counter behind which he hid his big figure. It had wooden desks for the visitors in the front, lined in formation.

He was busy jotting down another visitor's information when his concentration got lost to a waft of fresh air coupled with the scent of vanilla when a woman walked in. She swayed her petite form down the long passage to the front desk like she was on a mission: ready to take on the world and bring it down to its knees. Who was it who'd said that?

She was dressed in a tucked-in blouse, as white as summer roses, under a knee-high skirt, as black as her high heels. Every step her high heels made was as if she was stamping her authority that she was a phenomenal woman, and she loved every minute of it. Behind her, was a little boy, very cute, about three years or so, following with his tiny footsteps, naive and oblivious of his surroundings. She took a seat and the little boy hopped onto her lap as she waited for her turn.

"Next," Montie said, glancing at the bustling room, seeing her pull herself up like a lady, and striding towards the counter.

"I'm here to—" she said, in a huff.

"Excuse me, pretty lady," Montie interjected, "would that little man be accompanying you by any chance?"

"Yes, he is," she said as she turned and looked at the little boy with admiration, and then turned to face him.

"Well," Montie said, raising his eyebrows. "Kids aren't allowed inside."

She sighed.

"Fuck, I'll tell you what, you leave him behind. I won't mind looking after him until you come back." Montie added. "He seems like a good kid, aren't you little man?"

He nodded at the kid with a tilt of his head.

"Please mister," she said, lifting her body as if she wanted to jump over the counter, "I brought his father a special gift. You see, he doesn't know he has a son."

Montie's fingers played with a ball-point pen as he digested her words, occasionally glancing at the visitor's register book.

"You know, I've kept this from him for over three years now," she said, frowning. "You see, this has eaten me like a slow poison, all these years."

"Rules are rules, pretty lady," Montie said.

She turned her head and looked again at the boy, in a tiny black suit, and then back to him. Tears floated her eyelids.

"I just want him to see his son," she said, her hands fidgeting, "maybe he might've a reason to get out of this place, and turn his life around. You do understand, don't you?"

"I'm afraid I can't help you there," Montie said, his look betraying, feeling bad he was denying her a genuine request. "Fuck, I'll tell you what—"

"Yes, mister," she said, her tone very hopeful.

"You go up to the visitor's room first, and I'll follow you shortly with the kid. While you're with him, I'll sneak the kid in just for a few seconds. Fuck, I'd lose my job for doing this, you know."

"Oh thank you mister, you're very kind," she said, her eyes lighting up.

"In all my thirty odd years working here," Montie said, "this is the second time I'll be breaking the rules in just less than a week."

She knelt on one knee, and chatted with the little man, her hands passionately holding him.

"Okay, pumpkin, mommy's going up first. You see this good man," she pointed at him, "he's going to follow with you, shortly.

You're not going to cry, will you?" she said, smiling as the kid nodded.

She lifted herself up again, and turned to face Montie.

"What's the father's name, pretty lady?" Montie said, ready to jot it down in a register book.

She gasped as if a weight has been lifted off her shoulders.

"It's Sosobala," she said, "NoZulu."

Montie's breath was caught in his throat after hearing those words. The ball-point pen skidding out of his fingers, and thudded on the floor.

"I'll be damned. Who is it again?" Montie asked, trying to make sense of the name spoken with compassion.

"Sosobala NoZulu," she said, her voice proud.

Then there was silence at the front desk as if somebody had pressed the mute button of a remote control in the room. He took a long lingering glance at the little boy: the light complexion with a chiselled shaped face, and the brown eyes. It was indeed Sosobala's features.

"Sandy Gumede," Montie said, as if reading the name at a sign board.

"Did I tell you my name?" Sandy asked, doubting it.

"Not quite, pretty lady," Montie said, "Sosobaal did."

"Oh good, so you do know him," Sandy said, elated, "great stuff."

"I'm afraid I've some bad news," Montie said, his face melting like heated ice. "Fuck, Sosobaal died last week, a real tragedy. I have been trying to find you and his family for the past few days now."

He had the eyes of a poverty stricken man as she dizzily took a step back, like his words had just struck her like lightning. Her face seemed to crack with every word that he mouthed. Her eyes turned bloodshot as if coloured with a reddish crayon.

"You're okay?" Montie asked, leaning over the counter. "Hold on, let me come over there. Do you need anything, water?"

He skipped over the counter, and assisted her to a seat. Sandy clutched the little boy as a trickle of tears made its way down her cheek bones, to the corners of her lips, down her chin, warm and sticky.

"God no. What happened, how?" Sandy asked, her voice trembling.

His big built sat next to her, and engulfed her like a whale engulfing a dolphin. Montie relived that moment once again as he began to explain the circumstances that led to Sosobala handing himself over to the mob.

"All I'd say is, in the end, Sosobala did good," Montie said, looking remorseful. "Fuck, you know, a lot of lives were saved cause of his bravery."

"I have this guilt, it's killing me inside," Sandy said, her body shaking as she hung on to the little man like someone wanted to snatch him away from her. "How did I fail to tell him?"

"Don't punish yourself this way," Montie said, his tone comforting. "I have watched him all these years in here. Sosobala had a lot of hatred, and resentment, as if he was carrying the burden of the world on his shoulders. Fuck, he had turned into something else."

A monster, he stopped short of saying it.

"I'd have saved him maybe, if I'd been there for him, you know," Sandy said.

"Fuck, no, pretty lady. I can tell you this much, it was too late for him to be saved," Montie said, rubbing her back intimately. "In his last words, he left a message for you."

"For me?" Sandy asked.

"Yes. He said you were the love of his life. He was sorry for everything. And he hopes in the next life he'll come back as a better man for you. The man you and his mother could be proud of," Montie said, as if reading a love letter.

Sandy's shoulders slumped as she tightened her squeeze on the little man, her eyes gloomy. Montie paused for a while longer.

"Tell me, what was he like," Montie asked, curiosity getting the better of him, "did he have a favourite sport or something?"

"You know what, Soso was not into sport that much. Sure, he played soccer as a youngster, but that was it," Sandy said. "But there was a boxing match, if ever somebody mentioned the bizarre fights of all time, he'd never forgotten.

"Like I could see him now, talking about it. The fight between Mike Tyson and Evander Holyfield. I can't recall when the fight was broadcasted. But he'd waited anxiously for the fight that had been dubbed 'The WBA world heavyweight match of the decade.'

Clink!

The bell rang as Tyson in his usual style bulldozed Holyfield into the corners of the ring. Holyfield remained resilient, shrugging off whatever hard blows Tyson threw at him. Tyson had always made a quick meal of his opponents like two-minute noodles. But when the rounds had gone to three, the fatigue in Tyson had shown. Holyfield began jabbing with vigour, and throwing a few of his heavy blows that caught Tyson snoozing. And then Holyfield landed a right hook that caught him frolicking with his nuts. Tyson clutched Holyfield like he was pleading with his sweetheart for two minute shag. At that time, Soso had screamed for Holyfield to cease the moment. And Holyfield, maybe, he heard him because he tried to break free of Tyson's grip. And then Tyson bit into the ear of Evander Holyfield in that third round with just less than a minute for the gong to sound. Soso sprang out of his seat, astonished at what was the first… the only… and just maybe, the last in boxing history, an ear biting."

"I remember that fight too, like it was yesterday," Montie said, chuckling, "Maybe Sosobaal and me had something in common."

"Maybe, especially if you love fast cars," Sandy said. "Oh he adored Ricky."

"Who's that now?" Montie asked.

"His BMW 325is," Sandy answered. "I've never seen him so happy the day he bought that car, and took me for a spin.

"Soso pulled out at the parking as he slid in the first gear. Ricky choked at first. He joked that Ricky still needed a cough syrup to open the chest. He slid in the second gear, and Ricky sneezed as his foot fondled with the accelerator. He then revved the accelerator: Ricky accepted the third and fourth gear with a slight hum. By that time, the sound system was full blast in the cabin. He floored the pedal from the main road to the highway: Ricky begged for a fifth gear, and he obliged… Ricky whistled. He had taken a few sharp bends, maybe, to test the soundness of its cabin. Ricky sang, 'Hallelujah.' He sank into the sports seat until he pulled in back at my student residence parking. By that time, I'd fiddled with just about every button I could find."

"Guess he was a car enthusiast, like me," Montie said.

There was silence as they shared an intimate moment realising Montie could have made a lifelong friend, while Sandy could have found a lifelong partner.

"There's some stuff I'd like you to sign them off, its Sosobaal's things. If it's okay with you?" Montie said.

Sandy nodded; her look saddened, as she pulled herself up, lifted the little boy up onto her left hip side, and followed him.

"Was Soso that bad, even knowing he has a son couldn't have changed him?" she asked, her face distraught.

Montie sighed.

"Don't know about that," Montie said, "but all I can say is, in the end, he made an ultimate sacrifice."

"Soso once said to me, after I'd grilled him, you know, about his gangster life, 'Sandy, a man has got to do what a man has got to do to survive in this bubble called life, cause when it bursts, you cease to exist.'"

About the Author

Musawenkosi (Mso) Kheswa, grew up in Umlazi, a township prone to crime in southwest Durban, South Africa. He is a reformed gangster (jail-bird) who turned his life around and qualified as a Telkom technician.

Musa completed his Matric (with Exemption) at Ogwini Comprehensive High School in Umlazi. Post Matric, he studied towards a National Diploma in Electrical Engineering: Light Current from the then ML Sultan Technikon (now Durban University of Technology).

He followed it up with a Diploma in Business Management (with Distinction) from BMT College of Southern Africa. Years later Musa did a Bachelor degree in Business Administration (BBA – with Distinction) from MANCOSA (Management College of Southern Africa).

As the bug for writing bit him, Musa then completed a Creative Writing Certificate with the Writers Bureau, from UK.

And that was preceded by a Project Management Professional (PMP) Level certificate received through SQDC Business School.

He is a Professional Project Management Candidate, and former member of the Project Management Institute (PMI-USA).

Musa also have a BCom Honours (Management – passed with Upper Second Class) degree from the University of KwaZulu-Natal (UKZN).

He is a member of OnlineBookClub.org; Author/Publisher/Editor/Bookreaders; Aspiring Authors United; Writers Forum; Thriller, Mystery and Suspense Writers/Authors; Writers and Authors Promotions, just to name a few.

He also subscribed to both the Writer's Digest, and the WritersRelief.com.

www.ingramcontent.com/pod-product-compliance
Lightning Source LLC
La Vergne TN
LVHW091142080826
845145LV00008B/2226
9780620861380